T0086161

# The Boy Who Searched for the End of Numbers

# The Boy Who Searched for the End of Numbers

Danny Rittman

iUniverse

# THE BOY WHO SEARCHED FOR THE END OF NUMBERS

*iUniverse books may be ordered through booksellers or by contacting:*

*iUniverse*
*1663 Liberty Drive*
*Bloomington, IN 47403*
*www.iuniverse.com*
*844-349-9409*

*Because of the dynamic nature of the Internet, any web addresses or links contained in this book may have changed since publication and may no longer be valid. The views expressed in this work are solely those of the author and do not necessarily reflect the views of the publisher, and the publisher hereby disclaims any responsibility for them.*

*Adobe Stock images depicting people are used with their permission and for illustrative purposes only.*
*Certain stock imagery © Adobe Stock.*

*ISBN: 978-1-6632-5302-6 (sc)*
*ISBN: 978-1-6632-5303-3 (e)*

*Library of Congress Control Number: 2024900522*

*Print information available on the last page.*

*iUniverse rev. date: 01/29/2024*

The Universe doesn't like secrets. It conspires
to reveal the truth, to lead you to it.
—Lisa Unger

It is not the strength of the body that counts,
but the strength of the spirit.
—J. R. R. Tolkien

# Contents

# Acknowledgments

I want to express my profound thanks to Mo, my childhood best friend, whose extensive knowledge of biblical events was an invaluable resource during the writing of this book. Your friendship and insights have enriched this work in countless ways.

# Chapter 1

# Pleased to Meet You

My instincts didn't fail me. They only rarely do in situations like this. Something was wrong just above me. I knew what I had to do, and I had to do it instantly—or else.

I swiftly aimed my M-4, dropped a terrorist to the left, and immediately dispatched another to the right. I looked upward. A helicopter with six well-armed soldiers was hovering just above me. They were preparing to rappel down on me. The seconds were flashing by, but I remained calm. I aimed my RPG at the helicopter, making sure it was locked in. I squeezed the trigger. A whoosh sound told me the missile was on its way, and I watched it as it flew for two seconds until hitting the chopper and turning it into a yellow-red fireball. It veered awkwardly to the left, jerked downward, and crashed into a warehouse.

I felt relieved, but there was no time to pat myself on the back. A vicious battle was still raging all around me. Greenish-yellow tracer rounds flew by me, and I tracked them to a light armor vehicle to my right.

*Where the #%@! did this come from?*

I raised my M-4 and returned fire. A dozen soldiers jumped out of the back, took up tactical stances, and came my way.

*Trained solders. They know what they're doing. Hmmm ... well, so do I!*

Scores of angry tracers streaked past me. Another vehicle appeared on my left. More soldiers dismounted and headed for me.

*This isn't fair! Too many!*

I got hit again and again and knew I wasn't going to make it. I pursed my lips and prepared. I heard a solemn voice call out to me.

"Ty, maybe you can enlighten us with an answer to the question on the parashah we've been discussing?"

Rabbi Shmuel gave me a stern look. He recognized when I was in daydream land and enjoyed snapping me back to the classroom. He caught me, and he was going to take full advantage of it. I was doomed.

"Uh yes ..."

I was back, albeit reluctantly and incompletely. The images and experiences of the *Fallujah 2004* video game were powerful and gripping. They had me. Nonetheless, I had been ordered to leave the front lines. The terrorists would have to wait until after school to learn their fate.

"I'm thinking, Rabbi Shmuel. It will take a moment."

"Good! But we don't have all day."

He made a point of looking at his watch, and my classmates enjoyed the drama.

"Your moment has passed, Ty. Now that you are back from your deep thoughts, please be so kind as to share the knowledge you gained with the class and with me as well."

His lecture had wafted into my brain while I was doing battle. Unfortunately, most of it had wafted out too. A few words about Abraham and Isaac popped up, but no question came to me. I fidgeted in my seat and felt the stares of classmates. Some felt sorry for me; others enjoyed my plight.

The bell rang. I was saved. Rabbi Shmuel was disappointed.

"I have good news, class. Ty will explain everything to us tomorrow. I hope you can wait till then."

Everyone laughed, except for me.

"Yes, yes. I'll be prepared tomorrow." I closed my book and headed out of the room for lunch. I'd have to talk with Hannah. She was an excellent student, and I could count on her for help. She liked me. I could tell from her smile. And, well, I kind of liked her too.

---

Okay. Before I get to my numbers quest, I should tell you a little about me. My name is Ty Lev, and I was ten when the grand adventure began. That was a few years ago. I was born in Haifa—that's in Israel—but live in San Diego with my folks. They work a lot, which leaves me with time for exploration. My father is a computer engineer. He designs the little silicon chips that make all those cool things come to life and solve problems. My mom is a free spirit who does seminars on holistic living.

I was in the fifth grade when all this began. Good grades come easy to me. Everyone says that school is important, including my parents. *Especially* my parents. Religion is the heart of my schooling. Many classmates come from very religious homes. Everything is based on something in the Torah. They walk to services every Friday night, even in the rain. And Yom Kippur, well, that's a day of sadness and regret and soul searching. That's okay with me. It's okay with my folks. We don't live that way though. My friends' parents wonder about us, maybe especially about me.

Opportunity came knocking one day, loud and clear!

# Chapter 2

# Numbers

I t all started one day in math class. I was into numbers for years, but that day was different. We worked on addition and subtraction, multiplication and division. The numbers mostly kept getting bigger and bigger. Thousands, hundreds of thousands, and this mysterious thing called a billion. You had to pronounce the *b* so no one thought you were talking about a mere million. I learned to solve problems. I learned about the base ten number system and calculation strategies. I guess you could say my school was little bit ahead of most of the other ones in San Diego. All these were great, but then one big question arose in my mind.

I knew very well where numbers start, but where do they end? Easy enough, or so it seemed.

I raised my hand, and Mrs. Lerner called on me.

"Where do numbers end?"

"Numbers never end!" she instantly replied. Her smile told me she liked my question and the mind that came up with it.

"But how can that be, Mrs. Lerner? Everything in the world has a beginning and end. The hour, the day, summer and winter. Even TV shows. The same must be true of numbers!"

I might have sounded like I was challenging her authority, but I was curious, that's all.

"Numbers go to infinity, and that's endless. They go on and on—forever."

She smiled again, but this time I noticed a little wrinkle formed on her forehead. Now I knew that my time was probably limited to another one of two questions.

She saw that I still was not satisfied with her answer and added, "Imagine adding oranges to a big pile. You can add as many as you want. You can add every orange in California, then add every orange in Florida. You can always add one more."

"Okay, I guess. But eventually the pile will get larger than our planet."

"Then our orange pile will go into outer space. And, Ty, you know outer space is endless."

"But what if outer space has an end?"

Her smile disappeared, and she became punctual. "It doesn't."

I knew that my time was up. I'd learned the signs of an irritated teacher long ago, and they were clear as day just then. I had to be careful. I knew it, and so did everyone in class.

"Any questions from the others?"

No one else had one. Many classmates looked at me like I was weird. Maybe I am, at least a little. I remained puzzled, and it started to bother me. There was someone else I could ask.

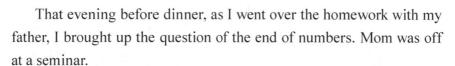

That evening before dinner, as I went over the homework with my father, I brought up the question of the end of numbers. Mom was off at a seminar.

"Well, there is no end. You can always add one to any result. It's that simple. It doesn't matter how large the number is, you can always add another one to it. Therefore, they go on forever—to infinity, as we call it." He smiled and patted my back. "And now let's see what's for dinner."

"But there must be an end to them. Everything in the world has an end."

I suppose he tried to think of something else that went on forever but came up with a blank. Poor Dad was stumped.

"You're right, young man. Our world has a start and an end. But there are some things that, according to our understanding, are defined as going to infinity. Maybe we simply can't comprehend these huge amounts. This is something that many mathematicians investigated for many years without any other results."

I nodded.

"A good example is the number pi. This is a small number with infinite decimal value. The numbers go on and on into infinity."

"Or they stop somewhere."

"Even if they are stopping at some point, our supercomputers churn and churn but are unable to find a stopping point. How about spaghetti?"

"Spaghetti? Oh, you mean for dinner."

"Yes, dinner. We are back to earth, Ty." He smiled and messed my hair.

"Spaghetti sounds great."

The evening routine started. Dinner, a little television, a lot of homework, and off to bed. The day was coming to an end. I lay in bed and determined to come to an understanding of this end stuff. After half an hour, drowsiness put things on hold.

# Chapter 3

# Reaching Out

The next night, just before bedtime, I was glued to my computer, especially since I got *Fallujah 2004*. But mathematics was more important than terrorism just then. Search after search revealed nothing more than what Dad said. A few more words and several big ones—that was all.

I wondered what a ten-year-old kid could add to the question. I mean, sure I'm smart and creative, but these people I'm seeing online are wizzes at MIT and Cal Tech with lots of letters after their names. I almost opened my war game. The cursor was in place; my finger was ready. Nope. I wasn't going to give up. There was something interesting and maybe even amazing in this.

I entered new search terms: "Who can help me with the end of numbers?"

I scrolled through pages of hits, but I'd seen most of them, and the others didn't help.

I typed "I want to know where numbers end."

I scrolled and scrolled, and only on the third page did something catch my eye. It was a chat room. I entered and asked the question. This time, I made a little change.

"My question is, why don't numbers come to an end?"

I waited for replies. After two minutes, one came.

"Why do you want to know that? Is this for a game?"

"Nope. Just curiosity."

"Don't waste our time. This place is for gamers, not philosfers."

Even I caught the typo. I ignored it.

"Okay, but it's very interesting to me. I want to know."

His reply was quick and short, but at least he spelled the F-word right.

I sent a quick and short reply of my own and logged out. I opened *Fallujah 2004* and locked and loaded my M-4.

# Chapter 4
# Religion

After classes finished on Fridays, the school let us have a Shabbat party in the auditorium. It took place before sundown, when religion took hold and demanded time for reflection and family life. We enjoyed the social gatherings and good food more than the other things. Families took turns providing the goodies for our parties, and this week it was my folks' turn, but Mom was away at a seminar in the Rockies, so Hannah's folks picked up the load. Her folks were better bakers anyway.

Mrs. Lerner supervised the lighting of the candles and smiled as her pupils chatted and joked and made plans for the weekend of fun and a little homework.

Rabbi Shmuel came in late. He was never the life of the party, I must say.

"Does anyone have a question regarding this week's parashah?"

The room fell silent. Oh, a *parashah* is the weekly reading from the Torah. See what I mean about him?

"Does anyone have a question about anything? Anything at all? If not, then enjoy the rest of the period and pick up your books and get on your buses. Shabbat Shalom!"

My mind was still on the weekend, but that one thing came to mind. "I have a question, Rabbi Shmuel!"

He wasn't happy to hear me chime in. He was halfway out the

door, and now he sensed delay from an annoying student. "Oh. Young man, what question has been vexing you amid the song and food this afternoon?"

"I actually have a question that I've wanted to ask you for quite some time now."

He looked at his watch. "All right then. What is it?"

"Umm … well …"

I studied his annoyed face and wondered about my timing.

"Young man, do you have a question or not?" Seeing my unease, he became more fatherly. "It's all right, Ty. You can ask. We're all here to learn. I'm listening."

"Where do numbers end?"

"Numbers end?" He looked perplexed and blotted his bald spot with a hanky. "They don't. They go on and on to infinity."

"But how can it be? We have a beginning and end to everything. Why not numbers?"

I'd thrown him. The room was silent. All eyes were on the rabbi and student.

"Well, mathematicians have asked that question for decades, for centuries. Descartes, Leibniz, many others. They found no end and found no reason there could be one. I'm not a mathematician, but I do know that numbers simply do not end."

"Is there any passage in the Bible that talks about this question?"

He raised a brow.

Uh oh. I'd done it now.

"The Bible is a wealth of information. Everything we need to know in life is in it. You know that, Ty. You all know that."

"I do know that. That's exactly why I asked. So the answer is in there somewhere?"

His face became peaceful and gentle, and he slowly nodded, as my grandfather did when he watched me play.

"It's very interesting that a boy your age would like to know about such a profound question. Why do you want to know?"

"It's very interesting to me. I wonder how the Bible addresses it."

"Young man, I will look into it and offer you clearer counsel next week."

"Thank you, Rabbi Shmuel!"

"Now pack up and go home for Shabbat!"

We erupted in cheers and headed for the buses. The weekend was on!

Monday passed without word from Rabbi Shmuel. Same with Tuesday. I wondered if he'd forgotten about me. Wednesday, however, he called me over just as I was accompanying friends to the lunchroom.

"Young man, your mind is on to something. I've looked through a few books in my personal library and made a few calls to colleagues, but no one has a firm answer. To be perfectly honest, which I try to be, no one has much of an answer at all. Yes, you're on to something. We just don't know exactly what."

Despite the praise, disappointment must have been clear on my face.

"However, Ty, we have a guest coming in two weeks, Rabbi Mordechai. He's a professor at Yeshiva University and a very wise man. I'm proud to say I studied under him. A former student of the Great Rebbe in Jerusalem himself. Very learned and respected not only in our religion but also in mathematics."

"Mathematics!"

"He has a PhD in math. That's the highest level of education you can get. He knows the science of numbers."

I knew these initials from my web searches. I was filled with joy.

"Thank you, Rabbi Shmuel! I can't wait."

He looked at me sternly, then laughed.

"Go enjoy your lunch. Play football or something. Don't try to solve the mysteries of the world right away. You're only ten years old for crying out loud!"

Off I went, practically floating on air. I was moving ahead, and I had help.

---

I did more and more web searches over the next two weeks but never found anything of interest. I even searched into mathematics books in the city's public library. They were too complicated for me. All the books dealt with numbers, but none of them showed where they end. I became more puzzled. So much mathematics with numbers but nothing about where they stop.

Rabbi Mordechai brought scientific articles with long equations and dozens of footnotes. Don't ask me what they were about. The two weeks passed, then two weeks and two days. On Friday, as I was packing up for the bus, a tall man in his sixties and wearing a dark suit came in the classroom. Sensing he would lecture on something and keep us after school, my classmates scurried outside. But I knew who he was before he said a word. He approached me and leaned over. His blue eyes and long gray beard instantly told me he was kind and smart. More than smart, he looked like a genius! He put a hand out. I leapt to my feet.

"I presume you are Ty. I am Rabbi Mordechai from the school in New York, where I had a gifted student who became Rabbi Shmuel. Yes, your inquisitive face tells me you are the gifted student he told me about."

I shook hands. "Yes, of course! Pleased to meet you! This is amazing. No, an honor. I mean—"

"Thank you, Ty. I understand. You are a bright and respectful young man. An increasing rarity in our modern day. Now, let us sit down and talk of things that matter."

He sat sideways in a student desk, and I sat in mine. He took out a small cloth and polished the lenses of his wire-rimmed glasses.

"Everything has a beginning and end, Rabbi Mordechai. Everything in the world. Except for numbers."

He leaned forward as best he could in the student desk, nodding his head and stroking his beard. "Yes, yes. Except for numbers. Quite true and quite perplexing. Now, that's a question I don't hear every day. It speaks highly of you. How old are you, Ty?"

"Ten."

"Ten years old. Such an unusual question for such a young man."

"It's very interesting to me. The more I learn about math, the more the question comes to my mind. Where do the numbers come from? Why do they exist? And ultimately where do they go? I really want to know."

"You are correct, Ty. Our world is made of life forms and objects that have a beginning and end. Numbers fall into a different category though. Mathematics is a science that started in the previous millennium. Because many mathematical discoveries were made as a result of necessity, it comes as no surprise that scientists believe that many basic mathematical functions, such as addition, multiplication, and the alike, appeared thousands of years ago in various areas at the same time, including China, India, Mesopotamia, and Egypt."

I didn't understand everything he said. But I was fascinated. I wanted to hear about mathematics and how it evolved throughout the years. The Torah connected to my question. It had numbers. I wondered how the Torah explained it. I planned to ask the rabbi about it.

"The oldest clay tablets with mathematics date back over four thousand years. They were found in Mesopotamia, which by the way is near the Holy Land, our Israel."

I nodded like I knew that. He continued.

"The oldest mathematical writings are on Egyptian papyrus. Ancient civilizations developed the basics of mathematics. Since then, we have learned a great deal and developed a richer understanding of the subject. This is what history tells us."

I remembered learning the story of Passover years ago. As a young child, it caused me not to favor Egypt.

"So the first mathematics was invented by the Egyptians? Our enemy?"

He smiled and nodded. "Back then, yes. Those were different times. Egypt, like many other countries, had good leaders who were friendly to our people and others who were not, as in the events surrounding Passover. But they had great thinkers too. Among them were mathematicians. Brilliant ones."

I imagined a guy walking around the pyramids with a calculator. I almost laughed out loud. "Awesome!" I exclaimed.

"Yes, they made remarkable contributions. You'll learn more about them one day. Perhaps in college."

"So did anyone find out where the numbers end?"

"No, Ty. They believed what we believe today—"

"That numbers never end."

"Exactly."

"Okay, so maybe I'll study math in college."

"An excellent plan!"

"Meanwhile, I can play with the math I know, and maybe that will open something to me."

"Play and investigate, play and investigate. And maybe a door will indeed open for you, and you can enter it boldly and come out of it wisely!"

"Thank you, Rabbi Mordechai!"

"You are more than welcome. I come back to San Diego every now and then. We can speak and see what doors you find. But, Ty ..." He leaned forward, and again a weariness came over him. "Your investigation may take many years. Many, many years. Life is a journey, young man. A long journey."

I wanted to know more about the years and the journey, but I sensed he had other things to do that day. After all, Shabbat was upon us. And I had to catch a bus.

That evening, when my mother came home from her seminar, she lit the candles, and my father recited the Kiddush. I said my own prayer. I prayed to learn. I prayed to solve mysteries. I prayed to find the answer to my question.

# Chapter 5

# Investigations

"I don't understand why we're doing this, Ty. It's *so* boring." Hannah sighed as she put down her tablet.

It was during math class when we were allowed to do stuff on our own. I could usually rely on her to help with every mischievous idea I dreamed up but not that day. I wanted to perform a bunch of math operations to see if we could get some ideas about the end. I'd found an intriguing website that published UCLA dissertations with long equations and something called algorithms. A little more searching, and I found out how to make sense of some of the equations, and I even leaned what algorithms were. They're computer commands with numbers inside them.

"Let's do something else, Ty. Let's throw paper balls at Seth and Myron over there!" Smiling, Hannah pulled out a piece of her notebook paper and crumpled it with glee.

"Not just now, Hannah," I said in an annoyed whisper. "Today, I need your help. Here. I'll write a few operations for these fractions. I want to see something."

She put the crumpled paper down. "Okay, Ty. I'll play along. But you have to get me some of the chocolates from the headmaster's office."

"On Mrs. Rosen's desk?"

"That's it."

"Okay. Deal."

I wrote a series of operations on her notebook and explained what needed to be done.

"Why do we need to do more math?" Hannah asked. "It's just going to give us one huge number."

"Exactly," I said. "We need a large number for a cypher."

Hannah's puzzled look told me everything. Hannah had no clue how to do this. To demonstrate the concept of a cypher, I said, "I am writing a sentence." I wrote on a paper,

*Madam, in Eden, I'm Adam.* "Now if I write it backward, using letter after letter, it spells the same."

Hannah looked at the paper. "Madam, in Eden, I'm Adam." Hannah was fascinated. "Wow … I love this!" Her eyes got big.

"Here is another one." I wrote on the paper, *Lipps, mri duh brx wsbub?*

Her forehead wrinkled. "What is it? I don't understand."

"In this sentence, each letter in the original message is shifted forward by four positions in the alphabet to create the ciphered message. The original sentence is *Hello, how are you today?*"

Hannah tried the concept, and her eyes sparkled. "This is very cool! We are geniuses."

"This is a simple example. Let's try to decipher what we have here."

And so we played with numbers and letters. It took us a while. As I said, she's a smart student too. Soon we were crunching numbers, feeding them into online math processors and hoping for … for something. I had a plan. I just needed a little help. Just before the end of math class, I combined Hannah's results with mine and wrote a long series of numbers, one after the other.

"What's this?" she whispered. "Are you trying to hack into the CIA?"

"Not today, Hannah. I don't really know what it is, but it's called a key."

"A key to what?"

"I don't know. It's called cryptography. That's the study of codes. I need it to get a link to a special website. I found it late last night."

"So you *are* you trying to hack into the CIA! That's exciting!"

"Not today, Hannah dear. Look! We have two hundred and fifty-six numbers! It's our key! We have the key, Hannah! We have it!"

My heart raced, but Hannah scanned the long line of numbers, and her eyes opened wide.

"So now we're off to Mrs. Rosen's desk!"

Wouldn't you know it. The office was locked. Hannah was understanding.

---

I couldn't wait until my parents went to sleep after the local news. I took a snack bar from the kitchen and went to my room, prepared for the long haul. With shaky hands, I turned on my MacBook and clicked on the bookmark that took me to a link I found on the UCLA site. It didn't have a name in its URL, just a lot of numbers. That seemed about right. A prompt came.

*Enter the key.*

I carefully typed in the series of numbers Hannah and I came up with.

*Incorrect. Try again.*

My heart sank. A series of naughty words ran through my head, but I didn't think they were the answer.

*You may have made a typing error. Reenter the key.*

Well, it was 256 numbers, it was late, and I'm not a typist. I reentered each character.

*Incorrect. Try again.*

Well, someone once said if at first you don't succeed, enter, enter, enter again. So I went through the numbers again and hit enter.

*Incorrect. But you've tried again.*

My heartbeat quickened, but I stared into the screen, not knowing what would come. Then it went black, and I thought the site was a joke or I got caught by the web police. Or was it gone forever? I was about to hit enter a few times when the screen suddenly displayed instructions, part in words, part in math. I followed them and hoped for the best.

A message appeared:

*Knowledge does not lie in complex calculations but in understanding their meaning. The trick is easy. It's so easy that no one ever saw it.*

*There are few steps to go through to unveil the secret. They will provide you with more cryptographic keys. This is the technique to find more information about the end of numbers—and other questions too.*

The technique?

*It's essential to trust this source. You'll have to do exactly as instructed. Each step is based on the previous one, like a tower of cards. Do not let standard thinking hold you back. One wrong move will bring down the tower, and you'll have to go back to the beginning. A second chance will be given only once. Another wrong move will forever bar you.*

*The process is long and complex. It may take months or even years. The reward is tremendous. You have no idea how it will change your life.*

*You may seek help from others, but only you can enter results.*

*Once you enter an answer, it will erase itself, and you must move on to the next task.*

*Think thoroughly and carefully before you begin. Once you begin, you cannot stop.*

A blue button blinked.

*Click here to start.*

I was pulled in but cautious. Any gamer knows from hard experience of sites that lure you in, then ask for personal information or money or both. I learned that the hard way. Every kid my age has. This site was so serious. No music, no bells, no hot women.

I stared at the screen for a while. I mean, it wasn't like I had found anything else that helped answer my question. What was the worst that could happen? I could always leave or tell my parents if it became a problem. Still, I was only ten.

I took a bite from my bar and chewed for a while. *What if this site knows? What if they know, and I leave, and then I never know the answer to my question?*

I looked around my room as though I was about to leave it and go on a long journey. I took another bite from my bar and clicked the button.

"I'm in!"

The screen went blank for just long enough to make me wonder what would happen next. I hoped my computer didn't just get a horrible virus that meant I'd have to explain what happened when I asked my parents to replace it. Then the words came on the screen.

*Stage one.*

*You must follow these instructions precisely and expeditiously. Don't question or doubt or hesitate.*

I had to look up "expeditiously." It means fast. Why didn't they just say that?

*According to the Jewish religion, there are weekly Torah passages, the parashah, to be read. In Hebrew, it's פרשת השבוע. You must do the following.*

*Every Shabbat, you must recite the parashah. It must be recited in Hebrew. If you don't know Hebrew, you'll have to learn it. There is an ancient meaning to every Torah passage. You don't have to know its meaning, only the words, at least for now.*

*The next thing is critical. Immediately after reciting the parashah, close your eyes and think of a number. Write that number down. You have ten seconds to do this; otherwise you'll miss the window. You must do this only once per week.*

*You'll start at the first week of the Jewish year (שנה עברית) and end at the last month of the Jewish year. Write each number one after the previous one. Assembling these numbers will make a cryptographic code. You should have fifty-three numbers.*

*The process will take one Jewish year. If you miss a number, the entire sequence will be broken. Be thorough, be dedicated, and believe.*

*Once you have the full code, you'll be able to go on to the next step. Good luck.*

The screen remained visible for another five minutes and then logged me out with this message:

*The site is now locked. Enter the code to unlock.*

I breathed nervously, took a huge bite from my bar, and tried to fight off sleep.

Did I just start a journey for the next year? I wrote down what I remembered of the instructions. *Maybe it's too big for me.* After all, I was only ten. *Well, why not? It can't hurt to try, and I just may get my answer.*

---

"Today we'll learn about a very important holiday in our faith," Rabbi Shmuel said as he walked between the rows of chair. "Does anyone want to guess which one it is?"

He had a mischievous expression that we all knew and loved. It meant fun. A few hands went up.

"Well! We have more interest than usual today. That's a welcome sight for this *rebbe*. Hannah, your hand was first."

"Rosh Hashanah." Hannah beamed.

"Very good, dear."

"My mother told me last night."

"Very good for your mother. And what is the meaning of Rosh Hashanah?"

I raised my hand and answered before being called on. "Oh, I know! It's the beginning of the Jewish new year. That's exactly what I was waiting for."

"I didn't give you permission to answer, Ty, but yes, you're correct. Next time, please do us all a favor and wait to be asked to respond—by me. Oh, and, Ty, may I ask why you are waiting for this great holiday?"

"I love the tradition with apples and honey."

"I see, I see. Well, we'll have plenty of apples and honey, as with every Rosh Hashanah. It's tradition. Till then, please open your *Chumash* book to this week's parashah."

"I have a question, please!"

"Ty, I must again tell you to first raise your hand, then await my permission to talk."

"When do we read the first parashah of the year?"

"Such eagerness from such an unlikely source! That would be the holiday we called Simchat Torah, the day we finish reading the Torah and start reading it from the beginning. The first parashah is Parashat Breshit, or Genesis. Typically, it's the last day of Sukkot."

Everyone in the class looked at me in puzzlement, then pondered the meaning of our teacher's words. I pondered them too, but it meant more. It would bring the day I entered a string of code and began the journey.

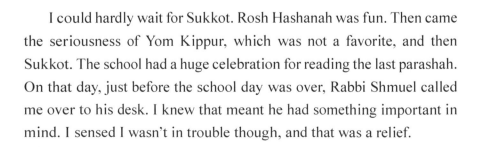

I could hardly wait for Sukkot. Rosh Hashanah was fun. Then came the seriousness of Yom Kippur, which was not a favorite, and then Sukkot. The school had a huge celebration for reading the last parashah. On that day, just before the school day was over, Rabbi Shmuel called me over to his desk. I knew that meant he had something important in mind. I sensed I wasn't in trouble though, and that was a relief.

"So, Ty, how are things?" He looked at me in a concerned, fatherly way. Despite my occasionally lapses in following the rules, he liked me. And I liked and respected him. He was knowledgeable and most of the time quite kind.

"Everything is quite good."

"You were asking for the past few weeks, when does Simchat Torah come. When do we complete the Torah and start anew. Why?"

"No particular reason."

His shoulders slumped a little, like he was disappointed. "I don't buy it, Ty. Not for a minute. What's going on in your life? It's related to your quest to understand numbers, isn't it."

"Yes, it is. You're right. It's just that I have to perform certain tasks." Me and my big mouth.

"Tasks, eh. Are you working with Rabbi Mordechai on this?"

"Well, I may need his help sometimes. If that's okay."

"Yes, it's all right. I must say, however, that you have to be careful. I'm here to help, and when Rabbi Mordechai is here, he can help as well."

"Thank you. It's good to know."

He looked at me as though he wanted me to tell more but respected my judgment. "Ty, you have a courageous spirit. You don't give up. Your quest may be long and difficult. Our faith has deep knowledge about science and more mysterious things as well. Stay safe, young man. Stay on track."

I bet he knew more than he was letting on. But then again, so did I.

That evening, upon completing the Torah reading, my classmates and I celebrated with dances and games. The whole time, I thought of the parashah and a string of code and that website. I looked at Hannah and Seth and wondered if they were far more sensible than I was.

Next Shabbat, I asked my father to take me to temple at noon. That's when the parashah is read. He looked up from his comfortable chair and tablet.

"You've never asked to do that before. Why now?"

"Well, I have to read the parashah every Shabbat throughout the year."

"I don't understand. Is this homework or something you're doing on your own?"

"It's a special project I've decided to take up, Dad."

He looked at me quizzically. "Do you want to hang out with your friends there?"

"Yes, but that's not the main thing at all. I have good reasons. It's a personal quest."

"Well, an interest in our faith is a good thing. Do you want to *walk* over there? It's pretty far."

"You're right. It is far."

It was easy to find a parking spot. Dad and I entered the modern gray structure and took our seats. Rabbi Shmuel, two other rabbis, and a cantor stood near the Torah scrolls in their tallits and began the davening. It was of course the opening words of Genesis. Rabbi Shmuel saw me and gave me a brief look before returning to the sacred text. I waited with paper and pen in hand until the book was closed. This was what I had been waiting for.

I closed my eyes and determined to think of a number. The first one that came to mind. One came in an instant, and I opened my eyes and wrote it down. That was it. But many more readings were ahead.

That night, I entered the number in a notebook I kept with a pile of books underneath my bed. I looked at the page with its single number.

I lay in bed and felt a sense of accomplishment and looked forward to the year, but how could a number I thought of have cosmic meaning?

That website had to be a scam that preyed on kids with a zeal for numbers. I thought about it some more. The website was so convincing. It insisted on faith and self-confidence, and it didn't ask me for money or any other information. I decided to continue. My guard was up though.

---

I learned in school the next week that Rabbi Mordechai was in the building, and I asked Rabbi Shmuel if I could see him. A meeting was arranged for after school in the auditorium. Right after class, I walked briskly to the hall and entered. It was empty and still, like a pharaoh's tomb. My every step echoed off the walls and ceiling. I wondered if Rabbi Mordechai had a more important matter to attend to and the meeting had been called off.

"How are you, Ty? How were your high holidays?"

The words came from the darkened stage where a few chairs and a lectern were. He had no microphone or PA system, but his voice filled the hall.

"My holidays went well."

"Come up here, Ty. We have much to discuss. And how are you progressing in your quest?"

"That's what I wanted to talk with you about. I searched online for answers and couldn't really find any. Website after website repeated the same things or tried to lure me into scams."

I didn't want to say any more.

"But did you did find any particularly interesting websites?"

"Well, yes …"

He took a deep breath, and his blue eyes sparkled. "Well, what do you think of it?"

"It asks me to do things—they're not bad things. I mean, it's not asking me for any kind of information. It's just … it's telling me to do something that I am not sure makes sense."

"Many things do not make sense in the world, Ty. Many, many things. You probably know safety rules regarding websites. I'm sure your parents have given you the warnings."

"Many times. I don't give my address, phone number, or any information about myself or others. That's not the problem. It's asking me to read all the weekly parashah for the entire year."

"Ah, and then you are to think of a number."

"How did you …"

He stroked his beard and looked into the dark hall. Several moments passed. "Well, what do you think about the instructions?"

"They don't make sense. How can the number I think of have any higher meaning?"

"An interesting question and an inevitable one. Now, Ty, I want you to do as I say. It's going to be interesting and rewarding."

He wrote something on a scrap of paper and placed it face down on a chair.

"Ty, say the number three."

"Three."

"Now say thirty-three."

"Thirty-three."

"Now say three hundred and thirty-three."

"Three hundred and thirty-three."

"Now say three thousand, three hundred and thirty-three."

The process went on in the dark hall till we reached 33,333.

"Now tell me the first profession that comes to mind. No time to think. What is the first profession that comes to mind? Quickly!"

"Carpenter."

He smiled softly.

"Now look what I wrote on the paper."

I turned the paper over, and my blood ran cold.

"Carpenter," I murmured. "But how?"

"The human mind thinks in mathematical patterns. It most likely will not work every time, but in most of the cases, it will. Maybe that's the whole idea of the task you have to perform."

"So should I continue with the website?"

"It's up to you. A wise teacher recognizes good students, and he also knows that the highest learning is done on their own."

Numbers could do all of this? It was about far more than just solving a problem like we did in math class. I was eager to repeat the number exercise with friends.

"I see you are already thinking of other things, Ty. That's not unusual with young people. I've learned that. You know where to find me if you want to ask me more questions—or to tell me something."

"Thank you, Rabbi Mordechai."

I headed for the door, listening to my footfalls reverberate in the dark hall. I looked back to the stage, but he was gone.

I tried Rabbi Mordechai's number game with several classmates. Almost all of them gave the same answer—carpenter. Hannah, however, said, "Baker." But I got the idea. There are patterns in our brains, and that played a role in my task.

Dad was perplexed when I wanted to go to Shul every Saturday.

"You're not playing sports or video games as much as you used to. Are you seeing friends at Shul?" he asked as we walked to the car.

"Not really. I'm on a quest. Remember when I asked you a long time ago about the end of numbers?"

"Of course. I'm beginning to think I didn't fully answer your question!"

"Your answer led me to a quest. I have a to read the parashah every Saturday for a year."

"Is this part of school? Punishment for daydreaming perhaps? Well, it seems like a quest that will simply lead you back to my answer. But, Ty, you are my son, and I want you to explore things in life. May it lead to amazing things!"

"I hope it does, Dad! In fact, it feels really cool already!"

We sat in the temple and listened to the davening week after week. I determined to assemble the code and solve the riddle—and go on to amazing things!

# Chapter 6

# Forward

Week after week, month after month, I attended Shul. Usually Dad drove me, but sometimes he was out of town or busy and I walked the mile and a half. When the rabbis and congregants saw me arrive by foot, they must have thought me especially devout—more so than my folks, more so than most of their children.

Time passed by, and I finished elementary school and moved on to middle school. Rabbi Shmuel taught upper grades too. My quest remained. Oh, there were times of doubt. Was I wasting my time? I never quit though. Scam sites come and go. This one remained there. Even if the pursuit led nowhere, it was fun—and a unique learning experience. I didn't torture myself about arriving somewhere; I enjoyed the journey. No, that's not true. I deeply wanted to arrive somewhere, someday.

Dad gave me a diary to jot down everything I was doing. I wrote down the numbers and instructions in my best penmanship. It was all there on paper, not floating around in my head. I felt accomplished and professional, like Dad and my teachers.

---

One weekend, Hannah came over to do homework and play games. More games than homework. She and I shared the bond of mischievousness. A few weeks before, she and I gathered jellyfish from the beach, put them in plastic bags, and brought them home. Well, what could we do with them? They're not something you put in an aquarium with other creatures, and you sure can't eat them.

"I know, Ty! We'll set them free in the community pool!"

Well, it was fun to see everyone scramble out, but we got caught and were grounded for two weeks. No more pool or beach for longer than that.

Well, it turns out that there are websites that have nothing to do with numbers and everything to do with selling small glass ampules containing a sulfuric liquid. Think rotten eggs. Think taking it to school to show friends. What could possibly go wrong?

I brought it to show Hannah and accidentally dropped it in Rabbi Shmuel's class. The quiet tinkling of glass preceded the horrible smell that spread across the classroom in less than a minute. Classmate after classmate groaned and complained as the stink bomb lived up to its name. Hannah looked at me in disbelief and horror of what was coming.

I'm sure I looked guilty.

Rabbi Shmuel was also sure I looked guilty. His eyes remained fixed on me, and I struggled to keep from fidgeting.

"Ty, do you, by any chance, have any idea regarding the interesting odor that is spreading here?

"Yes I do, Rabbi Shmuel. I am sorry. It was an accident."

"I see, I see. Well, accidents happen. Everyone can leave the classroom. We'll be finishing early today. Not you, Ty. You and I stay here."

He wanted to press the matter, but the redness on his face and even his bald spot indicated the stench was getting to him.

"You know, Ty, I think we both could use some fresh air."

Whew!

We walked down the hallway to the courtyard exit, our pace quickening with every step. We welcomed the fresh air.

"Now look, young man, this time only, I'll not make a big fuss. I don't want to see any incidents like this again. Not in my classes and not in others. Do I have your word?"

I could see a glimpse of a smile on his face.

"Yes, I promise this will never happen again. I never meant to drop it in the classroom. The bomb fell out of my hand …" I said amid noisy panting.

"Good. Let me know if you have any questions for me."

*Questions for him? That's odd.*

———————— ◈ ————————

I came close to losing all my work that weekend. Another accident. Hannah and I were playing on my computer when she came upon my diary. She can be nosy.

"Top secret stuff, Ty? Are you a secret agent? I get it. You name is Bond. Ty Bond."

"It's secret all right. It's my numbers project, related to those exercises we did in school last year."

"The crypt key?"

"Yes. Now I need that back right now." I tried to grab it from her, but she was too quick and hid it behind her back.

"Right now, I want to see what's in it. I helped you with the key, so the least you can do is let me in on your secret."

I learned early in life that there's no way to change a girl's mind, even if she's only eleven. She leafed through a few pages before coming to a stop.

"What's this? Your girlfriend's phone number?"

"I thought you were my girlfriend, Hannah dear."

"Oh, gross," she said. She made a face. "No offense." She laughed.

I decided to ignore that. "Actually, it's another cryptography code. I hope it's the key for the next stage. I'm proud of what I've done!"

"Ha! All I see is a bunch of numbers. And not one of them is my phone number!"

"I have a feeling that I'm embarking on a great adventure."

And with that, I waved my hand in a manly gesture—manly but clumsy. I knocked over a glass, and the contents splashed down on my notebook. Hannah shrieked and accidentally tossed my life's work high in the air. A few loose pages fluttered down. A few *wet* pages, I should say. We went through a few pages and saw the blue ink beginning to streak down the pages. We immediately tried using a pair of socks as blotters, but it was useless. The damage was done. Only a few characters here and there were readable. The rest were lost in a deluge I created.

"A year of my life wasted!" I was close to tears. Only Hannah's presence kept me from sobbing and pounding my fist on the desk.

"I'm so sorry, Ty. It was my fault. I was—"

"It was all my fault. It was my clumsiness."

I sat in near despair. Gone. There was no going back; once I started this quest, I had to finish it or start all over again. I thought about that. I really wanted to know. This was so interesting, much more than anything else I'd done with numbers. But I didn't think to back up the cypher outside of the notebook. Everything was in that notebook. The one I could no longer read.

Hannah went through the notebook. I watched her dejectedly, hoping for a miracle. And we got one, sort of.

"Ty? Ty, look. When you pressed down with your pen, you left indentations on the page. It's hard to see, but they're definitely there."

I was skeptical, but sure enough, marks were there on every page. The paper had the imprint of the numbers. The ink smeared and faded, but the imprint remained. I could clearly see indentations on the page.

"Hannah! You genius!" I jumped in joy.

"I'm not a genius, but maybe I am. It just seems that way to a clumsy boy like you. Now, I'll read the indentations, and you write them down. And please stay away from any glasses, okay?"

"You got it!"

So we set to work. Parts were easy to read, and others required a magnifying glass and holding the notebook close to a lamp. We even had to lightly color a page at one point. After three hours, our mission was accomplished.

"Hannah, Hannah, Hannah," I said in exhaustion. "That was a close call. A year's work was almost lost. I would've had to start over, and that would mean another year of work."

"So maybe you should share with your genius friend what this is all about."

"I can't tell you everything because I don't know myself. I only know there's something out there in cyberspace that is helping me answer my question about the end of numbers and infinity—and maybe something even bigger."

Hannah looked at me in a new way. I wasn't just her goofy friend from school. I was someone with a plan, a mission, a great purpose in life.

"Ty, that's amazing! It's like you're looking to understand the world in a new way."

"That's a great way of putting it!"

"It's … oh, I don't know. It's something weird but *spiritual*!"

"Yes! That's an even better way of putting it. You understand me, Hannah. You *get* me!"

Hannah looked at me again. This time a little sorrowfully. "I get you. I get you so well that I know this is your quest and I'm an occasional helper and supporter."

"Well … I guess I do feel like I need to lead the way. I just need a little help here and there."

"We all do, Ty. We all do."

We sat on the floor together, her head on my shoulder. Perfection.

The final reading took place a few weeks later. Dad was at home with work to do. I guess homework never ends. So I walked to Shul, sat at my spot, and listened. At the closing of the recitation, I dutifully thought of a number, just as I had the previous many weeks. As the congregants filed out, I counted up and … oh no! There were fifty-four numbers. I was only supposed to have fifty-three. I counted again. Same thing. One too many. What went wrong? Did we copy the numbers wrong, or did I miscount?

I closed my book, looked up, and saw Rabbi Shmuel.

"Why the long face, Ty? You still have another day of play before classes on Monday!"

"Oh, I'm fine," I said without emotion—and without being convincing.

"I see, I see. Let me give you a riddle. It's not an easy one, but you like difficult things. If you solve it, you are free to go. If not, you have to unburden your heart with me. Deal?"

"Sure."

"In the book of Job, 26:7, it says, 'He stretched out the north over empty space, and hanged the earth over nothing.' That's actually a clear statement that the earth is in space. How did Job know that more than three thousand years ago?"

I sat back in the pew and thought a while. Rabbi Shmuel stood silently.

"How did Job know that so long ago? No telescopes, no astronomers," I murmured.

"No archaeological artifact or document with related evidence to this has ever been found. But, Ty, it's in our Torah. Only thousands of years later did we reach the conclusion that our earth was in space. Someone must have told Job of this. Who was it, Ty? Who gave Job the word so long ago?"

My mind naturally went to space travelers, creatures from other worlds. Then I realized my surroundings and riddle master. "G-d?" I said in astonishment.

"That's the only conclusion I can think of. It was revealed to Job, one way or another. The Torah is filled with scientific knowledge, and each passage points us to G-d."

"So He had lots to do with science."

"Not only with science, many other fields of our lives as well, young man. Now, admit that I have won. You must let me know what's on your mind."

"Okay. It's the completion of the parashah. I counted fifty-four of them, but there should be only fifty-three. I'm one off. And that's not a minor problem."

"A discerning mind! You notice things, Ty, and I'm glad you do. In leap years, we join two passages together in order to make fifty-three. This is a leap year, so you counted fifty-four."

"Oh! Of course! I was so fixed on my project that I lost track of a very simple thing." I shook my head. Another close call, and I was just starting.

"But what do we do with the additional number? We simply add the last two numbers, the same as we do with the passages. We read them together. Now, if you'll excuse me, a rabbi's work is never done." When he reached the door, he added, "Especially on the Shabbat!"

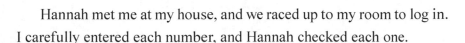

Hannah met me at my house, and we raced up to my room to log in. I carefully entered each number, and Hannah checked each one.

"Okay?" I asked.

"Okay. Hit it."

The screen went dark for a second or two. Then it came on.

*Correct.*

We shouted hurray and hugged each other. I think we both felt a little embarrassed.

"Now what, Ty?"

"How should I know? We'll find out though."

The screen answered us.

*Stage two.*

*Wait for instructions.*

"What?" I asked cyberspace.

"I feel like saying I can't wait, but that would be pointless—right, Ty?"

"Very pointless."

I tapped the side of the screen, just to be sure. But that was it. We had to wait … for something.

---

Every morning and every evening, Hannah and I would check to see if the cyber powers that be had sent us stage two or anything. Nothing but "Wait for instructions." But at least we weren't coaxed to send money, and that was a good sign. It ended my suspicions of being conned.

A year's work was on hold. There were doubts of course—from both of us. But we held fast. We were going to see this thing through. Fear of being hoodwinked was replaced by frustration at being delayed. There was occasional anger too. No one likes to wait.

---

Morah Sara was a grandmotherly figure at our school. She was short and stout with salt and pepper hair, and every sentence had at least one

Yiddish word, which she spoke with a thick Brooklyn accent. I came to know more Yiddish than my parents or my whole mishpachah. Oh, Morah Sara could be tough. You didn't run or shout in the hallway when she was around. That would mean detention. It was clear that she loved us though. Each one of us was practically a grandchild. At home, she probably told family lore of old New York and Poland. At school, she told us Bible stories and the meaning of holidays, like Tu BiShvat.

"Tu BiShvat is the day that each tree ages a year. In our religion, the age of a tree is important in determining whether you can eat the fruit from it. A tree's fruit cannot be eaten for the first three years, and the fourth year's fruit is only for G-d. After four years, it's ours to enjoy. That, children, is from our Talmud."

She noticed a classmate wasn't paying attention and ordered him to sit up.

"Everything has to be done in its time. Sometimes we have to wait a long time until things happen. The requirements for fruit trees remain to this day in essentially the same form they did in the Exile period. Fruit that's ripened on a three-year-old tree is *orlah*—forbidden to eat. Fruit ripening on or after Tu BiShvat of the tree's third year is permitted."

I was drifting off into numbers land. Where do they come from, and where do they go? And most important of all, where do they end? She noticed.

"Ty! Can you tell us what you understand from the story of Tu BiShvat?"

"Well, let me think. I guess it's this. Sometimes we have to wait a long time before the time comes to move forward."

"Excellent, Ty. We'll make a rebbe out of you yet!"

Everyone laughed, even Morah Sara. Hannah laughed so hard she had to be excused.

So I went about my day more calmly. I focused better on school but still found time to play with friends. San Diego is a fun place. Casual people, beautiful beaches. Of course I checked the website a few times a day. Still zippo. That's not Yiddish, by the way. Hannah told me over and over that stage two would arrive one day or one night. That helped. It really did.

Saturday evening, I came home from a birthday party for a neighbor who attended public school. I logged on and waited for the familiar message and was about to lecture the screen on Tu BiShvat in a thick Brooklyn accent. The screen blinked and stayed dark for a few moments.

"Dot's a little veird." I hoped it didn't mean I had been disconnected.

*Stage two. Starting with a riddle.*

"Wow!"

"What is it, Ty?" my father asked from down the hall.

"Just a game, Dad."

"Sounds like you reached a new level!"

"I have!"

*"G-d instructed Abraham in Genesis 12:1, "Now the Lord had said unto Abram, Get thee out of thy country, and from thy kindred, and from thy father's house, unto a land that I will shew thee."*

*"ויאמר יהוה אל אברם לך לך מארצך וממולדתך ומבית אביך אל הארץ אשר אראך"*

*There is a fact hidden in the text. You must summarize it in one word. What is it?*

"Dad, you got to see this! I need your help!"

"Can we do this tomorrow?" he said as he came in and peered over my shoulder.

"Look at this! I moved to stage two. I waited so long. I want to solve this riddle—tonight!"

"Ty, what kind of website is this? You know I warned you about the internet."

"This is the website I told you about that's helping me with my understanding of numbers."

"Oh, that one. Well, I'm not well versed in the Bible. You know my family was very secular. One of the rabbis can help you on Monday. Now, hit the hay. Oh, and good night. I hope you find your answers." He hugged me and left.

But how could I go to sleep? I reread the verse a dozen times but without any clue to the answer. I stared up at the ceiling till three or so and finally conked out. I woke up around eight and texted Hannah with the good news. We spent the day wracking our brains but came up with nothing.

"Ty, just ask Rabbi Shmuel on Monday."

Rabbi Shmuel lectured on the Ark of the Covenant and how it was used in battle against the Amalekites. I'd never thought of its military purpose before. I waited for the lecture to end and the class to file out. He was going over his notes for the next class when he saw me.

"Yes, Ty?"

"I have a question, please. It's about a specific verse."

"An interest in a specific verse, eh. Ty, we may make a rebbe out of you yet."

"So I'm told. May I read you the verse?"

"Please."

So I began to read the passage, and after a few words, Rabbi Shmuel said, "Genesis 12:1. Continue."

So I did until I came to the end.

"Ah, an important verse. Abraham is instructed to go to Canaan Land. I recall that we studied it in class recently, but then my memory is probably betraying me since all my students listen carefully."

"Undoubtedly true. My question is—"

"This is the beginning of the nation of Israel. Abraham was given clear instructions to go and begin a great nation. So what do you think happened here?"

"Well, I'm not sure how to add anything. Abraham is told to leave home, and his father's home, and go to the land. He'd be shown the way, I suppose … Wait! G-d instructing Abraham to leave his home for a place that He will show him. G-d will show him the way—north, south, east, and west. That's how we point the way. Geographic location? But this was thousands of years ago. There is only one explanation, Rabbi Shmuel!"

"Yes?" He raised his eyebrows and waited. I bet he was surprised by my reasoning and skeptical of my accuracy.

"They had geographic knowledge. So Abraham knew how to navigate."

"Well, this is not mentioned specifically."

"That's the only logical explanation. How would he know where to go without any navigation technology? It could be a simple compass but also like an advanced GPS system. No navigation technology is mentioned in the Bible, but it's understandable from the story content because otherwise he couldn't know. That's the hidden meaning in between the words. I got it! I got it!"

"Wait a minute, Ty. You might be jumping to conclusions. There's something else."

"But it's all clear to me! This is it! The answer to the riddle is one word!"

He looked bewildered by my boldness. I could see he wasn't convinced I was right.

"Scientific knowledge, Rabbi Shmuel. They had scientific knowledge and a sort of technology to use it back then."

"We know that there are many scientific facts in our Torah, but this passage … that's another thing."

But I didn't hear what it was. "I got to go. Thank you, Rabbi Shmuel. Thank you."

I got on the bus to go home, and Hanna and I ran upstairs to my room. I logged on, waited for the stage two prompt, and entered "Technology."

We didn't have to wait more than a second.

*Correct.*

*Stage three.*

*Where do the Gichon and Pishon Rivers lead?*

"What! They could have congratulated us at least! Bells and fireworks!" Hannah protested. "But no. Right on to the next round."

"They're no fun, but this isn't a game."

# Chapter 7

# Biblical Geography

"W e're stuck, Ty. I should say we're stuck *again*," Hannah whispered in social studies class. The teacher was talking about religious freedom in the colonies.

"I have a feeling the riddles will get harder from now on," I replied.

"Maybe we'll get better at solving them—or get better at knowing who to go to for help."

"Let's talk to Rabbi Shmuel after school."

"That's what I was thinking, Ty. Let's go to the mall after that. I don't want to become a computer nerd."

"All work and no play … all work and no play … all work and no play …"

"Stop, Ty! You're scaring me!"

"So how are my Torah experts doing today?" Our rabbi–code breaker was in high spirits that morning.

"We are well! Thank you for asking!" Hannah was laying it on.

"Yes, indeed," I added, not to be outdone.

The other students nodded.

"Let's begin with a question based on your homework. It should be easy. Any volunteers?"

Everyone looked down at their desks. The assignment had to do with geography. So did my most recent riddle. This could work out as long as someone knew the answer.

He walked up and down the aisles.

*Don't stop near me! Please don't stop near me!*

But he did. "Ty!"

*Oh no!*

"What are the names of the four rivers that went out of the Garden of Eden?"

*Oh yes!*

"That's easy! Their names are Pishon, Gichon, Hidekel, and Prat."

"Very good, Ty! You did your homework quite well. We may see you off to Yeshiva University one day!"

Several people laughed lightly. Seth's eyes rolled. Hannah covered her mouth and looked at me.

"I have a question about the rivers. May I please ask it?"

"What are teachers here for but to respond to bright minds with keen questions?"

"When we talk about the Garden of Eden, it seems like one place. Is this not so?"

"Yes. The word *garden* is singular."

"However, in the Torah, it indicates there was at least one other. I quote Genesis 2:8: 'And the Lord G-d planted a Garden eastward of Eden.'"

Rabbi Shmuel looked uneasy. I continued anyway.

"The Torah clearly mentions a 'Garden eastward of Eden.' This means that there was a garden named Eden and another garden eastward of it."

"I'd have to look into the various translations, Ty."

"A related question is about the four rivers. Today we know about the Prat and Hidekel Rivers, but what about the other two—the Pishon and Gichon? Where are they today?"

Our teacher thought long and hard, then finally nodded and smiled gently. "Yes, yes. Class, young Ty here is becoming a Torah scholar!"

There was some laughter, but a few looks of admiration came my way.

"And I am proud to say that this humble rabbi originally from New York has played a role."

"He's like that prodigal son!" Seth exclaimed.

"That's not in our Bible, Seth, but it may have relevance here," Rabbi Shmuel replied. He paced a bit, then sat down at his desk. "Indeed, we know the location of the two rivers, the Prat and Hidekel. They merge into one in modern-day Iraq. But young Ty's question—his very interesting question—is in regard to the other two. Scholarly opinion is divided. Some claim that they are the sources of the Nile—the Blue Nile and White Nile—and they are in the land of Cush. Others disagree and insist that the rivers are well to the east of Mesopotamia, perhaps in modern-day Iran or even India. I've spoken with esteemed scholars on the subject, and they've convinced me of the Blue and White Nile interpretation."

I jotted down as much of that as I could. Hannah did the same. We could look up what "esteemed" meant later.

"Thank you! You've been most helpful!"

"Glad to help, young man. And judging by the interest of Hannah, she too is interested in biblical geography. Why the interest, Hannah?"

"Sometimes I just get curious. I read things, and they make me look deeper."

"I see, I see."

I'm not sure he did.

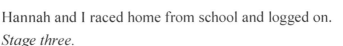

Hannah and I raced home from school and logged on.
*Stage three.*

*Where do the Gichon and Pishon Rivers lead?*

"So which is it, Ty, the Nile or those other places to the east?"

"Rabbi Shmuel's a smart man. He thinks the rivers form the Nile, so we should go with that. But where do the rivers go?"

"Egypt, of course!"

"Hit it!"

We held our breath while the screen went blank.

*Correct.*

*You have reached stage four.*

*The Torah talks about one person who was taken twice from the pit. Once this person was raised from a pit, and the second time, he was taken out of a pit. Who is this person?"*

"Joseph of Egypt!"

"Are you sure, Hannah?"

"Of course! Just hit it!"

I typed it in.

*Correct.*

"You're amazing, Hannah. Sounds like we have an Egyptian theme now."

*What exist in pits that don't have water?*

We looked at each other for ideas. I could only think of one thing.

"Sand."

*Incorrect.*

"Soil."

*Incorrect.*

"Rocks."

*Incorrect.*

We tried a few more but without success. We were stumped. We'd hit the wall. I felt like hitting my table in frustration but eventually decided to take a deep breath. I remembered a quote one of the teachers once told us. "Anyone can become angry. That is easy. But to be angry with the right person, to the right degree, at the right time, for the right purpose, and in the right way—this is not easy." It was by Aristotle. I had never understood that quote, but now I thought I did.

"Let's take a break, Ty. The mall awaits. Smoothies are on me."

But my mind never left the stage four riddle. Hannah and I walked down the mall to Smoothie Bazaar, got our drinks, and sat down near the escalator. Nothing came to us. We walked to the video arcade but didn't feel like going in. On the short walk home, I said we'd have to ask Rabbi Shmuel for help on Monday.

"Ty, didn't you hear? He's at meetings in Salt Lake City."

"Oy!"

"And the man knows Yiddish too!"

"Gewalt!"

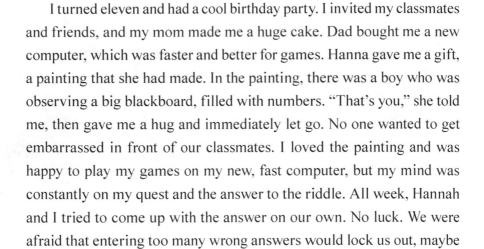

I turned eleven and had a cool birthday party. I invited my classmates and friends, and my mom made me a huge cake. Dad bought me a new computer, which was faster and better for games. Hanna gave me a gift, a painting that she had made. In the painting, there was a boy who was observing a big blackboard, filled with numbers. "That's you," she told me, then gave me a hug and immediately let go. No one wanted to get embarrassed in front of our classmates. I loved the painting and was happy to play my games on my new, fast computer, but my mind was constantly on my quest and the answer to the riddle. All week, Hannah and I tried to come up with the answer on our own. No luck. We were afraid that entering too many wrong answers would lock us out, maybe for good. At Wednesday lunch, Hannah came to my table, excitement in her eyes.

"Ty, I was in the office just now!"

"Lifting candy from Mrs. Rosen's desk?"

"Not today. Ty, this is important. I overheard Mrs. Rosen say that

Rabbi Mordechai would be here Friday! He'll be sitting in for Rabbi Shmuel."

"Great! We're in!"

The next two days passed slowly. Never before had we looked forward to Friday classes. Rabbi Mordechai entered the classroom in a black suit and matching hat. I think they're called fedoras. He placed it on the desk, opened his briefcase, and polished his glasses. It seemed like a ritual. He recognized me immediately and probably sensed I wanted to have a word with him. He spoke to us about the Exile period and the miraculous rescue from destruction in the holiday known as Purim. It led up to high praise for Queen Esther and faint praise for Persia, which he said was now known as Iran.

"Wonderful, class," he said. "Now pack up and enjoy the Shabbat with your families."

Students thanked him individually as they fled out into the hallway. Hannah and I stayed behind.

"Ty! Good to see you again. And who is your friend?"

"This is Hannah Stern. She and I are exploring the world of numbers together."

"A noble calling in our increasingly materialistic world. I sense a question coming."

"Correct as always! Our question is, what exists in pits that don't have water in them?"

He repeated the question softly as he stroked his long beard.

"Not an easy question. I presume this is somehow related to sacred texts and you're not just trying to stump me."

"We believe it is related to an important figure in the Torah. The answer isn't sand or soil or rocks."

I saw a flash of realization come across his face. He pointed a finger to the ceiling.

"The answer is scorpions and snakes. And the important figure is of course Joseph of Egypt."

"That's it!" Hannah all but shouted. "I think there's more to the answer though."

"Well, let's think together. When a person falls or is thrown into a pit in the Holy Land, he will be attacked by snakes and scorpions. He'll die."

"But Joseph didn't," I added cautiously.

"Very good, Ty. Joseph twice found himself in dangerous pits, yet he lived. Neither scorpion nor snake attacked him. He was protected."

"Because he was a very important person and destined for great things?" asked Hannah.

"Yes, he certainly was. Joseph was a very important person in Egyptian history and that of our people. He was the Pharaoh's adviser, the vizier. In Egyptian, this person is called *Imhotep*, and he is revered for great wisdom."

"Awesome! Thank you, Rabbi Mordechai!" we said together.

"You two young people warm my heart and fill me with hope. I encourage you to continue your investigations. You both have good heads on your shoulders. Alas, I must say goodbye for now. Shabbat starts at sunset, and I have to get to my friend's house. Shabbat Shalom!"

"Shabbat Shalom!"

Hannah and I scampered for the bus. I couldn't wait to get home.

Back in my room, I entered "scorpions and snakes."

*Correct.*

*Stage five.*

*Search about the pyramids. Who designed and built them?*

"Easy one!" we said, a little too soon.

"Joseph."

*Incorrect.*

"Pharaoh's Imhotep."

*Correct.*

*Who was the Imhotep?*

"Joseph."

*Correct. There is an inscription that states "seven meagre years and seven rich years." This refers to Pharaoh Djoser, who asked Imhotep to help him with the coming famine. Imhotep was Pharaoh Djoser's vizier and architect of the Step Pyramid Complex at Saqqara. The complex contains not only the Step Pyramid, which can be seen from afar, it also contains many buildings that adjoin the surrounding walls. Within the walls are open pits that are interconnected at the bottom and accessible from another pit that has stairs leading down to the bottom. These pits are similar to others found in other Egyptian cities from the same period. They were used to store grain.*

I typed, "Where is the location of these inscriptions?"

*Search for Pharaoh Djoser's inscriptions.*

We did a little research, and I typed in "Island of Sehel."

*Correct.*

I gave Hannah a high five. "Look at this! We have progressed so far today!"

"How many questions do you think there are?" Hannah asked.

I shrugged. The screen flickered with our next message.

*Stage six.*

*You have progressed to higher levels that require greater commitment. You must go to the Island of Sehel.*

"What?" we exclaimed together.

"How?" I asked.

# Chapter 8

# The Ancient Island

Hannah and I talked about how we would go anywhere. This was definitely a big step up in our adventure.

"But how do we handle this thing?" I mumbled. "How do we get to this place the website mentioned?"

"They're leaving that to us, Ty. It shows that they have great trust in us."

"What do I look for on the Island of Sehel?"

*Island of Sehel. Behind the rock, find a clue.*

"What clue?"

*Island of Sehel. Behind the rock, find a clue.*

*Search under the invisible, and you'll find it.*

"How the Sehel are we going to get there?" Hannah giggled.

"How the Sehel should I know. But I'll find a way. You stay here and help me as best you can. We can stay in touch."

"You think they have internet service in Egyptian pits?"

"We'll see."

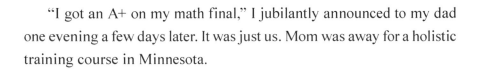

"I got an A+ on my math final," I jubilantly announced to my dad one evening a few days later. It was just us. Mom was away for a holistic training course in Minnesota.

"Great work, Ty. Proud of you."

My plan was working. "I will continue excelling in math—and all my subjects for that matter."

"Welcome news. We may make a mathematician out of you. Maybe even a chip designer."

"Yeah. A chip designer sounds great."

"I have a sneaking feeling you want some sort of incentive to keep up the good work and lofty ambitions."

It was working better than I thought. "There is actually something I had in mind. It's a bit out of the ordinary, but you and Mom are not ordinary parents. You're both a little ..."

"Screwy?"

"I was working up to unconventional."

"That we are, Ty, that we are. We want to keep you motivated, on the ball, ever searching for great things."

Way better than I thought.

"What is it? A new game? A microphone? Name it. It's yours."

"I want to go on a trip. A field trip."

"Ahh! A field trip. Now that's exciting. An outdoor activity. Although I'm a tekkie, I love the outdoor life and want you to appreciate it too. Where do you want to go? Sonora? Yosemite?"

"The Island of Sehel."

"Sehel? Where the Sehel is that? Pretty witty, eh?"

"Oh, that was very witty, Dad. Not sure how you do it."

"Is it near Santa Catalina?"

I shook my head.

"The Gulf of Mexico then."

"You're getting warmer but not much."

"I give up. Where is this enchanting getaway spot?"

"It's in Egypt."

"Egypt?"

"Yes. It's in North Africa."

"I know that, Ty! Remember, we used to live next to that country."

"Oh yeah."

"Egypt, eh. Is this about your numbers project?" He sat back and looked at me with interest.

"It's central to it. According to the instructions—the strict instructions—I have to do field research to continue. I've already passed several tests, and I can't give up now. You know, Dad, spring break is coming."

"Ty, there are many wonderful numbers associated with Sonora and Yosemite. For example, they're only a few hundred miles away and won't cost so many dollars to go there. Think of those numbers. I assure you I *have* to."

"What about the numbers in your frequent flyer account?"

"Well ..."

"Enough for two? You're finishing a chip project this week. It would be a dad-son outing but with numbers and archaeology instead of fishing and camping."

He didn't budge. Not that evening. But a seed had been planted, and with the right nurturing, it could grow. I played Middle Eastern music every evening. I thought about dressing up like Lawrence of Arabia and playing "Walk Like an Egyptian" really loud, but that might've been going too far. Dad often said that an empty feeling followed the completion of a semiconductor project, and a Middle Eastern adventure began to appeal to him. By the weekend, he'd come around. He'd explain to Mom somehow. She was off in western Massachusetts.

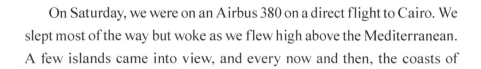

On Saturday, we were on an Airbus 380 on a direct flight to Cairo. We slept most of the way but woke as we flew high above the Mediterranean. A few islands came into view, and every now and then, the coasts of

Tunisia and Libya could be seen. The coast line was a magnificent view. Blueish-green water, white sand, and, in the background, modern, tall buildings were almost a complete contradiction to the desert view. I could see container ships that looked small from above, slowly making their way, probably to Cairo. I'd been reading up on history and knew there were Roman and Carthaginian ruins down there. Soon enough, the engines slowed, and we began a descent. I caught a glimpse of narrow, winding stretches of green with vast dry areas on each side.

"Dad! It's the Nile!"

"I never would've seen it if not for my inquisitive son."

"Aw, Dad!"

As we made our final approach, we saw the huge capital. It was an interesting mixture of old architecture, like mosques and public buildings, and modern office buildings and apartment blocks like those you'd see in the US. I looked for the pyramids, but Dad said they were quite a ways south.

A taxi took us to our hotel, where we stayed the night before taking a bus down to Sehel. I'd never had falafel and eggs for breakfast, and I might never again, but I was on an adventure, and so far, the food part was going well. Most people would love to spend a week in Cairo. My father certainly would have. But I was on a mission and couldn't wait for the bus that would pick us up at the hotel around ten in the morning.

The brakes squeaked and groaned as it came to a stop, and the engine made hammering sounds as it idled. I looked at my father as if to ask whether this was going to break down and leave us stranded. Dad said that diesel engines sounded like that. It wasn't anywhere near new, and dust already covered the metal exterior. The driver loaded our bags and those of a dozen others and launched into his tourist speech.

"My cherished guests, do not let the outward appearances of my bus deceive you. She is a very reliable vehicle, I assure you. I do welcome tips to make everything more accommodating. The good news, it has an air-conditioning system, which you'll learn to appreciate on the long, hot journey in front of us. I'll make a few toilet stops. If anyone needs to go urgently, let me know, and I'll make a special stop. I'll provide toilet paper and guidance to private spots off the highway. And please don't forget to tip!"

The seats were wood, and the aisles narrow. We found our places behind a large family and settled in for the ten-hour trip. The AC was working, but going up against the desert sun, it was no contest. Dad made sure to bring plenty of bottled water. We weren't accustomed to the local water and didn't want to make frequent stops to scamper out into the scorching hot sands.

Just after midnight, we arrived at the David hostel, where Dad had booked us while still in San Diego. I'm sure he preferred a big hotel, but options were few. A stout man with a gray mustache asked for payment in advance and showed us our room. We saw two bunk beds in the dim light, one of which was occupied by another guest who was sound asleep. Dad wasn't pleased with the accommodations, but it was late.

"I guess this is part of the adventure, Ty."

"That's how I look at it!"

I climbed onto the top bunk and looked out the window. So many stars! We were far from the light and smog of cities. I felt a little like Lawrence of Arabia and hoped to ride a camel. We swatted bugs every now and then.

In the morning, while Dad was out looking for a breakfast place, I spoke with our roommate. He was in his twenties, and his plaid shirt and LL Bean boots made him look outdoorsy. The moment he said hello, I knew he was American.

"I'm Sam Novotny from Sayre, Pennsylvania. I'm a graduate student at MIT taking time off to see a remote but amazing part of the world. What brings you here, young man?

"I'm Ty. Dad and I are interested in the local architecture and its relationship to mathematics."

"Fantastically weird, Ty. By the sheerest of chance, I'm entering the doctoral phase of my studies in, wait for it, mathematics. I'm specifically interested in encryption."

"A doctor of numbers!"

"Not yet. I'm working on it though. I have numbers running through my head even when I'm asleep."

"Me too!"

"So, Ty. How do you think architecture and numbers go together?"

"That's part of my research. All I can say now is that I think there are clues in ancient things. Clues about the end of numbers."

"They don't end!" said Sam.

"Well, even if that's true, there must be an explanation for it. Maybe they do, maybe they don't. Maybe no one's investigated the question thoroughly."

"That's far-out stuff, Ty!"

I didn't know how much I should say. Dad thought it best not to talk too much about my thing with numbers. But I was there with a doctor of numbers in the making, and I couldn't hold back.

"You know, in the Bible, there's scientific evidence about many things in life. Lots about mathematics. And there are signs of science in many biblical stories."

I think he was holding back a chuckle. He nodded, then said, "When G-d said, 'Let there be light,' he meant just that. He didn't want darkness, and that's it. Not sure he meant all the rest to happen. You know, the animals and plants and the tree and the snake."

"You forgot the apple! Well, I am going to a few archeological sites today and see what I can find."

"Look, I'm sorry. I don't mean to be insensitive, and I certainly don't want to discourage you. But trust me, numbers don't end." He touched my shoulder. "Maybe someday you'll study at MIT."

"And maybe I'll prove I'm right to all MIT!"

"That's the spirit, Ty! They're not as smart as they think!"

"Sam, do you do research on the internet?"

"Yes, of course. That's the way a lot of research is done now."

"There's one site I came across. It's leading me in the direction I want to go. It gives me questions, and when I answer them, I go on to the next stage. No, it doesn't ask for money or photos."

"Give me an idea of the sort of directions it's taking you."

"Okay. The Hebrew Joseph was the Imhotep who helped Pharaoh Djoser design and build the pyramids. He must have needed advanced scientific knowledge to do so, advanced mathematical knowledge. Tomorrow, I'm going to find more about that."

He paused in thoughts. I don't think he believed me, but he seemed to think I was on to something interesting. I love seeing that look on people's faces!

Dad came back. He'd found a breakfast place and, more importantly, the directions to the ruins. The three of us sat down for eggs and falafel and planned our trek to the island. Dad and Sam talked about algorithms in chip design and code making. Seems there's some overlap. Dad started to feel a little under the weather, perhaps from the food and water, so he said for Sam and me to go ahead and do some initial explorations.

"Go. Just don't go onto the island yet. We'll do that tomorrow when I'm better. Take a hat and a bottle of water. It's already hot out there. And stay away from mummy tombs. They can be cursed!" he said as he went back to the hostel.

"Cursed mummy tombs?" Sam said.

"My daddy has an odd sense of humor. So does my mummy."

"Yes, you're MIT material all right!"

Toward noon, the sun hit us with all its might, but I was undaunted. I lowered my cap down to my eyes, and off we went down narrow streets. Carts sold trinkets and rugs and food. Laundry was strung overhead from building to building. People shouted to one another. It wasn't in anger. Loud talk was just part of daily life. In a few places, we had to hold our noses and scurry. People went about their lives, ignoring the two American math scholars walking around their village that day.

Soon we came to a sandy road. It looked like years ago it had been a path for cattle and sheep, but a little motor vehicle traffic had widened it.

"I was down here yesterday. I'll show you something really cool!"

We climbed a steep hill, holding on to branches and roots to keep from sliding back. On the top, we could look out upon the Nile. The great river wound in parts and boasted of swift waters with whitecaps. Below us was the island I had learned of and become enchanted with thousands of miles away. As much as I wanted to race downhill and make my way to the ruins, I had to wait for the next day when my dad could come along.

"Do you know exactly where you're going?" Sam asked. "There are more than one archeological sites on this island."

"We're looking for the Famine Stela. It has an inscription in Egyptian hieroglyphs about a seven-year drought and famine during the reign of Pharaoh Djoser of the Third Dynasty. The Pharaoh asked earlier for advice from his adviser Imhotep, who I believe was Joseph of the Bible. Joseph advised to store food for a coming famine. I wrote a whole twenty pages about this place in my notebook.

"Ty, you are a most impressive young man. They should call you California Jones!"

"I love it! It's not necessary, but you can get me a cool hat and jacket if you like! I researched plenty before we left home. Pharaoh Djoser later asked Imhotep to build great monuments, and Imhotep found the scientific techniques to build the famous pyramids. Joseph was considered the smartest man of his time."

"We can see that in his amazing works! We're still debating how they were built."

"The Famine Stela was a granite rock carved into the rectangular shape of a commemorative stone. Sort of a like a big tombstone. The Ten Commandments were carved into stone tablets. The Famine Stela was in the same old tradition."

"Math or archeology or theology? Which is it going to be, Ty?"

"How should I know? I just turned eleven a few months ago!"

We continued eating, and Sam told us more. "The inscription in this site is written in hieroglyphs and contains forty-two columns. The top part shows three Egyptian gods: Khnum, Satis, and Anuket. Pharaoh Djoser faces them, carrying offerings in his outstretched hands. A broad crack, which was there at the time the Stela was made, goes through the middle. Some sections are damaged, so a few passages of the text are unreadable or missing."

"Why don't you come with me to the Famine Stela?" I said. "Who knows. You might be part of a great discovery!"

Sam smiled. "You know, I planned to go snorkeling a bit upriver before heading back to Cairo and catching a flight back home. But I'd rather see this Stela. It sounds more interesting than swimming around the sandy riverbed. Not sure about the great discovery, but who knows."

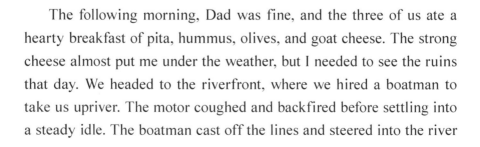

The following morning, Dad was fine, and the three of us ate a hearty breakfast of pita, hummus, olives, and goat cheese. The strong cheese almost put me under the weather, but I needed to see the ruins that day. We headed to the riverfront, where we hired a boatman to take us upriver. The motor coughed and backfired before settling into a steady idle. The boatman cast off the lines and steered into the river to begin the half-mile journey. We passed scores of fishermen with young children casting nets and shooing hungry birds. Once ashore, Dad studied a map, and we began the half-mile walk to the site.

I recognized it two hundred yards away! My heart raced! "C'mon, guys. Let's go!"

We ran the hundred yards or so to the great rock, careful not to stumble on the dry, rocky ground and startling a few tourists coming the other way. There it was, just ten yards away. Six feet tall with rows and columns of hieroglyphics. I was woozy. Not from the running or the sun though. Staring at the rock and the mysterious symbols made me feel drawn into it. Not drawn to it, drawn into it. I had to kneel down. I felt like I had drifted into another time, another world, another life. I was ...

"Ty? Ty! Are you okay?" My father knelt down in front of me.

"Oh ... yes, yes. I'm fine, Dad. Really."

My father and Sam helped me to my feet and steadied me. I looked again at the rock.

"What do all those things mean?"

Sam stared with boyish wonder at the rock. "You know, figuring them out is like code breaking. It's not a Russian naval signal. Nonetheless, cuneiform is a code—an ancient secret code. We studied it in grad school before moving on to other codes, like Ultra, which was a German code used during World War Two!"

He paused a little, using his finger to keep his place as he mumbled to himself.

"Do you know what it says?" my dad asked.

"Oh, I think so. The story is from the reign of Pharaoh Djoser. He was upset and worried, as his kingdom had been in the grip of drought and famine for seven years. Great hunger. Pharaoh Djoser asked his high priest, Imhotep, for help. Imhotep had dreams."

"This Imhotep was Joseph. He was a vizier to the king," I said, butting in. "Joseph was known for his dreams and his understanding of their meaning. This is about him."

Sam stood closer to the rock and ran his hand across a few lines. "There are details here saying that this Imhotep had a dream about the situation getting better and the Nile water nourishing the fields again."

"According to the Bible, Joseph's dreams came true. I guess we can call them predictions. And he made sense of Pharaoh's dreams too."

Sam stood back from the rock and sat down awkwardly. He never stopped staring at the cuneiform. Not for a half hour it seemed.

"It's like going to the bottom of the ocean and seeing a wreck with *Titanic* still visible on the stern."

*Behind the stone. That's what the website said. Look behind the stone.* I started walking away.

Dad asked where I was going, but I don't think I answered. I simply walked around to the back. The ground was rocky, and it was hard to keep my footing, but I had work to do. I wondered how many people had stolen small tokens from the great rock.

*Grave robbers ... grave robbers ...*

My eyes searched the rear area, looking in every crevice and underneath every small outcropping. I didn't know what I was looking for, but I was certain I'd recognize it the instant I came across it. My fingers reached into every small crevice no matter how small, hoping to feel something. I started to feel woozy again. This time it was the sun.

"Ty, we have to head back now. I think we've seen all there is to see."

"I'm afraid you're right, Dad. I thought there was more though. I thought I'd find a clue, a series of numbers, something to help me along." The thought of there being nothing made me want to sit down.

"It was a remarkable experience nonetheless," said Sam. "We saw a biblical story chiseled into ancient stone. Someone so long ago did amazing artisanal work to give us this. Someone with faith and hope for the future. We're lucky."

"We're blessed, Sam. We're blessed."

"Yes we are, Ty. Now let's—"

"Wait! There was more to the clue! 'Search the invisible, and you'll find it.' The clue is here, but I'm not looking in the right place, that's all." *What did it mean when it said it was behind the rock?*

"Ty, my inquisitive son, we can't very well search for the invisible. All we can do is look around the sides and top."

"What about beneath it?" Sam murmured as he shrugged his shoulders.

"That must be it! There's something under the rock. That's what the clue was trying to tell me!"

"We can't lift the rock, young man!"

"We can sure dig into the dirt around it, guys! Let's start here in the back!"

We made sure no one was around. After all, the authorities wouldn't want American tourists digging underneath an ancient national treasure. Then we each started digging a few yards from one another, using rocks, roots, and sometimes bare hands. We were in a frenzy. I came across an area beneath the great stone that was smooth and arch shaped. It had been carved by human hands. I dug deeper and deeper. At times, I felt foolish as I jabbed Egyptian soil with root and rock, and at times I thought I was on to something, only to have it be a boring rock or clump of dirt. But I kept at it. I dug deeper beneath the arch, pushing away centuries of sandy, clumpy dirt. It was rough, like the rocks were sharp, and the dirt was so dry it was like sandpaper. Until something felt different. What was it? I peered in, trying to see, but it was hard to make out. I pushed more dirt aside with my fingers. It was smooth. I was on the edge of a great discovery or an abyss.

"I found something!"

Dad and Sam scurried over and saw a smooth surface, then began digging on either side.

"Hieroglyphs!" shouted Sam.

"I see them too!" Dad added.

"I knew it! I knew it!"

After half an hour, we'd uncovered a tablet about the size of a large TV. That was the first thing that came to me. Sam took off his khaki shirt and slapped it against the tablet to get thousands of years of dirt off the face. We stood in awe.

"Well, Sam," Dad finally blurted out, "what does it say?"

"Whatever it is, it isn't on the internet!" I chimed in.

Sam studied the tablet, barely lit up by indirect sunlight.

"This is amazing. This part describes something technical—a formula. It's a mathematical equation! Not sure I understand all of this. It's clearly some sort of instructions to execute a calculation. It's an algorithm to calculate something. No … it can't be."

"What?" I all but shouted.

"I think this concerns the most famous constant in mathematics—pi."

"You were right when you said it can't be," Dad said. "The Egyptians knew nothing about pi. That was something the Greeks gave us many centuries later."

Sam wiped his forehead with his dirty shirt and caught his breath.

"The stone clearly describes a series of operations leading to 3.1415. It then gives a series of operations to continue the calculation. Here are the instructions. I have no understanding how it works."

He took a photo with his phone and zoomed in on the image.

"Every line describes a different operation with integers and floating point numbers. At the end of each operation, the results are to be added onto the previous one. Let me write it out on my notepad."

He handed the scribbling to Dad.

"I'll be damned. No doubt about it. It's definitely an algorithm—a flow."

"I don't understand it clearly, but I know how to check it out. We have a Cray DEROS supercomputer back at MIT. We'll feed these instructions to the computer and run it sequentially over a long period of time. I think we can extract the algorithm. But there's more written here. I think it says, 'Take me to the land of Canaan to be buried there. When you do, a miracle will take place.'"

"What do you make of that, Ty?" my father asked.

"This proves beyond any doubt that this guy Imhotep was Joseph. It is said in the Torah that when Moses led the Israelites from Egypt, they took Joseph's bones to be buried in the Promised Land. That was Joseph's request, and Moses saw that it was done. When he left Egypt, he ordered the Israelites to take Joseph's bones with them to the Holy Land so Joseph would be buried in the land of Israel."

"You continue to amaze me, Ty!" said Sam.

"See? I'm not just a little kid lured into an internet scam!" I could never have done this without them.

Sam patted me on the back, and Dad tousled my hair.

"I won't doubt you anymore, Ty. I'll write a letter of recommendation for you when you apply to MIT."

"You mean when I'm twelve!"

"My son may be there sooner! A lot sooner!"

"I have one more observation, gentlemen." Eyes turned to me. "I think we need to get dinner!"

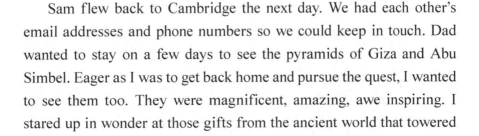

Sam flew back to Cambridge the next day. We had each other's email addresses and phone numbers so we could keep in touch. Dad wanted to stay on a few days to see the pyramids of Giza and Abu Simbel. Eager as I was to get back home and pursue the quest, I wanted to see them too. They were magnificent, amazing, awe inspiring. I stared up in wonder at those gifts from the ancient world that towered above us and told us they'd been there forever and would stay there forever. An eleven-year-old boy from San Diego was given a look at time and history.

When we got back home, I sat in front of my computer late one night. Nothing I entered into the computer from our trip got anywhere. I tried to enter "pi," and then I tried "3.14." Only the same blunt reply came:

*Island of Sehel. Behind the rock, find a clue.*

I sat back, frustrated. We did find the clue. But everything was wrong. Time to call Rabbi 911.

---

It was still spring break, and Passover was coming soon, but I knew he'd be at school, preparing lectures, meeting with other teachers and parents. You know, school stuff that goes on behind the scenes. He saw me the instant I reached the doorway to his class. No chance to knock or clear my throat to signal my presence.

"Ty! I presume you're not here to help me clean up the classroom. You must have a question."

"Yes, Rabbi Shmuel. As a matter of fact, I am looking for help. Can I ask you something?"

He looked at me sternly.

"I mean, may I *please* ask you something?"

"Much better. Now, as your generation says, bring it on."

"Well, you see, I went away on a long trip last week. Dad and I went to Egypt."

"Egypt! Our people left that land long ago! Haven't you heard of Passover? But I jest. Why Egypt and not a theme park? Ah, wait. It has something to do with the numbers quest. That's impressive, young man. Truly impressive."

"I visited the Island of Sehel. It's a small island on the Nile where there's a stone with hieroglyphics. They describe a very wise man, Imhotep, who was the Pharaoh's vizier."

"Imhotep. Yes, yes. Please continue."

"This Imhotep was said to be the wisest of men. Does this remind us of someone who was mentioned in the Torah?"

He nodded and motioned for me to continue.

"This wise man was an expert in dream interpretation and prophecy. His dreams came true, and he answered the Pharaoh's questions about his own dreams. One of them was about seven years of famine and seven years of wealth."

I paused, hoping for words but got only more nodding.

"I believe this Imhotep was our Joseph guy."

The room became still. I'd done it. I'd crossed the line. Our religious figures insisted our knowledge come solely from the Torah and not from schoolboy hunches. I was going to be struck by lightning or turned into a pillar of salt. I knew it. I decided to blurt out more before the end came.

"But there's more. An inscription mentions Imhotep's request. It's a very interesting request—for an Egyptian anyway."

"Go ahead, Ty. What was his request?"

"He wanted, upon his death that is, for his bones to be taken away. He wanted his remains to be buried in Canaan—the land of Israel."

My voice fell off into a whisper.

He nodded more. His face took on a look of wonder. A soft smile formed.

"And as every student here knows, that's what Moses did with Joseph's body. That's an important part of Exodus."

"Exactly! Can you believe it? It really happened."

"Did you have any doubt?"

"No, but still. It's one thing to read Exodus as a religious story and another to see proof, in stone, that it happened that way. Also, it shows that Joseph was truly the Pharaoh's wise man."

"Yes, it does. Yes, yes. It certainly does." He looked at me keenly. "I sense you have more to say."

"One more thing. According to other sources. Imhotep, our Joseph, was asked by Pharaoh to build extraordinary structures. That led to the pyramids, I think. He was a genius."

"A very wise man. An amazing engineer, we might say."

"Yes! He had to have incredible scientific knowledge to build the pyramids. Mathematics, physics, geometry …"

"Indeed." He waited.

"I found another piece of information. It's a riddle."

My teacher leaned forward.

"And you need my help with it? I'm very surprised about your passion to go that deep with this, Ty. Pleasantly surprised. I never imagined you would do your own research, outside of classwork, on our sacred texts. Frankly, you always seemed interested in other things while I lectured. In all candor, young man, you looked … well, bored."

"Well, to be honest, I was."

His eyes bulged. I instantly regretted those words, so I quickly continued. "Solving this riddle is important for my investigation. This is what I saw in stone: 'Take me to the land of Canaan to be buried there. When you do, a miracle will take place.' Joseph states that only if his bones are taken to the land of Israel will a miracle happen. What is that miracle?"

Rabbi Shmuel stood and paced about the classroom. I could see the gears were turning in his head. Sweat formed on his brow and bald spot. His footfalls clicked and echoed in the emptiness.

"Yes, yes. Most interesting. Most extraordinary. Clearly Joseph asks that his bones be taken to the Promised Land. Was this a prophetic dream? Did he foresee Exodus, though it happened many years after his death?"

"It seems to me that he did, Rabbi."

"I agree, I agree. You know the history that follows from Exodus? You undoubtedly have listened to the events from a learned teacher. Or were you too bored?"

"The ten plagues?" I asked.

"Plagues aren't what we're looking for. We're looking for miracles. The Israelites leave Egypt on their way to the land of Israel and ..."

"And they walk in the desert for forty years."

"How did they reach the desert?"

"They crossed the Red Sea. That's it! The parting of the Red Sea!"

"'Then Moses stretched out his hand over the sea, and all that night the LORD drove the sea back with a strong east wind and turned it into dry land. The waters were divided. וַיֵּט מֹשֶׁה אֶת יָדוֹ עַל הַיָּם וַיּוֹלֶךְ ה' אֶת הַיָּם בְּרוּחַ קָדִים עַזָּה כָּל הַלַּיְלָה וַיָּשֶׂם אֶת הַיָּם לֶחָרָבָה וַיִּבָּקְעוּ הַמָּיִם.'"

"That's the miracle," I whispered. "That's what I'm searching for."

I didn't mention that I was thinking of Charlton Heston and those cool special effects that they make in movies.

"See? Rabbis aren't always boring. But I don't understand why you are traveling the world, scratching around the desert, and yearning to solve riddles—all with such passion? Why, young man? Is this still about those numbers you asked me about a few weeks ago?"

"I can't say, Rabbi, But I can say thank you and see you in class soon!"

"Goodbye till then. Oh, Ty, one more thing."

"Yes?"

"Were you thinking of Charlton Heston a minute ago?"

"Well ..."

"I love this movie!"

---

We sat in front of my laptop.

"Ready, Hannah?"

"Ready!"

*Stage six. Island of Sehel. Behind the rock, find a clue.*

"The Red Sea crossing."

The screen went black for several moments, several painful moments.

"Ty, I think we—"

*Correct.*

"Awesome!" we both exclaimed.

We sat back and waited.

# Chapter 9
# The Holy Land

A response came less than a minute later.

*Stage seven. Find a location in the Holy Land and go there at the next day of the miracle, exactly noon time. Get the next destination you need to go to.*

I typed, "How do I find the location?"

*The Joseph Code.*

"What's that?" Hannah asked in annoyance and frustration.

"Search me. I'll have to ask, but I sense this guy's a little cranky." I typed, "What is the Joseph Code?"

*You found the Joseph Code on the Island of Sehel.*

"Hmmm. This is probably some type of mathematical information that Sam found. We entered the numbers, but they were wrong the first time. I remember my dad told me about geographical coordinates once. I didn't understand much, but I think it must be it."

"Is that the guy at MIT?" Hannah asked.

"It is. Now let's ask out cyberfriend what this place is." I started typing and pressed enter.

*A location in the Holy Land.*

"What city?"

*A location in the Holy Land.*

"He's definitely a little cranky, Ty! Ask in a different way."

I typed, "Any special instructions?"

*Find the location in the Holy Land and go there on the next day of the miracle, exactly at noon. You must not miss this day.*

We lay on the floor and tried to figure out what it meant.

"I think you need to talk to a higher power again, Ty."

"He'd laugh out loud if he heard you say that!"

---

"Again, Ty? You're here before me again? Twice during the last week. I'm not sure if I should be impressed, moved, or worried."

"Sorry to bother you so soon, Rabbi Shmuel, but I need your help with a very important question."

"And it can't wait until next week? For crying out loud, we have Passover next week, and I'm busy with preparations at the synagogue and my humble dwelling. You think my lectures and *derasha* just flow naturally from my learned mind and tongue? I am a repository of learning though—on the Torah and many other matters."

"It seems that way! But my question is urgent, and your knowledge is so awesome!"

He looked at me and sighed. "I've been wondering if you are going to be a rabbi or a mathematician. Last week, I added archaeologist to the possibilities. Now am I to add salesman? Maybe conman! Come tomorrow, morning to Shul. After the morning prayer, I'll give you five minutes—no more."

"Thank you!"

I went home and looked up "repository." It's a place where a lot of information is stored. Man, is he ever a repository! I hope to be one someday.

---

The next morning, I watched Rabbi Shmuel prepare for the davening. There were only a few people in the Shul, barely enough to create a minyan. That's the necessary number of congregants to conduct morning prayers. Many of them looked at me, wondering what I was doing there so early in the day during spring break. They knew their own children and grandchildren were at home or at the beach.

As I watched him pray, I felt admiration for him. I mean, I always did, but now I felt more. There was the learning of course but also the emotion he placed in his work. He wasn't mumbling stale words. He was so careful, and his movements were precise, not careless. I could see that each word had deep meaning to him and he wanted each word to have meaning for his people. He was a learned man, a wise man, a holy man.

He completed his prayer and saw me. He allowed a brief smile to come across his otherwise solemn face and motioned for me to follow him to the back area where he prepared for services.

"It's an honor to be in this part of Shul."

"You are a special student, Ty. I presume you don't drink coffee, but please help yourself to hamantasch. Although they are intended for Purim, she bakes them all year long. They're quite good. Mr. Rosenblatt's bakery sent them. But let's get down to the matter troubling you this morning."

"The last time I sought your counsel, we discussed the miracle of parting the Red Sea."

"Indeed, we did."

"Do we know the date of this great event?"

"Another interesting question. I'm becoming accustomed to being challenged by you. The event is of course related to our Passover observation, which is at hand, I might add. The seventh day of Passover is judged the day of the Red Sea miracle. Scholars agree on that."

"I see. Passover took place before our people left Egypt. Why was the miracle of the Red Sea already set by the religious leader?"

"Yes, yes. Another question from a keen mind. It's said that this special day, the last day of the holiday, is like a unique Shabbat and has to be celebrated with special attention. It is also customary to sing the song of the sea. It will happen soon enough."

"Oh yes! Passover is at hand." Something came to me. "Thanks, Rabbi Shmuel. I mean, thanks again!"

"I hope to see your acute mind at work in class in coming weeks!"

"Me too!"

*Acute? I think that's something good.*

---

I emailed Sam at MIT and asked to speak with him. His reply was fast and welcome. I called him twenty minutes later.

"Sam, I'm in a rush. I believe the numbers we found at the rock can be understood as coordinates. Map coordinates. Somewhere in the Middle East, possibly Israel."

"Ty, the numbers are from a rock chiseled on thousands of years ago. No one knew about GPS back then."

"Trust me. I know it sounds weird. I know it sounds impossible. But I think I'm right about it. Some things you just know are true."

"We call them hypotheses."

"I'll take your word for it. I need those numbers decoded into coordinates. I need it soon too."

"For your dissertation!"

"Maybe someday. For now, I need the coordinates. Sam, I beg of you."

"The Cray is booked solid by the NSA and NOAA, but I think I can sneak on to it late tonight."

"You mean hack into it."

"Such an unpleasant word, Ty. I'll get on it. Trust me."

"I trust you. Believe me. I have to know the location soon so I can fly over there and know where I'm going."

"I'm on it. I'll get back to you when I have something."

———————————❋———————————

I texted him the next morning.

"I'm on the case."

I texted him that evening, but he didn't reply. The next morning, I got this: "I'm on the case. Go ride some tasty waves!"

I was annoying him. At least that was my hypothesis. On the fourth day, he called me at about seven in the morning my time.

"I don't quite know how you knew it, but you were correct. The Cray worked on it for hours. The algorithm we found on the island is very obscure, but after numerous calculations that could have probably conducted much simpler—"

"Sam, you may be forgetting that it was thousands of years ago. We also may not exactly understand it as the original creator meant."

"Right. I figured that. Anyway, the code is an algorithm that eventually produced a set of numbers. And after close observation, this set provides coordinates. You were correct, my young friend. You were correct."

"My hypothesis panned out! My PhD is on the way! Where is the location?"

"So that you'll have the fun of the discovery, I'll send you the coordinates via email right now. Enter them into Google Maps and see for yourself. It's amazing! Unbelievable! I'm hitting send right … now."

I copied exactly what I saw in the text, 31.771959° N, 35.217018° E, into Google.

The Western Wall, Jerusalem, Israel.

I had to sit down.

*How am I going to get there?*

---

Again?" My father looked at me in utter disbelief. "No way!"

"But, Dad, this is extremely important to me. You know how long I've been working on this quest. If I'm not there at an exact time and day, I'll miss the opportunity—forever."

"Ty, I've supported you all this time. You know that. I even took you to Egypt. Do you even know how much that trip cost me?"

"You had a lot of frequent flyer points."

"Never mind that. And now you want to go to Israel? These trips are very expensive, you know. Hotels, flights. And I'd have to take time off work again. As much as I really want to help, I can't. How about we plan a trip for the summer? It'll give me time to regroup financially."

I stayed silent, unless you count the look of disappointment on my face as words. The room stayed silent. After a few minutes, I felt the tide turn.

"Ty, Ty, oh, Ty. I'll see what I can do."

I went to my room and looked at the laptop screen.

*Stage seven. Find the location in the Holy Land and go there at the next day of the miracle, exactly noon time.*

"There's only one problem," I said to the screen. "I don't know if I can get there."

# Chapter 10
# A Miraculous Trip

T wo days later, I sat forlornly at the breakfast table with Dad. Mom was at another holistic seminar in the mountains near Taos, New Mexico. I was chewing granola she brought back from Oregon as my mind wandered about the Middle East. Dad's phone beeped. He looked at the text message.

"It's a text from your school, Ty. It said for you to call this number. I'll forward it to you. I'm off to the salt mines." I'm not sure, but I thought he was smiling.

I called the number, and a familiar voice answered. I was expecting it—or at least hoping for it.

"Ty! Rabbi Shmuel here."

"Oh, how nice to hear from you."

"I have an offer for you. Something I think you'll like. Every year, we send a group of seniors for a field trip to Israel. We had one fellow who had to drop out. An untimely bout of appendicitis. He's doing fine, but travel for now is out of the question. I thought you might be interested. The school is paying for everything."

I was speechless. That doesn't happen to me much.

"Ty? Ty? Are you interested? Argh! I think the call dropped."

"The call didn't drop! I'm here! I'm right here! I'd love to go! Thank you! Thank you ever so much!"

"We will be visiting the Western Wall on the Seventh Day of Passover. Does that pique your interest any more?"

I was dumbfounded. I felt woozy, just as I did at the great stone on Sehel. It was all I could do to pull myself together to text Dad with the news.

---

So in a matter of days, I was off to Israel. This time I was accompanied by seventeen seniors. Rabbi Shmuel wasn't coming this year. Apparently, a family matter came up, and Rabbi Motti took his place. I didn't know him well. On first appearances, he seemed sterner and more demanding than the religion teacher I'd known so many years.

We toured the usual sites, such as the tombs of great medieval scholars. Tiberias has a wonderful view of the Sea of Galilee. The Talmud is said to have been written there. Not far from Tiberias is the Kfar Baram Synagogue, which was built about seventeen centuries ago. They were taking pictures and jotting down notes. They had to write papers when they got home.

I wasn't the only one who was eager to get to Jerusalem. After all, it's the capital of Israel and home to many sacred sites of Judaism, Christianity, and Islam. Everyone was excited about seeing the Western Wall but not for the reason that was bursting inside me. As much as I wanted share what I knew, I didn't want to cause anyone to wonder about me or distract me.

Every step I took, I thought of my directions.

*Stage seven. Find the location in the Holy Land and go there at the next day of the miracle, exactly noon time.*

I probably muttered those words in my sleep.

---

On the appointed day, according to the tour and my special instructions, we would board a bus to take us to the heart of Jerusalem and the heart of Judaism. In the distance, I could see the Temple Mount and the shiny golden Dome of the Rock. We were heading for the base of the sacred mount, the site of the Western Wall, the holiest site in our faith. It was, as every boy and girl knows, the remnant of the wall that surrounded the Temple that was destroyed almost two thousand years ago. There it stood, not a hundred yards away from me, the sand-colored rising against deep blue sky. It was huge, at least sixty feet high. It made me feel small.

Our group headed immediately for it and began to pray. Some touched the ancient stones and placed lovingly folded notes in crevices for friends and family members back home. I had a special purpose and an exact time, but I didn't know what to expect. How could I? I prayed with the others, placed a note for my parents, and looked at the time on my phone.

I remembered what it said. *Stage seven. Find the location in the Holy Land and go there at the next day of the miracle, exactly noon time.*

I touched the wall, expecting some great experience. There was nothing special, at least not yet, but noon was still a minute away. Moments later, I looked upward. A note, not the one I placed for my folks, fell from the crevice it had been tucked into by someone at one point.

It was lifted up by a breeze and fluttered higher, almost reaching the top of the wall before wafting downward, darting left and right, swirling in circles, then finding a home on my shoe. Strangely, the note hadn't been folded like the others. Should I read it? It was somebody's personal message, but it had made a special journey to me. The message was handwritten in pencil and was so faded that it must have been in the wall for a long time. Naturally, I read it. How could I not?

*Six days in a week, six days in the world's creation, six world's times.*

*We live in the sixth thousand years' time. Extinction and rejuvenation, in which biblical chapter? Go there. Find a clue.*

I looked around. Was anyone missing this note? Where did this come from? Which crevice? Who wrote it? When? No one seemed to be looking for a note. Everyone was focused on prayers. There was no way to know who had written it. I read it again, hoping its meaning would come to me. It didn't. The note was mine now. I placed it in my shirt pocket. It had been sent to me.

"So are you going to pray here or not, young man?"

It was Rabbi Motti. He was smiling, but I sensed he thought I wasn't as prayerful and solemn as I should be. I looked around, and all my classes were praying and nodding.

"After all, it's not every day you're at the Western Wall. Look at it! It goes back to the time of Herod and before! One day, young man, one day! And it will be magnificent! The whole world will marvel and come to their senses!"

I looked up again at the mighty wall, hoping again for a sign of the note's origin.

"Yes, of course I'll pray. This is an amazing moment for me—and for all of us here."

"And let's use the tefillin. It's a great mitzvah to use them near this sacred place. You may use this set. It was my uncle's." He handed me a small leather box with leather straps.

I donned the set and silently recited prayers—I davened. Although I was not yet of age, I knew of the powers of the tefillin and to some extent believed in them. Rabbi Motti glanced over to me before moving over to other students. I completed my prayer and looked up once more at the wall. I felt something, a sense of sacredness. I felt a little woozy and had to turn my head away from the Middle Eastern sun. My hand went to my chest and felt the paper in my pocket. I felt calm and safe.

"This is a special moment, isn't it, Ty? Some people have their lives changed here. I've seen it. More than once, I've seen it."

He looked at me intently. He sensed the extraordinary experience I was having.

"I have a question, Rabbi Motti."

"That is why I'm here."

"Can you please keep it a secret?"

"If that's your wish, then yes. Of course."

"Six days in a week, six days in the world's creation, six worlds' times. We live in the sixth thousand years' time. Extinction and rejuvenation. In which biblical chapter is this?"

He looked into my being several moments before speaking. "Interesting, interesting." He turned to the wall and prayed quietly. "A very interesting question, Ty. I am not going to ask you how you came by it. One thing I can tell you, it's a question that needs a formidable understanding of the Torah to answer. Are you aware of that?"

"Yes."

"I'll point you in the right direction, and we'll see if you remember your Torah lessons. The world was created in six days, and according to the Hebrew calendar, we are living in the sixth period, the year 5782. All this points to the number six—the Hebrew letter *VAV*, the sixth number. Is there a chapter six that comes to mind?"

"I don't know of one."

"Let's think further then. We're getting another clue here: extinction and rejuvenation. In what biblical event was there extinction and rejuvenation? The entire world was wiped out and then restored. Any idea, Ty?"

My mind called up so many teachings and readings and stories. Too many, really. The sun was strong, and the sounds of thousands of davening vibrated inside me.

"Sodom and Gomorrah?"

"They were only two cities. Think harder."

"Oh, I know! Noah's Ark and the Great Flood!"

"Very good, Ty!" He was pleased by my answer.

"And it fits perfectly with the question at hand since the story of Noah is given to us in Genesis—"

"In Genesis 6! Of course!"

He clasped my shoulder and once again looked deep into my being. "May I ask why you seek this information? It will be between us only."

"I need to go there," I said without thinking or understanding. I immediately regretted it. But it was too late. Rabbi Motti cocked his head to one side, his fedora staying in place somehow.

"Go where? This is important to you and perhaps to others as well. I sense it."

"Where Noah's Ark came to rest once the waters of the Great Flood went away."

His head came back to being centered, and he nodded. His eyes bore into me. "But, Ty. That's far way. Our finest scholars say it came to rest in the mountains of Turkey. Others say Tibet. I am convinced it came to rest on Mount Ararat in Turkey."

"Do you believe it's still there, Rabbi Motti?"

"Yes, of course."

"Then I must go there. Somehow I must go there."

"Maybe someday. Someday when you're a young man." With that, he returned to the other students. "Young men, you see that our faith is unique and alive!"

My shoulders sagged. How long would that be? I prayed once again.

---

I waited until we got back to San Diego before logging on
"Noah's Ark."
*Stage eight. Your next destination?*

I didn't hesitate. "Mount Ararat."

*Correct.*

*Find the exact location using the information that you received in the Holy Land. Go there and retrieve a key.*

You've got to be kidding me. I was pretty sure Sam wasn't going to help me much further. And I didn't know how much more I could solve without people really thinking I was strange. But I thought back to the wall. I thought about miracles, both the ones I saw and the ones I studied. "What is the key?"

*A code.*

"What code?"

*A code.*

Oh, man. Not again. Well, vacation's over. Back to work.

---

Rabbi Shmuel dismissed the class and sat at his desk. I stayed in my seat. He opened a brown bag. "Ahh. Corned beef on rye!"

I cleared my throat.

"Ty, my inquisitive though unruly student! Did you forget to bring lunch and hope your generous teacher would share his? Oh, but I jest— and you know it."

"Yes, I appreciate your humor almost as much as I appreciate your knowledge and wisdom."

"Oy! What is it now then? If you don't mind, I'll take a bite of my sandwich every now and then."

I walked up to his desk and placed the note from the Western Wall before him.

"I prefer not to put on my reading glasses at the moment. Perhaps you can read it to me while I enjoy my lunch to the extent possible."

"Six days in a week, six days in the world's creation, six worlds' times. We live in the sixth thousand years' time. Extinction and rejuvenation. In which biblical chapter is this?"

"Where the … where did you get this?"

"It fell from the sky while I was at the Western Wall."

He paused. I believe he was envisioning the message fluttering down to me and perhaps recalling amazing moments he had there. "Ah, the wall. Remarkable, most remarkable." He studied the paper, moving it farther into the light. "The paper is quite old. Hmm … Noah's Ark, eh?"

"Yes, Mount Ararat. But exactly where? It's a large mountain with many paths to climb up it. I need more information."

"You need a code." His voice fell to a solemn whisper. "It can be processed by a computer—a very powerful one. Perhaps you have access to such a machine?"

I didn't question how he knew about the code. "Yes, I do."

"I believe you need information on the Hebrew calendar. It can help you. I'll point you in the right direction, but you'll have to find the rest. The Hebrew year is 5782, and its length is 384 days. It started in *ALEF* in Tishrei, which is September 7, 2021, and will end at *CAF TET* in Elul, which is September 25, 2022. This year is of the Shmita type, and therefore its length is 384 days. It's the year of 1953 since the Great Temple was destroyed."

I scribbled down his words. The way he spoke told me, I'd get no repeat. He arched an eyebrow and returned to his sandwich. The help was over. He looked over to the door, and I took the hint. I thanked him, but he was busy with lunch. His eyes lit up when he found a pickle in the bag.

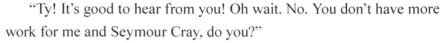

"Ty! It's good to hear from you! Oh wait. No. You don't have more work for me and Seymour Cray, do you?"

"As a matter of fact, Sam …"

"I'm working on my dissertation now."

"Well, I might be working on one now too. It's becoming longer and more complicated by the day."

"That sounds like a dissertation. I'm not good with religious material. I'm all numbers and science."

"That's my dissertation someday! Now back to the matter at hand. I believe—"

"You mean, Ty, that your hypothesis is."

"That's what I meant! My hypothesis is that there are other GPS coordinates in the material we found on the stone."

"Okay, okay. It won't be so hard looking for GPS data a second time."

"Great! But I have a question."

"A brief one I hope."

"Who's Seymour Cray?"

"He's the father of supercomputers, Ty. Now, it's back to work for both of us."

---

The following day, he called.

"Good news and bad news for you, buddy. First, the good news. I found it. I found another GPS code. The same algorithm that we used before but with slight modifications."

"I'm bracing for the bad news."

"The coordinates are in Turkey."

"Let me guess, Sam. In a mountainous part of Turkey."

"How the … You're smarter than you let on."

"So are you."

"Having that trait is essential to working on a dissertation. I should say it's essential to *completing* a dissertation."

# Chapter 11
# The Mountains of Turkey

"**N**o! No! No!"

"But, Dad ..."

"I said no, and I meant it. In fact, I said it three times. You're just back from Israel and recently back from Egypt, and now it's Turkey you need to travel to? Not just Turkey—it's the *mountains* of Turkey. Not Istanbul, not Ankara. You need to go to a remote mountain. Who knows how far it is from Istanbul? Oh, I suppose my son has looked into it."

"He has, Dad—and very thoroughly too. It's only eight hundred miles."

How I said the word *only* without choking I'll never know. From the look on Dad's face, he had the same thought.

"I received a very important message at the Western Wall. It tells me I must go to Mount Ararat."

"Why?"

"I believe Noah's Ark is there."

"There are certainly people—intelligent people—who are convinced the ark is there. But so many years have passed. So many expeditions have gone up the slopes. No one's found anything."

"I've read all that. I have something no one else has had. I have the exact coordinates of where the ark is resting."

"And you got them from a note that came your way at the Western Wall."

"There's a lot more to it, but yes. The message reached me there. It was an amazing, supernatural experience. Here's the message."

He looked at the paper, front and back. My hope that the skepticism on his face would vanish faded to nothing.

"Ty, this has become an obsession, and obsessions aren't healthful. In fact, they can be dangerous. I cannot take more time off from work to hike up a mountain *only* eight hundred miles from Istanbul. You have school to think of. And your education is very dear to me. I don't want to see it delayed or diverted or perverted by an obsession."

Silence fell. I had nothing more to say. Even if I did, it wouldn't have changed anything. He handed the paper back to me, and I put it in my pocket. Something would come my way. I couldn't quite know. There was something that wanted me to go on.

Two days later, Sam called. "Unless I miss my guess, you want very much to go to Turkey, but your father isn't on board with the idea."

"Your hypothesis is correct. I tried hard, but Dad did not budge. And I was out of ideas."

"So clever! Anyway, I've been crunching the data from the Sehel stone, and I'm finding more and more things. I've shown it to the department chair, and she showed it to the dean."

"So?"

"They're interested. Really interested. They've found some research funds and want me to go to Turkey—to Mount Ararat. The money will come through in early June."

"That's great!" I couldn't help feeling excited. Was this my answer? "On TV, they say, but wait—there's more!"

"But wait—there's more. I insisted on having a knowledgeable assistant accompany me. That's you, Ty!"

My head swirled. Events and forces were at play. I felt like that note fluttering in the Jerusalem breeze. "I still have to work on my dad though."

"Indeed, you do," my father said from the doorway behind me.

"Gotta go, Ty. Let me know what shakes out."

"What's going on?"

"That was Sam. I know you said we can't go to Turkey, but it turns out Sam is going there on a research trip." I looked at my dad, pleading. "He said I could go with him."

"He did, did he." My father appeared thoughtful. "Ty, you know I've been thinking about the stone and the Western Wall. I think we've got to see this thing though. You can go to Turkey with Sam, but I'm going with you. We can fly over to Turkey just as soon as school's over in a few weeks."

I fell back on the floor and stared up at the ceiling. Things were working out. Somehow, they were working out just fine.

---

The Bible said Noah's Ark settled in Mt. Ararat after the floodwaters went down. My being said the same thing. Noah and the others on the great wooden ship descended the mountain and started new lives on the fertile soil of what's now Igdir. They then migrated to the land between the Tigris and Euphrates Rivers, where a new generation of humans thrived and repopulated the world.

After flying to Istanbul later that summer, Dad, Sam, and I stood outside the terminal and gazed at Ararat. Dad and Sam were almost as awed as I was. They recalled stories from childhood and later speculations about the mysteries it held.

"The locals called it Mount Agri," I said, proud of my research.

"I never thought I'd see it," said Dad. "The mountain seemed more like a fable than an actual place."

"But there it is," said Sam. "It's been waiting for us thousands of years."

I would climb up the slopes that Noah came down. Me, a kid from San Diego! Well, me and two grown-ups.

Dad found us rooms at the Butik Ertur Hotel. It was a four-floor building, not new or old, nicely located near a busy, open marketplace. The rooms were small and not especially well decorated.

"We are definitely out in the provinces," Sam noted in good fun.

The restaurant on the ground floor was pretty good. Dad and Sam had local food. It looked okay, but I preferred my club sandwich.

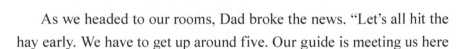

As we headed to our rooms, Dad broke the news. "Let's all hit the hay early. We have to get up around five. Our guide is meeting us here at six."

Sam was horrified. "I'm a graduate student. We don't sleep till three or four."

"Sorry, gents. It's a long way to the mountain, and especially far to the point where we ascend toward our destination. In fact, it's close to the Iranian border. We'll get to the base by jeep and from there climb up by foot."

Sam groaned.

"The coordinates and our boots will get us there. No Mount Everest stuff. I know we'll find something," I said. "Something important, something amazing!"

"Maybe some ancient text like at Sehel," Sam added.

"And I hope we find a semblance of sanity or common sense or something down to earth," Dad said. "Oh, I'm just kidding. It's going to be a wonderful adventure."

"And we owe it all to your gifted son. We wouldn't have seen the Nile or Ararat if not for Ty here."

That thought had occurred to me. Believe me, it had. Though only eleven, I was the center of things. We were on an expedition, a quest, and I was leading the way. Well, sort of. I felt important, almost like an adult, and with that came a sense of responsibility. I'd never felt that before. Not like this. Would I ever do anything else as important?

I started this quest wondering where numbers end. Now I had learned more about my faith, and I was about to learn even more about how numbers are the foundations of everything we believe in. I was so excited.

Sam went to his room, and Dad and I went into ours. I looked out the window and saw the snowcap lit up by a bright moon. It was the same moon that Noah and his family saw, the same one Moses and the Israelites saw as they wandered the desert, and the same one that shone down on the Temple Mount since the days of Herod and well before. The long day and jet lag put me under in minutes.

---

Abdel was waiting for us in the lobby at six. He was short and thin, and his face and hands showed the marks of strong sun and rocky terrain.

"Ah, my three mountaineers are right on time. It will be my pleasure to take you to the mountain and guide your way up. I have packed bread and jerky and water bottles. At a certain height, there will be snow to melt into cold drinks. Very cold drinks. My vehicle awaits."

In the gravel-covered parking lot was an old Land Rover. Where there wasn't mud, you could see dark green paint. It might've been an army vehicle years back.

"Yes, she is not new, but I keep her well maintained. I change the oil every three months and use only the best synthetic fluids. Air filters are changed monthly. We will get there. Of that you should have no concern!"

We tossed our backpacks in the rear, hopped in, and off we went down paved roads for a few miles and then on to dirt ones. We bounced around, but the seats were soft. In less than an hour, the way became hilly, and shortly after, we came to a stop at a visitor center. It was closed and looked like it had been that way for years.

I opened my phone and got a GPS reading.

"Gentlemen, from here on, we are by foot. I can have you near the place that people say Noah's Ark landed in three hours."

"Actually, we have a slightly different location in mind."

Abdel seemed surprised to hear that from a boy, but when the two grown-ups showed no objection, he bowed. "Show us the way then, my young friend!"

The GPS system led us up a winding path for half an hour, then on to rough terrain for a difficult ascent. It was all we could do to avoid tripping over rocks and roots.

"Many people have convinced me to take them to nearby places either by GPS or what you call the seat of their pants. But we never found anything. Are you sure you don't want to go to the place I mentioned earlier? It's not far."

"Quite sure," I said.

Dad and Sam agreed.

The terrain became steeper, and shrubbery gave us something to grab on to. We had to stop and rest every fifteen minutes. Sam and I checked the GPS and determined we were only about two hundred yards away from the goal.

"Let's go!" I shouted. I raced as fast as I dared.

In ten minutes, we were at the precise location, the one Sam found in the Sehel hieroglyphics. Abdel sat on a rock as we looked around for … for what? I guess something out of the ordinary, something amazing.

The three of us went off in different directions, never going far away from the spot, scratching the rocky soil and looking under rough bushes. Off to one side, then the other. A half hour passed.

We sat dejectedly on rocks near Abdel and drank water.

"No luck eh, my friends. She's a big mountain and knows how to keep her secrets."

"Let's try two more locations. The Cray provided three. This one had the strongest confidence interval."

"Why didn't you—oh, never mind. Let's go!"

Sam checked his phone and pointed to the west. "Just a few hundred yards. That's all."

There was nothing there either. The third spot came up empty too. Did I come all this way for nothing?

"Gentlemen, we cannot be on the mountain after dark. The risk of falling is too great, and you know the steepness of the slopes. I must insist we think about returning in an hour. That leaves us enough time to reach the spot tradition holds Noah climbed down from the big boat."

"We didn't find anything at first when we were at Sehel, but we kept looking. Same thing holds on this mountain. It has the secret I want to know, and I'm going to find it!"

We spread out again but again found nothing. We sat in silence. Sam finally spoke.

"The algorithm gave three locations by priority. We searched from the highest one to the lowest. There is nothing else to do."

More silence. My dad scratched the soil with a stick. I sat and watched him, my head propped up on my hand. What was the point of anything? All the puzzles, all the effort. We got here. And found nothing. Did I make a mistake in the numbers?

Abdel stood and was probably about to suggest the traditional spot again when my dad held up a hand for him to stop. He then poked the ground three times with a stick.

"Three locations, eh? The mighty computer at MIT gave us three locations."

"Right. The Cray DEROS."

"Perhaps it wasn't giving three locations. Perhaps it was giving us data to triangulate with."

Sam stood up despite the fatigue. "Of course! Triangulation is of course a metaphor derived from surveying and navigation, but it relies on the idea of using known points to locate the position of an unknown one."

I knew what was coming. An entire lecture from Dad. "It's also from radio emissions. Triangulation determines a transmitter's location by taking readings and plotting angles. Now let's make the analogy to our point of interest. This will be the transmitter. Now we must find our transmitter via the three given locations."

"Ingenious!" Sam exclaimed. "I can calculate direction and our transmitting source location based on the three locations priority. Give me a few minutes."

I stood up, hardly able to contain my excitement. "Dad, you've rescued me again!"

"Let's see what comes of this. We may need the Turkish army to rescue us in the morning!"

Sam was keying data into his phone. "See, if we are assigning for each location a priority, it gives it a weight value, and making analogy to direction, we can plot an exact location to our real coordinates."

He hit a key, and each location sent a dashed line, which instantly intersected and gave us a new GPS position.

"This way, men," he said.

In about half an hour, we came upon a flat, open area where tall trees had managed to grow.

"Never been here before," Abdel said as his pace picked up.

In the middle of the wooded area was a pile of rocks, and we immediately looked around it, then dug around it.

"Found something," Sam said softly, not trying to get our hopes up too high.

It was a flat rock underneath a few inches of soil. Smooth and oval shaped.

"Made by human hands," Dad said.

Sam brushed the surface with a branch, and with each motion, more of a symbol came into view.

"The lazy eight," I whispered. "It's the symbol for infinity."

"I'll be damned. Yes, infinity," Sam said.

"This may not be old, guys. It may be the work of hikers in recent years. Maybe a private joke about spending a lot of time looking for the ark but finding nothing or a prank for later searchers like us," Dad said.

"But it looks old. Very old. And look at the detail. This was done by a craftsman, not a mischievous hiker." He showed us the chisel marks indicating someone had used a fine, pointed tool to create it. It took a long time.

I brushed away dirt from the edges and found an arrow-like etching. "It's pointing to something!" I shouted.

We followed the direction of the pointer and came upon a jagged outcropping about fifty yards away.

"Look! There's an opening!" Sam said.

You would have missed it if you hadn't been looking for it.

"Did I mention the mountain has her secrets?" Abdel said as he joined us.

I ran to it and began tossing dirt away until Sam and I could crawl in. We soon came upon a deep hole. Sam tossed a stone in, and we listened as it brushed along the sides until finally hitting bottom a few seconds later.

"There's definitely something here," Sam said.

"My friends, the hour is late. Darkness is coming and with it cold and danger. We must head back now."

"We can get ropes and flashlights in town and come back for some serious exploration," I said.

"I can get them for you by early morning, but of course another day of my work ..."

"You will be compensated, Abdel," Dad said. "And you can bring tourists here by the dozen—once we figure out what's here."

"The Arrow Cave of Mystery I'll call it!"

I was hoping for "Ty's Cave," but I'm just a kid, and I kept my mouth shut.

# Chapter 12

# The Cave

The next morning, we reached the cave in good time, but I hadn't slept anyway. To be this close to something I didn't think I'd get to see was far more interesting—living a dream was better than anything I could dream. We secured our ropes around a boulder and, one by one, made our way down to the cave's bottom, illuminating the darkness with headlamps. The soft clinks as we went down echoed. It was about forty feet. Dad led the way, then Sam, then me. Abdel stayed at the top.

We turned off the headlamps to save the battery and used flashlights, shining them into a tunnel. We slowly walked down it, looking on the walls for writings or symbols and on the ground for snakes and scorpions. We saw none of those things. So on we went, the noise of our boots echoing eerily off the stone. I was scared. I have to admit it. But my fearless dad and friend were beside me, and a great discovery was just ahead. I knew it.

On we went for several hundred yards. It was hard to tell. The air became cooler and mustier. Every now and then, Dad would yell, "Hello." He didn't expect to hear anyone call back; he just wanted to get some idea of what was ahead. One shout sounded much different; it was a more hollow echo.

"There's something ahead," Dad said. "An opening maybe."

We all shone our lights and saw blue light shimmering off the walls and the mouth to a cavern about as big as a football stadium. The closer we got, the more open it seemed, the stronger the echoes, and the colder the air. We reached the cavern. We didn't need flashlights. It was illuminated already because the ice grabbed the light and held it, giving everything an otherworldly glow.

There in front of us was an enormous wooden vessel inside a foot or two of ice. We could clearly see a hull, bow, stern, and deck. It was here all right. Noah's Ark was right in front of us.

We stood there for a while, awed in silence.

"I don't believe it," said Dad.

"Neither do I," said Sam.

"It's here! It's really here! We found it!" I was excited and ran to touch the ice, as if I could feel the mighty ship inside. "According to the Bible, the Ark was three hundred cubits long, fifty cubits wide, and thirty cubits high, which is approximately four hundred and forty feet by seventy-two by forty-three," I recited from religion class.

"That's what this is—give or take a cubit!" Sam said. "We've made an important discovery that will make us famous. But right now I feel honored. No, that isn't it. I feel … I dunno, *holy.*"

We ran our hands across the icy surface in utter awe. I felt like I had been pulled back in time. The guys probably felt the same. A closer look showed portals and gaps in the planks filled by a resin of some sort.

"I don't understand something. How come the ice hasn't melted?" I asked.

"Yeah. It's chilly in here but undoubtedly above freezing," Sam said.

"There must be writing here. Symbols … numbers. Something," I murmured.

We split up and looked along the dark hull. As I neared the bow, I saw something.

"Dad! Sam! Come quick! Shine your lights up there."

The three lights lit up the bow nicely. There was writing! I pulled out my phone and took pictures. The numbers led me here! I found the *ark*! The stuff we studied at school, all those scriptures—they weren't boring! They were true. And the depth of things meant even numbers were included!

"Can you see it?" I asked Sam, the flashes from our phones illuminating the cavern periodically.

Sam was on the case. "It's in an old language called Akkadian. As with Babylonian, it uses positional numerical system based on sexagesimal, base sixty. We see the same in Sumerian. Very interesting."

"Can you tell us what it says?" I asked, eager to put the lecture behind me.

"It seems like a series of numbers. I can write them down and run them through an app." He pulled out a pencil and jotted things down on paper, then slipped it into his pocket.

"You have an app for that?" Dad laughed. He, too, was taking photos with his phone.

"Well, I knew we were coming to this region, so I loaded up. You'd be amazed what MIT people come up with. Okay, okay … got it. It seems like some type of dimensions based on preoccupation with the number sixty—the same number characterizing a vessel mentioned in Babylonian history. Beside numbers, there are symbols in here. Hmmm … the three symbols here, I believe, represent heaven, earth, and the underworld."

We sat down. We had to. Even though the ground was cold, we had to rest. We nonetheless continued gazing up at the wonder. The story that so many people thought was a fable, a children's story, was true. Towering above us was the proof. What would happen to this cavern and the ark? Would it become a sacred shrine? Would it become a tourist spot? *Step this way! Step right this way!* I didn't want that. My mind shifted to presenting my story to Rabbi Shmuel and my religion class.

We heard a voice calling from afar, and for a moment I thought another amazing event was about to take place.

"It's Abdel," Dad said. "He probably wants us to come back. He's right. It's getting late, and the weather report this morning called for rain and cold. Our flashlights won't last forever anyway."

"I've taken photos. We all have. We can analyze them later," Sam said.

We made our way back to the opening where Abdel was waiting anxiously.

"Was fortune with you, gentlemen?"

"Let us say that we will retain your services for tomorrow as well," Dad said.

"Then fortune is with us all!"

---

That evening, Dad and I sat in our room and discussed how to go about letting the world know about our discovery. We were also eager to examine the photos. When I opened my photos app and saw the first photo, it was just a blue blur. There was nothing recognizable. No hull, no wood. I scrolled down, and each photo was a blue blur. I was about to tell Dad when he looked at me with a long face.

"They're all useless, Ty. Nothing but blue haze. They look like abstract paintings, and bad ones at that. No world-changing discoveries."

Sam knocked on the door and peeped in. One look, and he knew.

"Oh. So you have the same problem. Nothing. Not one damn cubit. Even the Cray DEROS can't help with resolution. A blur will always be a blur."

We looked at one another's phones, then sat in puzzlement and dejection. Finally, Dad spoke up.

"It wasn't the light down there. There was enough with our flashes. The photos at the cave opening prove that. They're fine. Something,

something in that cavern, distorted our photos. Maybe an electromagnetic field."

"We have to go back, Dad. We just have to."

"I'll bring my Nikon," Sam said. "It's analog. I brought it for touristy stuff and didn't want to risk damaging it out in the rough, but this is too important."

"I'll call Abdel. Maybe he'll give us a frequent-climber discount." Dad's humor was intact.

---

We knew the way and could've rented a jeep, so we didn't really need Abdel. But Dad wanted someone to stay above ground just in case. I guess any number of bad things could happen underground. Up the slope we went, then on to the flat area with the trees. I raced to the spot but couldn't find the opening anywhere.

"Where is it?"

Dad and Sam looked around carefully but found nothing. We dug around the surface, but nothing was there. There was no mistake. We knew the place by then and could've found it in the dark. It simply wasn't there.

Who would believe us now? I wanted the world to know what I saw, and now we had no photographs and no proof.

"Something's up," Dad said. "Holes just don't disappear. There's definitely some strange power at work here."

"A strange power?" Abdel said. "What did you find in there anyway?"

"Oh, just some interesting caves. We thought they might have led somewhere," Dad replied.

"I can call upon some people to come up here with equipment. They'll find your cave. Naturally, their services ... well, an agreeable arrangement can be found. On the other hand, I can still lead you to the place where local traditions and many archaeologists say the ark came to rest."

"That's quite all right, Abdel. There's nothing more to be found. I think our exploration of Mount Ararat was a great experience, and it's come to a successful conclusion," Dad said.

I wasn't so sure, but I nodded along with Sam. Abdel thanked us for the pleasure of serving us and asked us to leave a review on Yelp.

---

Sam called two days later and said that he and the Cray found something in the writings he jotted down in the cavern.

"It's an eighteen-character numeric code. No words that I see. But we have a high probability of a few words. Hope it helps, buddy. I'm hitting send now."

After I saw the email, I went to the site.

*Stage eight. Enter a code.*

I hesitated as I felt anxiety. What if all this experience in Turkey was just some type of a hoax? What if there was nothing there? For a moment, I felt doubts about the entire event, but then I remembered very well. There was an ark in that cave. And I was not the only one who saw it.

I took a deep breath and with shaky hands typed the eighteen-character code, then hit enter.

*Correct.*

I felt great relief.

*Stage nine. The generation that came after Noah committed a sin, which they were punished for. Where did the sin take place?*

I typed, "I don't know."

*Find the place and retrieve a key from the cornerstone.*

I sighed. Back to my teacher.

# Chapter 13

# The Tower of Babel

The morning service was coming to a close, and Rabbi Shmuel noticed me sitting in a back pew. As the congregation filed out, I went to the back area, where I knew he'd be relaxing.

"Ty, I see you're back. Back from your summer travels and back in Shul to see me. Alas, we have nothing to nosh on today. You have a question. Is it about entering rabbinical school or the other matter?"

"For now, it's about the other matter. In a way, that is."

"I see, I see. Perhaps the two matters will merge into one someday. Do you want to say the morning prayer first?"

He had never asked me that before. "Yes. Yes, please."

"That's a good start." He handed me the Sidur and Talit. "You should know your prayers."

And for the first time in my life, I earnestly recited the morning prayer.

"Well done, well done. Every morning prayer is a private conversation between you and Ha Shem. There are things that are only between you and him."

I didn't understand why he said that, but it struck something in me.

"So what's on your mind, Ty?"

"Rabbi Shmuel, remember you taught us the Noah's Ark story in Genesis?"

"Of course, I remember. I was there. In the classroom, I mean. Not … well you know."

"I wanted to tell you that … that …"

"What is it, Ty? What is it you want to tell your teacher?"

"I wanted to tell you that the story, the story of Noah and the flood and the ark, is true."

He looked at me in a puzzled way. "Did you have any doubt?"

"No, not really. But in class, it just seemed like a story. It was like many other stories that we heard about and just accepted. Not with our hearts though. Not with our *beings*."

"Yes. There's more. What is it?"

"I know it happened, Rabbi Shmuel. It all really happened. We saw it. My dad, a friend, and I saw Noah's Ark. It was in a deep cavern inside Mount Ararat."

He stared at me, gauging me, probably looking for signs of mischievousness or deception or anything but honesty. He leaned forward. "You know, Ty, you've had an extraordinary experience. Such a great privilege. You've earned it. You've been blessed. Absolutely."

"I know. It's humbled me. Made me grow up."

"And with extraordinary privileges and blessings come extraordinary responsibilities. Do you understand what I am saying?"

"Yes, I do."

"Good. I understand that this is related to your number's quest. Am I correct?"

"Yes."

"So are you making progress?"

"A great deal of progress."

"Good to hear."

"I have one more question, Rabbi Shmuel."

He leaned back.

"I think Noah was a scientist. To build an ark of such size and precision was a quite complicated thing."

"Extremely complicated. He certainly had great knowledge."

"Not only Noah though. His sons and wives were also knowledgeable of science. They helped build the ark. It was a family effort."

"I would agree with that as well."

"After the flood, Noah populated the world again."

"Indeed."

"Rabbi Shmuel, Noah's descendants committed a major sin. Something that was selfish and materialistic. What was it?"

He leaned back in his chair and breathed deeply in and out, as though he'd been disoriented. "These questions convey a more profound understanding of our faith than I've ever encountered in anyone your age. Are you studying the Torah with someone? Or does it all stem from your quest?"

"I have no other teacher but you. I need no other teacher but you. My quest is giving me insights about mathematics and our faith."

"I see, I see. We discussed Parashat Noah. Did we not?"

"Yes, we did."

"Well, this leads to only one event. After Noah's time, people fled the land again. Then they did something that was selfish and indeed had a materialistic, vain nature. They were punished for it. They built a structure. What was that structure, Ty?"

"The Tower of Babylon."

He leaned back and breathed in. A lecture was coming, one I wanted to hear though.

"Now, beyond your knowledge of the Torah, which I am proud of, you just gladdened my heart. I was afraid you were the most inattentive student in class. At times, it seem your mind was on a video game or a television show. But to your question. Yes, the people sinned by gathering together not for the benefits of all humankind but in vanity.

They sought to make their name great, to make themselves above all others. Selfishness, materialism. Activity such as this brings no good to humankind. It leads to nothing but failure.

"They called it a symbol of great unity. Great unity. Bah! The tower brought failure, divisions, disunity. The results spread around the Middle East and around the world. Then, Ty, their sin was building a tower in the name of vanity. There is your answer. Spiritual unity! It is essential we strive for that. Absolutely essential!"

"The Tower of Babylon was built for the wrong reason—vanity."

"In a nutshell, yes."

"Thank you."

"Deep thought and passion. Always remember those things. They go well together. Now, if you will be so kind."

He looked to the door. The lecture was over. The answer found. I left—or started to.

"An additional question comes to mind, Rabbi Shmuel. If these people wanted to build the highest tower, why did they build in a valley, as the Torah tells us in Genesis: XI:

וַיְהִי, בְּנָסְעָם מִקֶּדֶם; וַיִּמְצְאוּ בִקְעָה בְּאֶרֶץ שִׁנְעָר, וַיֵּשְׁבוּ שָׁם.

"It translates as, 'And it came to pass, as they journeyed east, that they found a valley in the land of Shinar; and they dwelt there.' So, if they wanted to build so tall a building, why did they begin in a valley? Shouldn't they have begun on higher ground?"

Rabbi Shmuel leaned back again. "An expert in any field can only benefit from challenges. Perhaps they were so arrogant that they thought the low valley was an obstacle easy to overcome."

"I have to be honest with you, Rabbi Shmuel. The entire story sounds to me like they wanted to reach somewhere they shouldn't—— maybe conquering another place, maybe something else. But someone didn't like the idea and messed with their plans or maybe stole them so they could never succeed."

"A fine insight. You're developing your own interpretation of the passage. You're finding your own way to understand things."

I thought really hard about where I should go next. I needed more information, and where better than a school? "Again, I am extremely grateful. I'm going to the library at the University of California. The one here in San Diego of course. They have excellent books on the Tower of Babylon."

"University books?"

"I believe I'm up to it, Rabbi Shmuel! At least for some of them!"

"I believe you. I truly do."

I found a great book that was filled with information on the tower and a dozen or so sketches of the structure. Some of the drawings were from the Middle Ages and had a strange beauty to them. Things from the past can be like that. One passage hit me:

> The Tower of Babel stood at the very heart of the great city of Babylon. It had open squares, broad boulevards, and narrow, winding lanes. The city was considered one of the most beautiful places at the time. The site has not been clearly identified, but many archaeologists believe that its ruins are in the Great Temple of Nebo in the archeological site of Borsippa in modern-day Iraq.

Iraq? That's going to be a problem!

I kept reading:

> Archaeologists wondered all throughout the years where the Tower of Babel was. The Bible mentioned the valley of Shinar, a territory in south Mesopotamia. Yet an historical, geographical, and geological analysis shows

that Shinar cannot have been in the south but in what is northeastern Syria today. The analysis points out that the remnants of the tower must be located in the Upper Khabur River triangle, not far from Tell Brak, which is the missing city of Akkad.

The most thrilling part of the book was a debate about where the tower was built. Lots of debate. Conclusions—not so much.

"Sam, I need your help. Again."

"Well, Ty, I must say you've got me into some interesting experiences. What's up now?

"My rabbi told me that the sin we're looking for involved the Tower of Babel story."

"Okay, okay. My knowledge of the Bible is minute. You need many decimal points to comprehend it."

"The problem in front of us is to get another code from a cornerstone."

"Dare I ask what cornerstone?"

"The cornerstone of the Tower of Babel."

"Oh man! You've got to be yanking me. That thing was built thousands of years ago. We don't even know if it really existed."

"After our last trip, I am sure that everything mentioned in the Torah is true. Do you have any doubt?"

"Well, you know, that cavern was quite a trip. I haven't mentioned it to any of my professors here. They'd say I was high on something. But okay, let's say the tower story is true. How do we know anything is left of it? And if there is, how do we find it?"

"I've been on the case, Sam. I've been reading books—university books. Archaeologists have tried to find the location for centuries. It's like the search for Troy or Jericho or—"

"Or the fountain of youth or the holy grail! Some things just don't exist, Ty."

"Many things do exist though. Some specialists say the location is in modern-day Iraq. Others say Syria."

"Those are tough places now. Really tough!"

"Yes, when I do a web search of those places, I see there's a lot of soldiers and tanks. But first, we need to know if there's anything in your drawings of the figures on the ark that will give us an idea of where to go."

"Well, yes, buddy. These figures translate to numbers."

"Did you find it using the Cray DEROS?"

"Yes!"

# Chapter 14
# Finding a Way

"There must be some way, Hannah!"

We strolled down the mall, occasionally looking into windows but headed for the food court.

"Can't we just enjoy the day without obsessing about old stuff and hieroglyphics and a quarterstone?" Hannah quickly turned and ordered a smoothie for herself and one for me.

"It's a *cornerstone*. That's the first stone put down when a building or monument is built. I'm convinced there's important information on it," I said over the whir of the blender.

"Ty, it was built thousands of years ago. What makes you think the cornerstone is still in existence? And even if it is, how can you find it in all that dry and dangerous land?" She began to happily sip her smoothie and started to walk away.

I took my smoothie from the counter and followed her. "I can't be sure if I don't try. I've got to try. I've got to follow the clues."

"Iraq is a dangerous place now. It's a huge, dangerous place!"

"I agree. It is very risky. I have help from this guy at MIT. He and his really powerful computer have given me exact coordinates. I just have to get there."

We sat at a table away from the crowd and sipped blueberry and pineapple concoctions.

"You're thinking, Hannah. I know that look. It's the 'I've got great things going on in my head' look. Out with it, young lady!"

"I do have an idea. A pretty good one, if I do say so myself."

"Did you plan on sharing it with your friend and classmate?"

"Yes, but you have to get me another smoothie."

"What flavor?"

"Blackberry mango."

"Done! I'll be right back. Don't run off with a strange archaeologist."

"Better hurry! I see one coming my way now!"

A few minutes and a few dollars later, I placed the drink before her and sat down.

"Now, out with it!"

"Google Maps, Ty."

"I better get more for the drink than that."

"Find the coordinates that smart guy gave you and zoom in. Use the best hi-res screen you can find and zoom in. I've seen this done on TV. See what you can see."

"As much as I like the idea, it has limitations."

"Yes, I know. The stone may be underground. Or the code is too small to be read. Or it's too worn away after a gazillion years. Lots of rain and cold since those days. But you can try."

"Even if the stone is sideways or upside down, we'll see nothing."

"But there are super apps that may do better than Google. I know cuz my friend used one to find her lost dog. They have a really tiny pooch, but they found it. It's worth a try."

I gave it a thought. What did I have to lose? "Hannah, you are a genius!"

"I know. Maybe I can get a cinnamon bun from you now."

"Such chutzpah!"

"Dad, there's something more I need to do."

He was relaxing in a soft chair after dinner. The news was over, and he was about to look for a movie to stream.

"Let's see. Travel to Egypt? No, we've been there. Same with Turkey." He gave me a skeptical look.

"This one doesn't involve travel. Just some amazing high tech. You know, the sort of thing you work on every day. I need to get some information that may be engraved on a piece of stone. The stone is in Iraq, and I know it's too far."

"Too far and too dangerous! What's the stone? Oh, this is going to upset me." He put his hand to his head. "I know it. Go ahead. I know it's related to numbers and the Bible. Go ahead. Your old man is sitting down." He closed his eyes and winced.

"Yes, it's related to those things. You see, I'm convinced there's an important code engraved on the cornerstone of an ancient building."

"Well, I know there are ancient ziggurats in Iraq. Sumerian, Bronze Age, as I recall from college anthropology. Did I get it right? Hah! I'll bet I did!"

"Actually, no."

"Oh ... all right. What is it then?"

"The Tower of Babel."

He winced harder. "The Tower of Babel. Oh. For a minute, I thought it was going to be someplace hard."

"Dad, please take this seriously. It's important to me. I have its exact GPS coordinates."

"You do? I assume Sam helped you?"

"Yes. We can't go there. I know that. What I need is—"

"You need an app that can zoom in like a sophisticated spy satellite. Got it. When I did some work at PARC a few months ago, they showed me an app that worked with low-orbiting satellites. They called it

Bullseye. Ahem! I improved on it. No, your old man improved greatly on it."

"I'm sure you did. What's that park thing?"

"P-A-R-C, Palo Alto Research Center. It's a basic research institute."

"Oh yeah. Isn't that where Steve Jobs got some cool ideas that got Apple rolling?"

"Indeed, it is. In preliminary testing, Bullseye produced astonishing results. I can get hold of it, I believe. It's not secret. The only thing is that I'll need immense computing power. I'll check into it tomorrow."

"I'll remind you in the morning, Dad."

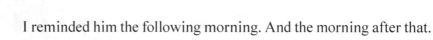

I reminded him the following morning. And the morning after that. And the next one too. He said he was very busy and that PARC was dragging its feet about letting him use Bullseye. Anyway, it needed needs a lot of power to run effectively. He said it wasn't like Pong or Pac-Man. I had to look up what they were. So seventies!

It must have been a week later that PARC authorized Dad to use Bullseye. Then we had to contact Sam to download the program and run it on the Cray DEROS. We arranged to get to work on Saturday when the mighty computer was open. Dad and I went to his office, where we could use a ginormous Linux-driven workstation with two hi-res screens. Sam was on speakerphone.

Dad opened a window named "xTerm" and linked to Sam and the Cray and Bullseye. Now Sam would see what we saw.

"Okay, execute the Python scripts, and we'll be in business," Sam said. "The satellite will be over Iraq in a few minutes, so we mustn't tarry."

Dad typed away and hit enter. I didn't ask what a Python script was. I could see machinery was at work by the progress bar and the sudden, noisy whirring inside the workstation.

"Never heard the fan run like this. Believe it or not, the Cray is doing most of the work. Sounds like things are proceeding though, Ty!"

"My friends, you should see it right about … now!" Sam said with delight.

A window popped up, and a map of the world appeared. The detail was amazing.

"Wow!" I gasped.

"Incredible resolution! I could see a mosquito in the deepest jungle with one of these Crays!"

"Your birthday's coming up, Dad. For now, can we enter the coordinates?"

A few keys and enter.

"Okay, my friends," Sam said, "the low-orbit satellite has the data. Now brace yourself for quite a show."

Bullseye processed millions of frames per second, and we could see the progress bar refreshing quickly with every zoom. The Middle East became Iraq, Iraq a province, the province a district, the district a patch of arid land with roads and trails, cars, and, yes, the occasional herd of sheep. My mind reeled. I had to hold on to the chair.

"I see ruins!" I shouted.

"I see them too," said Sam, more calmly but with a trace of awe.

Dad consulted a map.

"Those are the ruins of the Ziggurat and temple of Nabu at Borsippa. This may well be where the Tower of Babel was. Now, the tricky part is to find the code you want."

"The coordinates should zero in," I said with a little annoyance.

"Yes, well, with any GPS coordinate, there are margins. It's not accurate to the millimeter. It can be off by a few feet. Let's start to scan around."

The camera zoomed really close to the ground, and we could see rectangular blocks. Lots of them. Wind was blowing sand off of them, revealing fine detail. More and more blocks came into view as the camera moved around.

"I don't know why," said Sam, "but I believe it's here somewhere. Call it … I dunno. Call it faith or something."

"Let's me kick in my program scanner. I wrote this routine as a module to Bullseye so it can automatically scan in a ten-foot radius around a designated point. It will scan until it finds something out of the ordinary; then it will stop. Its pattern recognition technology will identify symbols, numbers, letters, and any other mark. Let's call it Bullseye 2.0."

Bullseye 2.0 started to scan in circles around the center. It progressed slowly but consistently. It stopped occasionally when it found broken brick or anything else out of the ordinary pattern of stones. The workstation was whirring and occasionally groaning like a horse asked to carry too heavy a load. The enclosure was hot to the touch.

"Let's keep going … keep going …" Sam was urging the great MIT horse on.

The camera suddenly stopped.

*Anomaly found.*

"Broken brick," I said. "Nope! There's something there!"

"There sure is," Dad said. "Looks like erosion has worn the images down, but there's something there."

"I'll take screen shots and run them through image enhancement and Middle Eastern languages programs," said Sam. "Something will show up. Have faith. I'll call you when I get it."

Sam didn't call Saturday night—or Sunday morning. I wanted to call him, but Dad said to sit tight and do some homework "for a change." He's so witty for a guy who played Pong. Noon my time, 3:00 p.m. MIT time, Dad's phone rang, and I sat nearby.

"Bingo, Ty! We got the code!"

"What did it say?" I all but shouted. Dad motioned for me to calm down.

"Well, something very peculiar. I don't understand it, but maybe your rabbis would be able to shed some light on it."

"Tell me! Tell me!"

"The carvings are symbols and numbers. I am not sure what the numbers are, but the symbols say something very odd. Numbers and days. It says, 'Forty days.' That's it."

"Forty days? That's it? Are you sure?"

"The rock was heavily eroded, and that presented problems for even the greatest technology. But with a fifty percent probability, there's another word—*mountain*."

"So we have mountain and forty days," Dad said.

I repeated the words over and over. It came to me rather quickly. It was obvious. Moses went up Mount Sinai for forty days and forty nights. But how to put these things together? Nothing came to me. Luckily, it was Shavuot holiday again. That meant a conference with a certain rabbi.

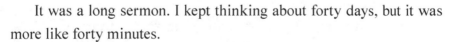

It was a long sermon. I kept thinking about forty days, but it was more like forty minutes.

"And that concludes today's lesson. I see many interested faces, and that's very gratifying. Very gratifying indeed."

My hand flew up.

"I have a question!"

Rabbi Shmuel sighed. No one could hear it, but a few saw it. I knew it was coming. "Ty, Ty. I didn't open things up for questions yet. I was expecting applause and praise. But piquing an eager young mind is a form of praise. What is it then?"

"Moses went up Mount Sinai for forty days and forty nights. This was to prepare the Torah for him."

"Yes, indeed."

"Would it be logical to assume that Moses went up the mountain to learn things? Maybe not just moral laws. Maybe science and other things? It's like he took a course up there. Also, maybe these forty days and nights were not enough, so he went up there for another forty days."

"Well, the Torah makes no mention of it, and we can't assume it. The passage states that when he saw the children of Israel worshipping a golden calf, he broke the tablets and went up Sinai to get replacements."

"I found a verse. Exodus 25: 'According to all that I shew thee, after the pattern of the tabernacle, and the pattern of all the instruments thereof, even so shall ye make it.'

«And in Hebrew:

.כְּכֹל, אֲשֶׁר אֲנִי מַרְאֶה אוֹתְךָ, אֵת תַּבְנִית הַמִּשְׁכָּן, וְאֵת תַּבְנִית כָּל-כֵּלָיו; וְכֵן, תַּעֲשׂוּ

"In our words, 'come, learn and copy.' That's a course. A course that Moses received on Mount Sinai. Moses was a student. And then he took the information and the tablets and gave it to the nation, to Israel. Exodus 24: 'And he took the book of covenant, and read in the audience of the people: and they said, All that the Lord hath said will we do, and be obedient.'

"And in Hebrew:

".וַיִּקַּח סֵפֶר הַבְּרִית וַיִּקְרָא בְּאָזְנֵי הָעָם וַיֹּאמְרוּ כֹּל אֲשֶׁר דִּבֶּר יְהוָה נַעֲשֶׂה וְנִשְׁמָע

Rabbi Shmuel fidgeted. Sweat formed on his bald spot. He was a little ticked at me.

"We can discuss this further in a little while. Class dismissed."

He motioned for me to follow him to his office. He pointed to a chair and exhaled.

"Har Saini was a sacred event, probably the most sacred event in the Torah. We can't really take it as scientific event. It has more of a religious and even political meaning to it."

"Of course, Rabbi Shmuel. I don't think there's a contradiction between the religious aspect and the science involved. I think the Torah doesn't give *all* the information around events. I am in search of more scientific facts, and so far, I found many. Oh, Rabbi Shmuel, there are so many. It's amazing."

"I am sure you did, and I'm equally sure you will find more. I am just asking you to remember there's a line between religion and science. Although they go together, sometimes it's easy to be dragged into directions that are not welcome in our faith. Now, I have much to do."

I thought about his words as I walked down the hallway. He was right. It can be real easy to drift into science or even science fiction. But I had seen things, things that couldn't be coincidence. I saw the ark. I found codes in places, as instructed. I knew that I was on the right track for something, and I was determined to continue with all my abilities.

---

Hannah and I sat in my room and stared at the screen.

"Ready?" I asked.

"Yes."

"Tower of Babel."

*Correct.*

*What is the number in the code?*

"Forty."

*Correct.*

*Stage ten. What is an important location connected with the number forty?*

"Mount Sinai."

*Correct.*

*You must be there at sunrise during summer.*

I thought a few minutes. "But where exactly?" I said loudly. "Mount Sinai is a huge place."

115

"Why are you asking me, Ty?" Hannah said as she rolled her eyes and pointed to the screen.

"Where exactly on the mountain?"

*The coordinates are in the code.*

My eyes rolled. I missed something. There was more information that I thought.

"I have to get back in touch with Sam at MIT."

"I hear MIT's on a river. Sounds beautiful. I'm gonna go there someday."

"Yeah. That sounds cool, Hannah. Maybe I'll go there with you."

"Aw, Ty. We'll be classmates again."

# Chapter 15

# Mount Sinai

66 "Ty, listen to me. I told you everything we got out of that stone in Iraq. And when I say we, I mean Cray, the software, and yours truly. There's nothing more we can do, and I have classwork to do."

I was talking to Sam, hoping he'd help me again. "I understand. Believe me. I don't need anything this instant or this day, but I do need more information out of the stone before I can go ahead. And you know how important this is. Not just for me. I think you see its importance too."

"You're right. You're right. I'll see what I can do in a few days."

Nothing more for me to do. So I did class assignments and worked on them harder than ever. I found myself leafing through the Bible and reading the page where my finger randomly stopped. Maybe I'd get a message that way. Maybe. In any case, I enjoyed the readings. There was beauty and wisdom most of the time. I realized that while I was at the beach. While most people were enjoying the sun and surf and listening to music, I lay on a blanket reading sacred writings. More and more, I was reading them in Hebrew. As I prepared to go home, the sun was coming down, and gulls flew by noisily. An old couple passed by carrying a grandchild. I looked out onto the horizon and stared as ship after ship sailed west, then disappeared.

I came home, brushed the sand off my shoes, and headed for the shower. My father vacuumed behind me. My phone rang, and I knew who it was. I just knew. Who needs caller ID!

"Sam! What have you learned?"

"Well, I played around with the images. The program rearranged the number combinations, converted symbols to numbers, and guess what?"

"Tell me!"

"I found coordinates! My program checked hundreds of millions of combinations and produced only one set of viable coordinates. Science ends here. Now you'll have to check with your religious people about the location. It's completely accurate, and the topographic conditions make sense."

"Where is it?"

"I researched the location for the past few days. Amazing! As a kid, I always accepted the Exodus story but later took it as a myth. Now? I amazed myself. First, a few facts. According to the coordinates I found, Moses and the Israelites crossed the Yam Sufh in a completely different place."

"Crossed the what?"

"Yam Sufh. It gets translated or mistranslated as the Red Sea or the Sea of Reeds. I've concluded that the crossing had to be at the shores of Nuweiba. That's the only place that's blocked by mountains and has a land path across the sea."

"I don't understand, Sam. Mount Sinai is in the desert of Egypt."

"Not according to the coordinates we found! They point to a different mountain, located in northwestern Saudi Arabia. The locals call the area the Land of Jethro. That's the biblical land of Midian. The tallest mountain near it is called Jabal Al Lawz, which means the Burnt Mountain. The reason it's called that is because it has a blackened top. It can be seen from far away. Miles and miles."

"The fire of G-d?" I whispered in awe.

"It's the best description for it I can think of! Locals also call it the 'Mountain of Moses. The coordinates and the locals are telling us something, Ty! We've got to look into this!"

"That's a problem. The mountain is in Saudi Arabia."

"I know, but we'll have to make it somehow. What are we supposed to see there at sunrise?"

"I don't know, but this will never pass my father's oversight. No way."

"Don't give up, buddy. We'll think of something. We always do."

---

The news was thrilling but saddening at the same time. The satellite and software worked for the Tower of Babel, but the newest challenge required me to be there at sunrise. How?

I went from hoping another break would come my way and thinking I'd run out of my breaks and back again.

My mom was home from her conference in Colorado. It was wonderful to see her, and it took my mind off the quest for a while. Never completely, but you know how wonderful moms are. We spent the day together at the beach and came home to have dinner that Dad prepared. Mom had asked for vegan cuisine.

As we finished the stir-fried soy and broccoli, Mom asked, "What's wrong, Ty? You seem down. I guess life is dull after seeing Mount Ararat."

"I'm fine. It's not that really."

"Your father and I discussed your newfound interests in math and its relationship to religion and ancient history. That sounds so beautiful. You're discovering the oneness in life!"

She has a way of seeing things in New Age terms.

"That may be so, Mom. There are many things in the way of my discovery."

"Indian texts say, 'The sharp edge of a razor is difficult to pass over; thus the wise say the path to salvation is hard.' That line inspired a great book."

"I don't know how hard it is to pass over a razor, but it might be relatively easy compared to going to Mount Sinai."

"Ty, we were in Egypt only a few months ago," Dad said dismissively.

"According to the information we decoded from the stone in Iraq, Mount Sinai isn't in Egypt. It's in Saudi Arabia."

Mom's eyes lit up. "There was a man in my seminar last month who said the same thing! The true place where Moses received the Ten Commandments was in Saudi Arabia—the Burnt Mountain! He was an archaeologist from the University of Chicago!"

I couldn't even get excited about that. "I have to be there at a certain time—sunrise during summer. I will get a message for my next step."

"I was hoping Sam would get you to ease up on this and study mathematics in a more, well, conventional way," Dad said.

"Dad, Sam wants to go there too. He's as convinced as I am that there's something amazing ahead. Well, he's almost as convinced as I am."

"Visualize it, Ty," Mom said with eyes closed. "Visualize it."

---

The weeks passed. Rabbi Shmuel said readings would serve me in my quest and in becoming a good man too, so I spent time reading books on ancient history and religion. But I had just about given up on going to Saudi Arabia for the Burnt Mountain. There was just no way to go.

It was in mid-May that my folks and I gathered at the table. I sensed there was an announcement coming. My father seemed excited, but my mother seemed bored. After talk of school and mowing the lawn and the like, Dad settled down to business.

"Ty, I have good news."

My heart swelled. I might have dropped a fork.

"My firm is sending a team to a conference in the Middle East in a few weeks. And I will head the team."

"What's the conference, dear?" My mother perked up.

"It's the Saudi High Performance Computing Conference."

I definitely dropped a fork.

"The Saudis are gathering tekkies to make their country a high-tech hub for the region. And this year, yours truly is making a presentation."

"That country isn't safe!" Mom objected. "You know what your place of birth is on your passports?"

"Haifa, Israel. We'll be met at the airport by an official or two."

"I'm not sure that's a good thing," my mother said.

"Yes, it is. The officials will see us through customs and the like and take us to and from the conference."

"I'm sure the Saudi government will make the conference safe," said an eager boy with no knowledge of the matter but a keen interest.

"I think that's true," my dad said. "The conference is held every year, and there hasn't been any trouble. So I have obtained a ticket for a young man to accompany me."

I jumped up out of my chair. "Wow! Thanks so much! I visualized something like this, Mom!"

"Oy! Then it's part of a plan, I suppose. Some strange plan with many twists and turns. Be careful, you guys."

"As always! We've arranged visas and passes for the Burnt Mountain area. The authorities don't like tourists there because locals feel the area is sacred. Some people in the government agree, but others are eager for high tech and prestige. I work with the second group, and they're on top. So we're booked. We're booked for the plane, and we're booked for the mountain! Oh, and tell Sam he can come along if he's able to swing it."

"I will! I'm sure he's almost as eager to go as I am!"

"The first week of June."

"Oh, Dad. I can't. I'm busy that week. It's a friend's birthday," You should've seen their faces.

---

"Mom wouldn't like it here," I said. We arrived in Riyadh, the capital of Saudi Arabia. Sam arrived on a different flight, and we met at the airport.

"Good to see you, young man." Sam high-fived me. He shook hands with Dad.

"I am always happy to see you, Sam. We'll have a great adventure here."

He laughed. "Based on our history trips, I have no doubt. I brought plenty of scientific equipment to analyze things. It'll be fun."

The airport was dazzlingly clean with people in sparkling white attire and colorful headscarves. The women wore coverings, and they were always accompanied by men. I mean *always.*

"Good thing your mom's not here, Ty. She'd organize a women's consciousness seminar."

"It might be popular, but it wouldn't work out well. Maybe you should buy her one of those strange outfits."

"Abayas, Ty. Those strange outfits, as you called them, are called abayas."

"I can't see her in one of those things!"

When we reached the passport control desk, the man saw our names and birthplaces on our passports and made a quick call. Two security guards quickly came, and I almost panicked. But Dad was calm, and the guards welcomed him courteously and by name. They took us to a lounge where we helped ourselves to beverages and bread. Then a man in flowing white attire greeted us and led us to a shiny Mercedes with a chauffeur. As we rode in the back, he gave us the papers we needed to travel freely in the mountainous area. We were designated "researchers."

We had a few days before the conference began, so off we went in the Mercedes. Its air-conditioning protected us from the desert heat. It must have had a supercharger. Three hours later, we arrived at a small villa in the foothills where we would stay.

As we relaxed before the hike, I looked at a map and got my bearings a little better. "You know, Dad, we're only about seventy-five miles from Eilat."

"Ahh! We used to vacation there. Best beaches anywhere."

"I swam with dolphins!"

"You swam with dolphins?" Sam asked.

"I sure did! There's a park specially built for it. They're amazing creatures. Gentle and playful."

The villa was on the edge of a quaint town of no more than a few hundred. The food nearby wasn't appetizing to me, but Dad and Sam seemed to think it was okay. Pita and olives, pita and olives. Ho-hum. We turned in early.

Around four in the morning, we awoke to meet our guide. Nasir was quiet and not the friendliest chap, but he brought hiking gear and lots of bottled water and nuts. We hopped into his Hongqi SUV and headed for the hills, where donkeys would carry us up the steep inclines. Hongqis are made in China, by the way.

"I not along with you on climb," Nasir said in broken English and pointing up to the summit. "I stay here. You take radio. I stay here with radio. Trouble? You call. Drink water. Not forget. Drink water. At night, cold. Desert hot in day, cold at night. Blankets for you."

They were thick, scratchy wool with broad stripes. I didn't like the feel of them, but it was part of a researcher's life.

"People here no like tourists. This place … holy. Stay away them.

Drink water. Take care of radio. Cost money. Three maybe four hours to top. Let donkeys rest. They get mean."

He helped us pack our gear on the donkeys and said goodbye. "See you in three days. No more. Take care of radio."

We loaded our donkeys with food and gear and started our ascent.

"This is so much fun!" I exclaimed as I bounced from side to side on my steed. "Way better than all my class field trips."

"If your mother knew exactly what we were doing, I'm not sure she would share your enthusiasm. I can't picture her on a donkey. No—wait. I *can* picture her on a donkey. She's wearing an abaya!"

"I never pictured myself on a donkey," Sam said. "But this is great fun."

"Wait till the afternoon sun is on us. It's like a blast furnace!"

Despite my father's complaints, I could see he was into it. He wasn't having a ball, but he was intrigued. He wanted to know more as much as Sam and I did. I looked over to my father and imagined telling my own son one day about this adventure. He'd think his old man and grandfather were really cool guys. At least I hope so. You can't tell with kids!

Our little caravan followed the winding path that led upward. The donkeys were dutiful, despite all the flies. I'll tell you in on a secret: donkeys poop a lot, and you should try not to be downwind.

By late afternoon, the sun was indeed a furnace. Behind us was the trail, and around us were the hills, bathing in the light of the late afternoon. Ahead of us, only more trail and stillness. Vegetation was sparse, to say the least. We checked the coordinates and knew we were only a few hundred meters from the objective. Our donkeys covered the distance in a few minutes.

A small, flat area of land, less than an acre, jutted out of the mountainside, giving the impression of a shelf carved out thousands of years ago for a great purpose. I sensed it. It seemed the shelf knew it too but kept it secret.

"This is it," I murmured. "Mount Sinai, where Moses received the commandments from on high."

Dad nodded in awe. Sam bowed his head, maybe in prayer. I can't say for sure.

"Something world-shaking took place here long ago," I said. "And something pretty amazing is going to happen at sunrise."

Dad did a radio check with Nasir, who told us to tie down his donkeys and prepare for the night. We made a campfire, spread out the blankets, and prepared a meal of beef jerky, beans, and figs. The sun fell, the shadow of the sacred mountain fell over us, and the chilly air came down hard and fast. We finished our nibbling, drank a little water, and settled in for the night. Not a word was said. We all had to wait till dawn—or try to.

Rustling sounds startled me a few hours later. A bobcat? A wolf? We'd been warned. It was Dad.

"It's only four, but we have a lot to prepare," he said.

Sam heard us and roused from his blanket.

I shivered as I reluctantly got up and hastily pulled on my U Cal San Diego sweatshirt. Dad made some last-minute calculations on his tablet. Sam set up a hi-res video camera that would sweep 270 degrees. He smiled proudly.

"I have an app that will analyze the video with astonishing accuracy. You're gonna love it!

We threw more sticks and brush into the fading campfire, and the guys made an herbal tea. Coffee and regular tea are banned in Saudi Arabia. They're still to be found, but we didn't want to rustle any feathers with the locals in case we came across some—or, more likely, they came across us. We let the fire extinguish itself and waited for the first glimmers of dawn to come.

I was on my second cup of herbal tea, which I didn't like, when a hint of light appeared in the east. The rays displayed the contours of hills in the distance and then the dry plain behind them. I looked around for a brief moment and saw cracks in the boulders around us. I didn't notice them at all yesterday, but my senses were on high that morning. The sun slowly rose like a red flame. It promised great heat but something else.

Each of us was looking for something remarkable, but none of us wanted to say a word. We waited … and waited. And then something happened.

The craggy slope beneath us became eerily illuminated, and a soft mist lifted out of the rocks and cracks.

"The sun … the sun is heating up gases in the rocks!" Sam whispered.

"But so quickly," Dad added. "How?"

"My question is *why*," I said.

The mist rose and swirled ever so gently, forming vague shapes beneath us.

"What are they?" I said as I trembled.

"They're signs. Akin to those we saw on the Egyptian island. This mountain is forming signals for … I don't know what for."

"For us!" I said.

"Yeah. For us! I'm trying to translate them, but there are so many! I'm taking notes, but we'll have to rely on the camera."

The symbols formed rows, one after the other, one on top of the other, stretching for hundreds of meters in the distance. In less than a few minutes, the symbols began to spread out into the morning sky, slowly becoming more shapeless until they vanished into the new morning.

We stood there in complete silence as each of us tried to comprehend what we'd just been so fortunate to see. The sun hit us hard for the early morning, and we knew what was coming.

"Let's look at the video."

The three of us huddled around Sam's tablet as he loaded the file.

The time stamp and run time were shown in red. Sam hit play. The remarkable sunrise was well recorded. The same for the gradual light on the rocks. Nothing else though. No mists, no symbols. Sam replayed it from the start and adjusted the contrast and highlights. Still nothing but the sunrise.

Sam was mystified. I wasn't. "Remember the cave on Ararat? There's something truly supernatural going on with this," I said.

"So, my fellow explorers, what do we do?" Sam said more to the sky than to us.

"We have two more nights before we have to go back," my father said. "Sam, set your camera up again. I'll use my phone to record video."

"And I'll take still images!"

"And while my camera is filming, I'll scribble down notes as fast as I can," Sam said.

"Right! Now we have to prepare for the afternoon sun. Oh, and let's be mindful about our water. No convenience stores up here."

We sheltered ourselves beneath an outcropping. The overhead rock was in the shade and relatively cool. Relatively. It must have been 106 by late afternoon. After another dinner of jerky and fruit, Nasir's voice crackled on the radio for a routine check. He was pleased we were doing well and repeated concerns about the heat and water and of course his donkeys. Before signing off, Dad posed a question.

"Nasir, old friend, do people ever report anything mysterious up here?"

The receiver was silent for several moments. "No, sir. Nothing out of the ordinary. Just beautiful scenery."

"Okay. Over and out from up here."

"Over and out, sir."

The sun lost some of its fury, and a light breeze came and went through our shelter beneath the outcropping. We made a fire for tea and to ward off any animals that might have sensed our presence in the last day. An hour or so later, we heard the chattering of jackals and the roar of bobcats; at least that's what we thought they were.

You've never seen so many stars until you've camped out in the Saudi desert. Not even in the deserts of California or Nevada. The canopy above reminded me of scenes from a spaceship in a sci-fi movie. You could even see white blurs of the Milky Way—thousands of distant suns, their light sent our way millions of years ago for our wonder. And we were seeing it that night on the mountain where Moses received the Ten Commandments. The children of Israel were camped below and looked up and saw the same wondrous sights.

"None of this would have happened without you, young man," Sam said as he chewed the last of his jerky. "We scientists are typically so enveloped in our scientific world that we tend to forget the rest of the world, its nature and its beauty. Well, here we have more than just beauty. It's a borderline miracle in my book."

"I just hope to find the answer to my numbers quest. There must be a meaning to numbers, more than what we see. There must be a meaning to the fact that they never end. Or maybe they do and we just don't know it? We've seen so much so far. Way far beyond imagination. Clues, evidence for biblical events—sometimes I wonder if all this is real or a dream. But its reality indeed, and last night we witnessed another miraculous thing. We have to get to the point of this. We have to solve the riddle. We have come very far, and I'll settle for nothing but a resolution about the nature of numbers."

Sam didn't mull it over a second. "Numbers go on to infinity. We don't even have computers that can count where they go, and we have pretty strong ones nowadays."

"Like our Cray DEROS friend, for example!" I said. "Maybe there's something we don't know yet. Maybe we have to do some mathematical operations that lead us to the end."

"With what we've seen the last few months in our travels, I'd say we have to keep open minds. Remember the island and the cave? And whatever happened this morning? Our outlooks can't be fixed anymore. We're working on something unknown and amazing. Let's keep our eyes and souls open." Dad spoke more somberly than I'd ever seen.

The three of us, the small band of searchers, fell silent. We looked out on the dark plain below and the glittering sky above and had our own thoughts. We slipped under our blankets and settled in for some sleep. We were well prepared for the morning, but I had my doubts about what we were about to witness. Was it real? Did it have any meaning at all, or was it just a glitch of nature? I was afraid of disappointment. What if we missed what we were supposed to see?

The sky was still inky and mysterious. A few animals snarled in the distance as we breakfasted on figs and herbal tea. I was starting to like the stuff. You have to learn to like things when you're hungry up on a mountain. We set up our gear and waited. Sam tested his pen and kept a spare in his shirt pocket. Not many words were said. We just waited for the miracle to repeat itself.

The fingers of dawn rose in the east as they had since time began. The plains could be seen and then the foothills. We watched the rocks and crevices for the mists from the warming rays. They did not disappoint us. It was happening again. The haze became wider, and shapes formed, then lines of fairly distinct symbols. They dissolved quickly, more quickly than yesterday.

"Too fast. I can't draw them all," Sam muttered as he scribbled furiously. "They're gone!"

They were gone all right. Was it higher air temperature? Our imaginations? Or the trickery of some supernatural force?

"Let's check our cameras," I said rather unenthusiastically.

We looked at all our recording gear, and to no one's astonishment, there was nothing.

"I wrote down a good deal of it," said Sam hopefully. "I'll get the rest tomorrow."

Dad set the agenda. "We have one more morning. We must change tactics. No cameras or videos. They don't work and will not work. Something's seeing to that. Something we don't understand and won't understand. We'll all have notebooks, and we'll all draw what we see." We talked about how to divide up the rows so we could capture as much as we could and decided on a plan.

And that's how it was.

The following morning, we were all ready with notes and pens in our hands as the sun started its way up. We decided to give every symbol no more than three seconds and then move to the next one. Sam would later try to fill in what we missed, then run it through character-recognition software back at MIT. The sun heated the rocks below, images rose, and we furiously sketched what we saw. Sam collected them and put them in order.

"Thirteen rows. What could that number mean?" I asked. "Maybe something to do with coming of age in our religion?"

"Sounds like you're looking forward to your Bar Mitzvah!" Dad said.

The material wasn't understandable, but it was promising. Dad radioed Nasir to expect us in a few hours.

On the way down Mount Sinai, I felt we'd made progress. I was part of something. Something big. I wasn't a kid in his pajamas surfing the internet, playing games, or engaging in arguments with other creatures of the web who might be bots. I was an explorer, a mathematician, an archeologist. I was on the threshold.

# Chapter 16

# A Famous Battle

Several days passed back in San Diego. Mom was in town for a while, and she pampered me with dinners and high praise for my powers of concentration on my task. Hannah asked question after question and enjoyed the photos I was able to save. All the while, I waited to hear from Sam and MIT's supercomputer. One morning, I received a text from him suggesting a Zoom chat with Dad and me at 3:00 p.m. our time. We were elated. We logged on ten minutes early and waited. Sam came on early too.

"First off, you guys will not believe what these symbols say! I was able to recover all the symbols, all thirteen rows. We all get high grades for drawing skills. Assembling them into a clear message … well, that's another matter. Anyway, this is what Cray and I got:

*"Six inner corners*

*"six outer corners*

*"marching form*

*"thirteen circles*

*"Find the connection and place.*

"Do you know what this means, Ty?"

I read the words over and over, to myself and aloud. Nothing came to me. "Afraid not."

"There was another piece of information. A standalone piece of data

I assumed to be another piece of information but couldn't figure out where it fit. The Cray could not find any viable meaning:

*"Five steps lead to pillar."*

"Still nothing, Sam. I'll have to consult some religious experts. I have a feeling they'll be expecting me!"

"Please do! This is bugging me! I'm going nuts here!"

"Give me a few days. I'll let you know."

We logged off.

"Rabbi Shmuel?" Dad asked.

"Who else?"

Rabbi Shmuel was away in New York. He texted me the night of his return and said to meet him at school the following morning.

"It's good to see you, Ty. Are you ready for the new school year in a few weeks?"

"Yes, I am."

"What of your quest? I sense you have questions for your esteemed mentor."

I looked puzzled.

"An esteemed mentor is a respected teacher, which I trust I am to you."

"Yes, you indeed are. While my esteemed mentor was in New York, I was on Mount Sinai!"

"I presume you mean at Mount Sinai Hospital."

"I mean the mountain in the Middle East. Not the one in Egypt. My research has led me to conclude the mountain was in northwestern Saudi Arabia."

He stood up and paced about the room. "Yes, yes. Many scholars believe the mountain where Moses received the Ten Commandments was located in what's now Saudi Arabia. The Burnt Mountain, as it's called by the Muslim faithful of the region. I, however, am not one of them. And few of my colleagues attach any belief to that finding. Moses and the children of Israel were in the Sinai Desert, not the Nafud desert of modern-day Saudi Arabia!"

"I respect that view, Rabbi Shmuel. However, I believe the true location was the Burnt Mountain. You see, I received the exact coordinates."

"And from where did you get the exact coordinates?"

"From the Tower of Babel's cornerstone."

"The cornerstone of the Tower of Babel? You received a message from the cornerstone of the Tower of Babel." Rabbi Shmuel was taken aback. One might say he was exasperated. "What is that connected to?"

I was ready for that question. "May I tell you the entire chain of events, Rabbi Shmuel?"

He sat down and took off his black hat. He looked uneasy as he prepared for a lecture from an unlikely person. "Yes, yes. I'm ready to hear your findings. Oy! If my fellow rabbis could see me now!"

"The reason I didn't tell you everything, Rabbi Shmuel, was because you told me that some things were meant for me and me alone."

"Well, I think it's time that I hear everything, Ty."

And so I told him everything. I started with the first trip to Egypt, then the cave with the ark, then the Tower of Babel, and ended with Mount Sinai experience. He simply nodded and occasionally said, "Yes, yes. Go on, please. Go on."

When I finished, he sat in silence. For a moment, I thought he wanted me to leave him alone. He cleared his throat.

"You know, Ty, you are very privileged to have experienced these things. Many great, righteous people never got this honor. But with great privileges come even larger responsibilities. You are aware of this?"

"Yes."

"Obviously, you cannot control the men you are working with, but we can hope they keep things confidential. Nothing to the media."

"We all agree we are on special quest and are keeping everything under our hats. Anyway, Rabbi Shmuel, we have no pictures, no videos, just ideas and claims. No one would believe us."

"Fair enough, fair enough. I guess someone or something takes care of these things. You know, Ty, I used to think of you as a smart student but a wise guy whose gifts would go into trivial, mundane pursuits. That is, into ordinary pursuits. But now I see discipline, focus, an eye for important matters. I see, if not wisdom, at least a foundation for it."

"Awesome! Thanks so much! That means a lot to me!"

"You've earned it, and you have not yet come of age."

"Almost. In about a year and few months, I'll be thirteen! But till that day, I need help with another mysterious set of words."

"Shoot, as they say."

"What could this mean?

"*Six inner corners*

"*six outer corners*

"*marching form*

"*thirteen circles*

"*Find the connection and place.*

"Can you help?"

He leaned back and looked above.

"Repeat the passage, please."

I read the words again.

"Once again."

I read it two more times, but Rabbi Shmuel was no closer to an answer.

"Your esteemed mentor has hit a wall. Bupkis, as we said in rabbinical school. Fortunately, I myself have an esteemed mentor."

"Rabbi Mordechai?"

"Who else?"

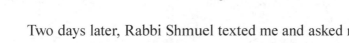

Two days later, Rabbi Shmuel texted me and asked me to come to Shul. After the service, we'd meet with Rabbi Mordechai. I immediately recognized him from his classy black suit and long gray beard. Rabbi Shmuel was especially precise and proud. It came to me he was pleased that his esteemed mentor was there.

At the conclusion, Rabbi Mordechai motioned for me to follow him to the back, where Rabbi Shmuel was relaxing with a cup of tea.

"Ty! Rabbi Mordechai! Welcome, my friends. Let me get some herbal tea for us older folks. Have you ever tried it, young man?"

"As a matter of fact, I have. I'd be delighted to share some with you this day."

"Tea and a deep exploration of our faith!" said Rabbi Mordechai. "A wonderful afternoon we shall have! Now, our colleague here has told me of your search and how it has taken you to many places in and around the Holy Land. You have made discoveries that awe me. Great people never had this honor, so my guess is that there is a reason you are given all these miracles. And your search has brought you many vexing questions. That is the sign of a worthy search and a worthy mind. How can I help, Ty?"

"I am honored by your presence. As you know, I find lots of science in the Torah. As a matter of fact, that's how my fellow searchers and I found all these wonders. I think that many of the simple verses in the Bible describe technology and other scientific things. Some of the ideas may be beyond our knowledge today."

"And there is nothing wrong with that," Rabbi Mordechai explained. "There is no contradiction between the Torah and science. G-d is the one who created all, including science. As long as you always keep this in mind, then everything is acceptable."

They both looked so serious, as if they wanted to make a point.

"I think we have an answer to your most recent clue," Rabbi Shmuel said.

"We thought about the information for quite some time and consulted Talmudic resources," Rabbi Mordechai continued. "It is a very interesting riddle. Very interesting. One that requires us to investigate deeply before arriving at an understanding."

"Six inner corners, six outer corners, marching structure, thirteen circles. What is the connection and where is the place?" Rabbi Shmuel's face brightened. "I must admit, I simply love Ty's riddles. They've intrigued me for months now!"

Rabbi Mordechai gave him a stern look, and Rabbi Shmuel became more serious.

"Here is the explanation that we came to. The tribes of Israel walked about the desert for forty years. They had to defend themselves against nomadic tribes and other potential foes. They had to develop a strategy—a military strategy—in order to defend themselves."

"By the way," I boldly interjected, "I think the forty years in the desert had a purpose. I think Moses instructed the children of Israel during those years."

"But of course!" Rabbi Mordechai was very much pleased. "Survival, respect for G-d, obeying G-d's will."

"Not only that. Moses brought lots of knowledge from Mount Sinai—knowledge he received there for forty days and forty nights. He then went up again for another forty days and forty nights and gained even more knowledge."

Both rabbis looked at me with interest. It was like I had them hooked.

"See, I think Moses was carefully instructed on the mountain and for an important reason. And not only him. It is said in the Torah that another seventy elders went up with him to study as well. It was like an academy. And they all learned science, morals, and probably other things."

Rabbi Shmuel started to pace about the room.

"The knowledge was brought to the people in the form of tablets, but it could be any other documentation. It was put in the Ark of the Covenant, not to be touched. Anyone who touched the ark died in fire. Can it be that the ark produced some type of electrical field?"

"Now wait, Ty," Rabbi Shmuel protested. "We can't start explaining all these events as science. It's more than that."

"Yes, it's more. There is the religious explanation, but as you said, there is no contradiction. G-d provided everything, including math and science. The people of Israel went through extensive education while in the desert. They were trained in military matters to prepare them to enter the land of Israel and makes it theirs. Does this make sense?"

The two mentors looked at each other and nodded.

"Yes, it makes sense. It also doesn't contradict what I am about to tell you," the older man said.

He breathed deeply and looked intently into my eyes. I was eager to learn from him.

"The twelve tribes walked in the desert and then into the land of Israel in a formation of the Magen David." He drew a six-pointed star on the board. "There were six tribes marching at the top of each outer vertex, and another six tribes marched at each inner vertex." He marked each vertex on the board. "This is a solid defensive formation. It protected the people, and it also protected the Ark of the Covenant, which was in the center of the formation."

"This is very cool!" I gasped.

"There's more, Ty," Rabbi Shmuel continued. "Now we understand the marching structure. It's the children of Israel's marching formation. But what are the thirteen circles?"

He looked over to his elder.

"Here is what comes to mind—and it's the only thing that relates to thirteen circles. The nation of Israel marched around the walls of Jericho once a day, for six days. On the seventh, they marched around the city seven times. Six plus seven is of course thirteen. That relates well to the defensive formation they roamed in. They also walked in this formation around Jericho."

"So the signs point to the conquest of Jericho, as described in the Torah," the younger Rabbi said.

"We learned it in your class!" I exclaimed. "But now I know so much more! That reminds me. I had a question in my mind back then and couldn't quite express it."

"I'm sure you've learned to express it now."

"I have! The battle for Jericho started on the first day, when Joshua met the messenger from G-d who told him about taking Jericho. But the actual attack was on the seventh day, Shabbat. How come?"

Rabbi Shmuel looked over to the senior Rabbi and smiled. "Ty, one day you will become a renowned commentator on the Torah!"

"That means a famous and respected writer, young man," Rabbi Mordechai added.

"Indeed, it does! The siege of Jericho was an exception and permitted on Shabbat for the sake of *Milchemes Mitzva*—to conquer the land of Israel. It's very similar to the verse *pikuch nefesh*. The preservation of human life takes precedent over all other commandments in Judaism. When life is involved, all Shabbat laws may be suspended to safeguard the health of the individual. The principle is *pikkuah nefesh docheh Shabbat*—saving a life in danger takes precedent over the Sabbath. Same with the battle for Jericho. This war was important above and beyond."

"Pikkuah nefesh docheh Shabbat," I murmured over and over. "Yes, yes." After a moment, I said, "Another thing about the battle makes me wonder. Do you think the Nation of Israel had some type of technology to knock the walls down? The description sounds like an acoustic weapon."

"We've never said that there is no description of technology in the Bible. The reason there is no specific description lies within. We may not know it, but what's in our Torah was put there for a reason. We don't question this reason because it is for our greater good," Rabbi Shmuel patiently explained.

"It makes sense. Thank you very much, esteemed mentors."

"You're welcome—and remember, use your knowledge wisely," Rabbi Shmuel said.

I was about to leave when the other words Sam found came to mind.

"If I may, one more matter. We found another few words that might or might not be related to the others: *five steps lead to pillar.* Do you know if this fits with anything?"

The two men pondered the words and tried to see a connection. They looked upward, they nodded, they mumbled. Rabbi Mordechai finally spoke. "A very wise rabbi was once asked a very difficult question, and after some time, he looked at the young man and uttered words I shall never forget. He said, 'Beats me.' I will have to give it further thought."

"As will I," said Rabbi Shmuel after chuckling a moment.

"Once again, I thank you for your time."

And with that, I raced home to my laptop.

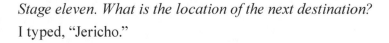

*Stage eleven. What is the location of the next destination?*
I typed, "Jericho."

Please don't make me do any more traveling! Oh please don't make me do any more traveling. You see, my father—

*Correct. Go to that location. Find the key.*

I came close to breaking the commandment about using a certain name in vain.

# Chapter 17
# Jericho

The folks, Hannah, and I went to La Jolla beach in late August, just before school was about to begin. My folks waded along the shore and let the gentle waves run across their bare feet. Hannah and I tried our luck with boogie boards. We didn't have much luck but improved slightly after an hour. Dad bought us snow cones to enjoy beneath an umbrella just above the beach. Hannah and I poked fun at the fruit stains around each other's mouths. As you can imagine, a question was dogging me all day.

"Someday you will understand the joy of seeing your children enjoying themselves," Mom said, looking over to Dad. His face all but glowed.

"I already know the joy of seeing my father playing with model cars he claims he bought for me!" I said.

"Guilty. That recollection makes me travel back in time," he said.

He said *travel*, and I had to pounce on it.

"You know, speaking of travel. I'm still on that numbers quest."

"Good to hear!" Mom replied. "Persevere. Always persevere."

"It's a one-of-a-kind learning experience," Dad added. "Such wonderful field trips."

"Yes, they are wonderful. One right after the other has been amazing. I've grown immeasurably from each of them."

"He's grown enough to use words like *immeasurably*!" Mom said.

"Well, there's another field trip in store."

"And I presume it'll cost a lot more than a snow cone."

"Umm … probably."

"Back in the Middle East, I presume."

"Yep. Specifically Jericho."

"Jericho? That's in the West Bank, I believe."

"Yes, but we can visit the ruins. I read about it. No restrictions for us."

"What for?"

"The usual. We need to find a site and some clues."

Dad looked over to Mom, and they chuckled.

"Here we go again …"

I wondered if this would be the point where Dad said there was no more travel. But he surprised me.

"You know something, why not? Just give me a little time to budget the trip. In the past year, we've been jetting around like the Kardashians. I need a second job."

"I have a lot of people who've registered for a seminar in Colorado this fall. I can contribute to your budget."

"Thank you, Mom, thank you." I gave her a bear hug.

---

In the end, it was just Dad and me. Sam wanted to come along but had to teach a grad course. We would stay in touch of course. Rabbi Shmuel called me shortly before we left San Diego.

"Ty, I wish you a fruitful trip, but the main thing is to be safe. Jericho is not a friendly place. You and your father have to be careful."

"Will do, Rabbi Shmuel, and thank you."

"It's believed that Jericho is among the oldest cities in the world. It's the site of amazing miracles for our people. The army of Joshua seized it—the first city east of the Jordan River to become ours. The land is sacred. Always treat it that way."

"I will. Of course."

"One more thing, Ty. I'm proud of you. Very proud."

"Thank you. Thank you so very much!"

"Never hesitate to call or text me with any questions, at any time. Good luck, and G-d bless."

An hour later, my father and I were winging our way back to the Holy Land. We went over the information we received on Mount Sinai, but it wasn't at all clear what it meant. As with the cave and mountain, we didn't have exact coordinates. We didn't really know what we were going to do. We decided to cover any and all the old sites and trust in … well, in something. We did have one thing going for us. Dad had a college friend who taught archaeology at the Hebrew University in Jerusalem. He knew the area and was interested in helping out when he could.

I felt grateful for all I had learned, but I wasn't yet satisfied. I hoped to find out more and looked forward to Jericho. I felt excited about the new adventure. I'd been to the Western Wall, seen the ark, and visited Mount Sinai. It had been a great adventure that was more than most people experienced in a lifetime. I was very privileged. But all those clues made me more curious. What was at the end of all this? I was sent to all these places to solve riddles for a purpose. What was it? I felt determination inside me. I had to complete this mission. I felt that this mission had become the mission of my life.

After a pleasant sleep, I awoke to see the beautiful beaches of Tel Aviv below us. The sun shown on hundreds of early swimmers enjoying calm Mediterranean waters. Even from that altitude, I could see it was crowded. Another thing. I realized that I had been born in Israel. It was my country. My place of birth and whole life were intertwined. No matter where I was, I was an Israeli.

We rented a car at Ben Gurion Airport, drove fifty miles east to Jericho, and checked into the Steele Honey B&B. It was a fairly simple place, but the hosts were pleasant and eager to help any way they could. We conked out and prepared to meet our guide in the morning.

We woke to the Muslim call to prayers that boomed from a loudspeaker. I didn't realize they would be so loud. In the cozy lobby, we enjoyed fruit and baklava. Soon enough, Dad's friend met up with us. He was tall and lean with a serious look and a Tembel hat. That kind of headgear was very popular in the 1940s and became a symbol of the hearty settlers who built farms and eventually the state of Israel.

"Tal Amir, my old friend! Good to see you after so many years. This is my son, Ty."

"Ty, I've heard so much about you and your interests in ancient sites. You may be a future archaeologist!"

"I've already seen some remarkable archaeological places in Egypt, Turkey, and Saudi Arabia, so I have a good start in that direction."

"So you enjoy archaeology then!"

"Yes, but I am also into math and religion."

"You have plenty of time to decide. I suggest we hop into my truck and head for the first site. We'll have to do a lot of walking, so I'm glad you're wearing sturdy boots."

Off we went. Dad and Tal chatted about families and past times. I suspected they were omitting a few events from their college days. Half an hour later, we came to a stop.

"We are now at Tell es-Sultan. It's a remarkable site, as you shall see and as I shall explain."

He began a tour guide presentation in accented English as we looked at all the buildings made of tan mudbricks on stone foundations. There were a lot of fences to keep visitors back. As I stood amid the captivating archaeological site of Jericho, I couldn't help but feel a profound sense of wonder and connection to the distant past. The ancient city, often referred to as the City of Palms, exuded an aura of mystery and history that enveloped me. The sight of the towering mound of Tel Jericho, with its layers of history dating back over eleven thousand years, was awe-inspiring. Walking among the remnants of this once-thriving city, I marveled at the Neolithic wall, a relic from around 8000 BCE, one of the oldest city walls in the world. The atmosphere was thick with the echoes of countless generations who had called this oasis home.

"Jericho is one of the oldest continuously lived-in cities in the world. Its Arabic name, Ārīḥā, means fragrant. There are freshwater springs here and there. If you look around, you will note how dry and brown everything is. Those springs meant life and a little prosperity. There are gentle hills in every direction, and underneath most of them is an ancient structure covered by dust and sand. Some walls go back eleven thousand years." Tal seemed infatuated with history.

"How many people lived here when the children of Israel settled here?" I was curious.

"Between two and three thousand."

"We're actually searching for a specific structure, Tal," Dad said. He rubbed his hands together, as if he was eager to get down to business.

"A little historical background could be of use, my friends. Jericho is famous as the first town conquered by the B'nai Israel under Joshua."

"That's in Joshua 6," I said.

"Indeed, indeed. After its destruction by Joshua's forces, the fortress was abandoned until Hiel the Bethelite set up there in the ninth century BCE. Herod the Great established a winter residence at Jericho. He died there in 4 BCE. Excavations in the 1950s revealed a magnificent façade that's thought to be part of Herod's palace. The style shows Roman influences. Newer areas date back to the Crusades, a mere thousand years ago."

"That's what goes for new around here!" Dad said. "I notice that there is no access to the site itself, as it's blocked by fences."

"Right. It's off-limits, mainly because it's dangerous. People have fallen and hurt themselves. Okay, maybe I've lectured too much. What are you guys looking for?" Tal sat on a rock and awaited our reply.

"We're looking for a specific monument that has five steps or stairs. They lead up to a pillar," I said.

"That's very specific. Why?"

"We believe there's vital information in the area. You know, like an inscription or some symbols. We don't really know."

"So you're playing a hunch or following some inner voice."

"That's pretty much it," Dad said.

"Oh … well, I am a bit disappointed, I have to say. I could have told you plenty of interesting information about the site, but my knowledge doesn't seem to be called for in this situation. I'm a lonely man with meaningless knowledge!" He bowed his head in pretend self-pity.

"Tal, please don't take this personally!" Dad said. "It's just that we have a specific task. And of course we need your help."

"I'll hide my tears for now! And maybe after you find what you're looking for, you'll allow me to blather on about the Romans and the Crusaders!"

"Deal," I said.

"Let me think about the five steps or stairs. Let me think. We are currently at Tell es-Sultan. Let's go over to the Tower of Jericho. That's a tall stone structure, about eight meters high. It's thought to be the world's first stone building and maybe the first monument. Oh, am I lecturing again? Anyway, it's only a short walk from here. Look! You can see it from here."

"Very cool! Let's go!" I said.

As we walked, the lecture started up again.

"The tower contains an internal staircase with twenty-two steps. It must have taken years to build. Most of the tower was destroyed along with the walls by B'nai Israel."

We arrived at the site in just a few minutes, and Dad and I inspected the ruins and the small bricks it was made of. A look of surprise came across Tal's face, and I thought he was suddenly reminded of another obscure detail about the site. Happily, I was wrong.

"Now that I think about it, I might know where your site is."

"Lead on!"

"It's this pillar here. It was one part of the walls."

"I see stairs!"

"But they're behind a fence," Dad cautioned. "But I'll be darned. This is exactly what you described. Five stairs into a pillar. I am astonished—again!"

"Well, I don't know if it's exactly what you seek, but it seems to fit. Let me tell you about it. The site was excavated in the fifties and—"

"We need to go down there. There's no one around!"

"Whoa! We're on the West Bank now. We've got to be a little mindful of local laws and officials."

I looked at Dad. He seemed to want to do the same thing I did. Dad and I pleaded with our eyes.

"Okay, okay. You guys have come a long way and feel there's something behind that fence."

"We know there's something waiting for us, Tal. We know it!" Dad said.

"Can you help us?" I added.

"You Americans sure can be pushy! We can work something out, I think. This place is usually deserted at night. Too many rocks to stumble over and too many pits to fall into. We can come back tonight—late tonight—look around, and find our way to the stairs. How's that sound?"

"You're a mensch!" Dad said. "We'll dine near where we're staying and return under cover of darkness."

I thought about Lara Croft but stayed silent. We were going to look at some stairs, not rob a tomb.

"Gentlemen, I know a place in town that has excellent kabobs."

He was right. The kabobs and rice were delightful. We bought flashlights, walked around the old town till nightfall, and hopped into Tal's car for the drive back to the tower. He dimmed his lights as we neared the site.

"Okay, no flashlights until we get to the stairs," Tal whispered.

We walked around the fence's perimeter, lit only by the moon, until we found a part we could crawl under. Tal pulled the fence back, and Dad and I scrambled underneath. Then Dad returned the favor. We brushed off the dirt and followed Tal to a gaping hole in the ground surrounded by rocks. Down we went, one flashlight on now. The footing wasn't easy. The rocks and bricks were loose, and some of them crumbled beneath our boots. The noise was alarmingly loud in the dead of night, and a dog barked in the distance. Down we went until we were at the base of the pillar.

"The steps! Five of them!" I whispered.

Dad and I shone our flashlights all around.

"So you don't know exactly what you're looking for, but I'll help," Tal said. "I guess I'd spot something out of the ordinary fairly well. Let's get rid of these weeds and shrubs."

We pulled them out by the roots and used stones to break the sturdier brush.

"What's this?" Tal said.

Dad and I went over to him. A clay fragment was sticking out from the dry soil. Dusting it with some shrubbery showed it to be pottery. So we dug around it carefully with sticks and hands and a pocketknife that Tal had.

"You know, if you scratch around Israel, you're bound to eventually find something old and intriguing," he said. He dug more deeply while Dad and I held our flashlights on the area. More and more of the clay came into view.

"It's a pitcher, a bit like a Greek amphora but much older than anything from the Mycenaean era. My question is, will it go to a museum or my office?"

"Our question is, can we see any symbols on it?" Dad countered. Those were my thoughts too.

"Let's dig around a little more. Then we'll head back and examine this treasure more carefully," Tal said.

We did just that, but aside from a few shards, there was nothing. So we went back to our hotel, where Tal ran water over the pottery's dirty surface.

"There's definitely something there!" I said. "What does it say?"

"It's peculiar. It seems like a set of numbers."

"Can you translate it?"

"Afraid not. But let's take photos and send them off to language experts."

"We know one at MIT!" I said.

We took plenty of pictures of the artifact from all angles, and I made sketches of them in case something intervened again. The photos came out well though, and we sent them to Sam, who quickly and enthusiastically acknowledged receipt.

The three of us spent the next day further exploring Jericho. With our mission done, we were much more interested in his lectures on history and archaeology, especially the ruins of Jericho's walls. Along the way, we mentioned our interests relating events in the Bible to science and mathematics. I couldn't help but let out what we'd found in Egypt and Saudi Arabia. When I started to mention our trip to Turkey, Dad gave me a look saying I was going too far, that Tal might think we were—what's the word? Oh yeah, *meshugenah*.

"That's intriguing, Ty. If I can be of any help, let me know. I can dig around here so you gentlemen don't have to fly over here and run up bills."

"Whew! That is a most welcome offer, old friend. Thank you," my father said.

It was very welcome news. The team was now my father, Sam, Tal, and me. Four brave searchers, thousands of miles apart.

That night as I lay in bed waiting for sleep to take hold, I realized I wanted to come back to Israel. In fact, I wanted to stay there forever.

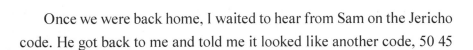

Once we were back home, I waited to hear from Sam on the Jericho code. He got back to me and told me it looked like another code, 50 45 40 30 20.

I entered it into the computer.

*Incorrect.*

*Two numbers missing.*

*Enter code.*

I entered the numbers, even though I was sure I'd done them right.

*Incorrect.*

*Two numbers missing.*

*You have three more attempts. Upon third unsuccessful attempt, your effort will be terminated.*

*Enter code.*

What the …

I checked the numbers once more. Nothing was off. How could we miss two numbers? I came close to panic. My journey might be coming to a swift and unsuccessful end for want of two lousy numbers. I texted Sam, and he set to work.

Wait, wait, wait. That was all I could do. I played video games, even *Fallujah 2004,* but they didn't hold my interest. The mall with Hannah was a pleasant diversion but my mind was elsewhere. Same when we went to the beach and boogie boarded.

Sam got back to me the next day.

"It's not a mathematical series of some sort. At least we can't estimate based on these numbers. Maybe it's a series, but the number forty-five breaks the series theory. One option is that the number before fifty should be sixty, assuming decrease operation by ten."

I went to work.

*Incorrect.*

*Two numbers missing.*

*You have two more attempts. Upon third unsuccessful attempt, your effort will be terminated.*

*Enter code.*

Oh no.

I stared at the screen. What if I asked for a hint? It wouldn't be considered an attempt. Maybe the system would give me a break.

With a shaky hand, I typed, "Hint," and waited several painful moments.

*Hint: the first number is three.*

I wrote down on my paper: 3 50 45 40 30 20.

I was more confused. So I called for help. He did say I could contact him anytime!

# Chapter 18

# Sin Cities

"Ty?" The groggy voice seemed to still be asleep. "Oh my … do you know what the time is now?"

"Yes, Rabbi Shmuel, but there's a crisis. I have two more attempts to figure this out. If I fail, my whole quest comes to a terrible end. Can I ask you something now please?"

"Oy … let me go to the study so my wife doesn't make me sleep on the couch."

I heard footfalls as he headed down a hallway. I told him of my trip to Jericho, then read him the numbers. He jotted them down and mumbled them over and over.

"These numbers have no connection as far as I see. Maybe it's the late hour. Let's talk tomorrow, all right? Over and out."

"Over and out."

I ran the images through an enhancement program on a camera enthusiast website but got nothing. It was pointless, but it helped me sleep.

---

This time, it was Rabbi Shmuel who woke me the next morning.

"I think I have it."

I was alert immediately.

"Rabbi Shmuel, remember we have to be very careful. Two more mistakes, and I turn into a pillar of salt or something like that."

"Well, few things in life are certain, Ty, unless they're given to us in scripture. However, I called Rabbi Mordechai, and he called a colleague, and we arrived at something. Are you in touch with the man in Israel who is in possession of the object?"

"Yes."

"Good. Before we try anything, please confirm with your friend that there's nothing more on the artifact. Then we can continue."

"I'll contact him today."

I Zoomed Tal when it was early evening there and told him of the numbers. I watched as he scribbled the numbers on his office blackboard.

"Two wise rabbis want to know if there're possibly any more symbols on the item. Something we missed or couldn't quite make out."

Tal switched on an ultraviolet light and took out a large magnifying glass. It made him look like Sherlock Holmes.

"Let's see, let's see. Nothing … nothing … still nothing. Wait." He bent in farther. "Well, I see something that might be another symbol, but it's extremely worn. I can't make out anything."

"Can you please take a photo of it and send it to me? We can run it through some programs here in the States."

"Yes, Ty. Give me a minute." I heard a few clicks. "They'll be on your way over WhatsApp in two minutes."

"Thanks, Tal! Over and out."

"Is that how they say goodbye now in California?"

I eagerly looked at the picture. I saw worn-down swirls and lines but nothing I could make out to be a symbol.

"Off to MIT for you!"

Sam acknowledged receipt and got to work on it with the Cray. An hour later, he called.

"The symbols are too worn to make them out with any certainty, but the program identified seven possible symbols. I've rejected two of them as highly unlikely, so we're down to five."

"We have only two chances left. After that … *pffftttt!*"

"That's all I can do on my end, Ty. Truth told, the two rejects might be right. I just doubt they are though."

"They are seven, twelve, ten, eighteen, and twenty-one."

"Thanks, Sam."

Rabbi Shmuel and I were in his office on a Zoom call with Rabbi Mordechai in New York. He had been sent the numbers via email earlier and spent an hour pondering them.

"A difficult case. A very difficult case. I looked at all these numbers and combinations, but I can't reach a conclusion with confidence. The numbers seven and eighteen are significant in the Jewish religion, but they don't match the initial sequence. You'll have to look inside yourself, Ty, and seek some sort of guidance beyond what two rabbis can offer. But your friend from Israel gave you more information. I would check with him one more time. Maybe he can look harder."

I had a sinking feeling as Dad and I began to speak with Tal. He'd obviously just gotten up and was sipping tea in an IDF sweatshirt.

"Isn't it rather late where you chaps are?"

"It's one in the morning, Tal. But unless we get some more data, Ty's mission may come to an abrupt end."

"An esteemed rabbi suggested the numbers seven and eighteen might be what we're looking for, but we wonder if there's anything else on the pottery. Anything at all that can help."

"Well, I'm quite certain there's nothing more on the artifact. However, I know a thing or two about numbers and what they meant in ancient Israel. Let me give it some thought. I'll check back with you when the sun comes up on Southern California."

"We'll be up a while longer," I said. "If anything comes to mind, give me a holler."

"A holler? You mean an email. Okay. Over and out."

Not an hour later, Tal hollered.

"Your rabbi suggested either seven or eighteen, correct?"

"Yes, but his confidence wasn't high."

"Hmmm ... this is a tough situation. The best I can come up with is the number eighteen. It's the closest to the others. We have only one number, three, which is small. The rest are larger."

"Thanks, Tal. I appreciate your thoughts, and I will make the decision."

"Over and out—oh, and good luck, young man!"

After Dad went off to sleep, I sat in front of my computer and stared at the blinking cursor.

What to do, what to do. I was almost sure about the number eighteen. But Rabbi Shmuel told me to listen to my heart.

What was my heart telling me?

Nothing.

What if it wasn't seven or eighteen?

Tal was thinking it was eighteen. He knew archaeology. My heart wasn't on board though.

Nonetheless ...

Zoom interrupted me. It was Tal.

"Nothing further to report on the artifact, but I thought you and I might be able to think things through. Can you think of anything in the Bible that involves a sequence of numbers?"

"The creation of the world took place in seven days."

"True, true. But seven just isn't in the vicinity of the sequence we have. We're dealing with fifty, forty, twenty—larger numbers."

"There were forty years of wandering the desert. And Moses was on Sinai for forty days."

"That's a candidate. It's in the vicinity. Let's take another look at the first group of numbers we found."

"They are three, fifty, forty-five, forty, thirty, twenty."

"And then we have seven, twelve, ten, eighteen, twenty-one. Which one can be our missing number?"

"Originally, the number three was not provided. It was given to me by the website as a hint."

"Aha! So originally, we had the numbers fifty, forty-five, forty, thirty, twenty."

Tal fell silent, which distressed me. But I perked up.

"Tal … what if the three is not really part of the sequence? It may be additional information, like three days, or three events, or three people, or something like that?"

"Excellent, Ty! You may be on to something. It doesn't look like it belongs to the sequence; it might well be additional information. What do you recall of the number three?"

"Well, three fathers, Abraham, Isaac, and Jacob. Then we also have three mothers, Sarah, Rivka, and Rachel. This comes to mind quickly, but I don't see any connection to our numbers."

"That's okay. What else?"

"I dunno, I just dunno … One more thing. G-d sent three messengers to Abraham. One to heal *brit milah* problems, the second to tell him his wife, Sarah, was going to have a son, and the third to tell him about the destruction of Sodom and Gomorrah. Three angels, Rafael (רפואה) to heal Abraham, Michael to speak of Sara, and Gabriel to Sodom and Gomorrah."

"And how does this relate?"

"I got it! It's the sinful cities of Sodom and Gomorrah! Abraham negotiated over them. He asked for mercy if fifty righteous people could be found in these. G-d agreed. Then Abraham asked what if only forty-five righteous people were found? And then thirty and twenty until ten. G-d was willing to spare the cities if ten people were found."

"And the righteous people were not found," Tal said.

"Exactly! The missing number is ten. That's it! It must be. The three is the three messengers, and all other numbers refer to the righteous people. The missing number is ten!"

"Go do your thing. I'll be waiting to hear what happened!" Tal smiled.

I typed, "3 50 45 40 30 20 10."

*Correct.*

*Sodom and Gomorrah.*

*In ten days, there will be more instructions.*

I turned back to the phone, screaming, "Tal! We did it!"

"Wonderful! Your scream made me half-deaf ... but I'm elated. I'm proud of you! Now, young man, you can rest for ten days!"

"I will!"

"Over and out."

# Chapter 19

# Hero

I 'd become deeply interest in the ancient world, especially Israel and
Egypt, Babylonia and Persia. I knew each nation's history and myths
and how they rose and why they fell. I could look at an image of a pillar
or relief and tell you what century it was made. Just call me California
Jones. But there was always the question of technology in ancient Israel
and the divine role in getting it. It was exciting to see it so clearly in
person. Numbers, math, and science are everywhere.

The more I thought of Sodom and Gomorrah, the more I wondered
about the technology used to destroy them. I read that traces of sulfur
and other chemicals were found in their today's location recently, and
that meant intense heat long ago. The more you learn, the more you
know how little you know. Some smart guy said that.

I logged on exactly ten days after my previous entry.

*Lot's wife was transformed into a pillar of salt during the destruction
of Sodom and Gomorrah. Not too far from those cities, there was
another event involving pillars. Who was the main character?*

It sounded familiar, but the hour was late. So I did a web search and
found several relevant passages.

I entered, "The pillars of cloud and fire. Book of Exodus, shortly
after Moses leads the Israelites out of captivity in Egypt."

*Incorrect.*

I scrolled through more web results and found something else. "Samson was tied to a pillar."

*Correct.*

*The number three and its derivatives are directly connected to Samson. What are the events connecting three and Samson?*

Okay, I did another web search.

"Three wives."

*Correct.*

"He challenged thirty Philistine guests to answer a riddle."

*Correct.*

"The thirty suits of clothing challenge for the riddle."

*Correct.*

"He killed thirty Philistines in Ashkelon."

*Correct.*

*More.*

"He caught three hundred foxes, tied them in pairs, placed burning torches on their tails, and let them loose, setting the crops ablaze."

*Correct.*

*More.*

I typed, "End."

*There is one more connection.*

"Hint."

*The land of Israel.*

Web searches got me nowhere. Same with sitting back and letting my mind think it through. An hour later, it was clear I needed help, but it was far too late to call Rabbi Shmuel. I opened WhatsApp and found Tal.

I summarized the most recent replies and the hint.

"Hmmm … well, we know that Samson lived in Timnah and was one of the major judges of the tribes of Israel." He pointed his camera at a huge map covering a wall to his right. "This is a map from that time. If we look at it, we can see a few things that I believe will be helpful."

"I'm all ears."

"What?"

"It's just an expression meaning I'm eager to hear you."

"Got it. Samson was from the tribe of Dan, which lived near Philistine cities. He was involved with those places. His first wife was a Philistine from Timnah. She converted to Judaism, and then he married her. He also went to the city of Ashkelon, where he avenged his wife's honor. And lastly, he carried the heavy gates of Gaza. Three Philistine cities. Maybe this is your answer?"

"I'll see."

I typed, "The cities of Timnah, Ashkelon, and Gaza."

*Correct.*

*Connect these cities, go to the middle, find a clue.*

I shared the screen over Zoom.

"Okay, okay. I'm working on this, Ty. Let's look at my map again."

He drew three lines on the map, connecting the cities and forming a triangle.

"Now we have to find the triangle's centroid. Let's draw a few more lines and … here it is. The center is the village of Mash'en. Interesting that the name means *brace*. Back in ancient times, it was known as a trading hub and—"

"Tal, is there any way—"

"I'll pack now!"

"You're a mensch!"

"So I'm told. So I'm told."

In the morning, Dad loaded the data into a program and got precise GPS data. Well, reasonably precise. Dad explained that the centroid was based on less than exact data.

"It might be a few hundred yards away at least, Ty."

"But it's the best data we have. So we work with it."

"You got it, son. I'll send the data to our colleague."

Tal was streaming on WhatsApp as he walked around Mash'en, a small village in Israel. I saw palm trees and, now and then, the sea. It didn't look very crowded or old.

"You know, it's a small town, maybe a thousand people, and rather new. It was established by Jews who emigrated from Yemen in 1949. The name comes from Isaiah 3:1. Okay, I'll reach the coordinates in a few minutes. I brought a metal detector. It might come in handy. You never know."

His camera showed him in sunglasses and tembel hat, then shifted to a few acres of open, rocky grassland with dry brush, some with menacing thorns. In the background was a filling station with a convenience store.

"I don't see anything of significance yet, but my experience is that in the Holy Land, many things aren't instantly visible. I'll walk around more. Aha! Never mind. It's only an empty bottle of Tempo. That's a beer, Ty. You're too young. Your dad and I—"

"Tal! Please!"

"Okay. Let's switch on the metal detector. Okay, here's a sardine tin. Someone had a snack out here."

The search went on and on. An hour passed.

"I need a break. Maybe that gas station has Popsicles."

"Or a bottle of Tempo!"

"Wait! Hold my beer! My metal detector found something."

We watched as the detector beeped over an area, and he dug through the dirt.

"It's a coin." He held it to the camera, and I could see it was old. I got that woozy feeling.

"Maybe at this angle you can see the image of a man's head."

"Yes, I see it now."

"Well, it's ancient, probably a few thousand years old. As you would suspect, I have a lot of old coins. This one, though, doesn't look familiar. This is quite a find!"

He got a Popsicle, then continued the search for another hour, going over the area in a grid pattern. Nothing showed.

"Tal, maybe that coin is what we were supposed to find. I feel it is."

"Maybe. Maybe just a coincidence. I'll examine it more closely at home and consult sources online and in my archeological network."

"Please let me know."

"Good night, Ty."

When I got home, I decided to gamble.

I typed, "I found the clue. It's a coin."

*Correct.*

*You must identify the coin's meaning in order to reach stage twelve. You can do it only after your twelfth birthday.*

I slumped back in my chair and stared at the blinking cursor. I knew I was on my way.

Wait! How did it know my age?

*What is the coin's meaning?*

"Hint."

*The last stage hero was defeated by the Philistines.*

*The man on the coin won against them, starting at a young age. Who is he?*

The last stage hero was Samson. He was defeated by the Philistines. After Delilah shaved his hair, they captured him and chained him. Those guys won, but Samson eventually beat them. He died doing it, but he still won. I decided to do a web search.

An hour later, I entered, "King David. He defeated Goliath and the Philistines as well."

*Correct.*

*Tomorrow at midnight you'll be given special instructions.*

*You must be there.*

Midnight, huh? Very mysterious.

Wait! This whole thing is mysterious!

*You have done good work so far and reached the twelfth stage.*

*It is the second to last stage and a most challenging one.*

*It is divided into two parts, and you must pass both to reach stage thirteen.*

*You have up to one year to complete stage twelve. It must be completed before your Bar Mitzvah; otherwise, you'll never get your answer.*

I hoped for more. I desperately needed more. It came.

*You must follow the path of a great leader.*

*Once started, you have to complete the assigned tasks within one year.*

*Are you ready to start now?*

I felt excitement. I felt obsessed.

"I am ready!"

*Good luck.*

*Follow the path.*

*Kind David was chosen by G-d.*

*The prophet Samuel was sent to Yishai's house in Bethlehem.*

*What was key to David's selection?*

This should be easy, I decided!

I quickly did a web search for King David and thought things through.

So Yishai thinks that David was not even his son. To protect him, he has him become a shepherd. The prophet Samuel was sent to find the next king. He was impressed with Yishai's handsome son, Eliav, so Samuel thinks he may be the chosen one. But G-d tells Samuel it's David.

The key to David's selection must be …

I typed, "Bravery."

*Incorrect.*

"Wisdom."

*Incorrect.*

Okay, okay. You know where I went.

---

Rabbi Shmuel listened attentively, occasionally nodding his head. When I finished, he stood and paced about his office.

"David was chosen in a unique way. Samuel was sent to Bethlehem by G-d's command but claimed to be there to worship."

"That was so Saul wouldn't suspect anything was up."

"Precisely, precisely. Samuel goes to the house of Yishai to select one of his sons to succeed Saul but has to do this without Saul's knowledge. He goes to Yishai's house and asks him to present his sons. He is impressed with Eliav, who was tall, strong, and handsome, but G-d tells him not to be deceived by appearances."

"He wasn't the one."

"Right. So Samuel considers the other sons, then asks Yishai if he has more children. Yishai answers he has another son who is shepherding. Yishai calls him in, and when Samuel sees him, G-d tells him that he is the one."

"David!"

"Right again. The wise men explain that Yishai suspected David was not his. He did not resemble him and even had red hair. Yishai kept him away from the others for fear they would slay him. So Samuel anoints David with olive oil."

"I don't understand the key to the choice."

"Think about it, Ty. How was he chosen?"

"He was brought from the field and … I dunno."

"Samuel wanted to select another for strength and appearance."

"Wait! There's a key verse, but …"

"G-d tells Samuel that he sees with his eyes."

"Got it. I remember now: ' הָאָדָם יִרְאֶה לַעֵינַיִם וַיהֹוָה יִרְאֶה לַלֵּבָב '—'For man looks at the outward appearance, but G-d looks at the heart.'"

"You are an exceptional student, young man!"

"You are an exceptional teacher!"

"An esteemed mentor?"

"That's what I meant!"

---

And that was what I typed, "For man looks at the outward appearance, but G-d looks at the heart."

*Correct.*

"Yes!"

I took a bite out of a Snickers bar to celebrate. The screen began to fill line after line. I was getting a lecture. Fortunately, I was sitting down.

*In 1993, there was a significant archaeological discovery. Three stone fragments were found with several lines of Aramaic. Archaeologists considered them proof King David existed. Four more pieces of the stone have not been found.*

*You must find the other four fragments and assemble the message inscribed on them. The message will send you to another place, where you'll have to find more clues.*

"Where is the place of excavation?"

*Find it.*

"No Snickers for you!"

I found a few articles online and enjoyed other bite of chocolate-peanut goodness as I began to read.

Math … theology … archaeology … and candy bars.

> The 1993 discovery was the Tel Dan Stele. It dated back to the ninth century BCE. The inscription details that an individual killed Jehoram of Israel, the son of Ahab, and the head of the House of David. It corroborates passages in the second book of Kings. The stele was probably erected by Hazael, an Aramean king mentioned in the second book of Kings as having conquered the land of Israel, though he was unable to take Jerusalem. One piece was found in 1993, and another two pieces were found in 1994 excavations. Its pieces are currently on display at the Israel Museum.

So the place was Tel Dan in Israel. I could ask Tal to go there. He probably knew the place. But finding four more pieces would be hard. At least we had Tal on board. Could be a long journey. A very long journey.

I ate my dinner slowly that evening. It would be more accurate to say I moved the chicken and mashed potatoes around my plate with only a few morsels making the trip to my mouth. Mom was talking about the herbs and crystal for her upcoming seminar in the Cascades of Washington. Dad was listening attentively but looked at me from time to time. He knew something was up. Mom excused herself to prepare for a conference call. It was quiet until Dad spoke.

"Ty, do you need any help with your homework tonight?"

"Not really. I can handle it."

"What's bugging you?"

"Nothing."

"Ty, Ty, Ty … I'm your father—and part of the team. I have a feeling you have something on your mind. Let's whisper. Your mother is a little weary of the archaeological expeditions. Out with it."

"I'm working on the last problem. The very last one. If I solve it, the quest is over. If not ... well, this one's too big for me."

"I doubt there is such a thing! What is it?"

"I need to find four pieces of an old stone that has an ancient message on it. I don't know where they are. On the bright side, I have until my thirteenth birthday to solve it."

"Well, that doesn't sound harder than what we've tackled already. And your birthday is a ways off."

"Yes, it is. But the items. I have no way of knowing where they are. I think the website made me run round the world as a joke, then hit me with an impossible problem. It played me."

"Alternately, Ty, the website prepared you for this last task. It believes that if you handled the previous ones, you can handle this one too. It was like grade school and high school preparing you for college."

"I've learned a lot since this thing began. About numbers and religion and the ancient world. It was all like a prep school."

"A very demanding prep school, which you excelled at, young man. No one else could have done this. You and I can handle this final challenge."

"With help from Sam and Tal."

"The team."

"What about Mom? I think she's concerned with my fascination."

"It's true, though she calls it your obsession!"

"Obsession?"

"Well, maybe once or twice. But she's supportive. She believes in finding one's own path and seeking ... well, seeking oneness or something like that."

"This is the deal. There's an archaeological site in Israel called Tel

Dan. Three pieces were found there. I need to find four more. We have Tal in Israel, so I thought to ask him to help."

"You know he's on board. He can do the digging. That would save us the trip, I hope!"

"It won't be easy. The site is big. An acre or more. And the fragments are, well, they're fragments. They're most likely underground, and they're not metal, so Tal's metal detector won't help."

"Ty, you are a remarkable young man. I'm so proud of you."

"I'm proud of the whole team—you, me, Tal, and Sam."

"With a team like that, we can't lose!"

We went over the location on a Zoom call with Tal.

"Of course I know the Tel Dan site! I've been there a dozen times. It's not a small place, you know. In fact, it's about two hectares. Oh, that's about five acres to you guys. And what am I looking for again?"

"Four stone fragments. None of them more than a few feet by a few feet. Maybe even smaller."

"So my trusty metal detector probably won't help, unless I'm looking for more beer cans. I was afraid of that. I really was. Anything specific you can tell me about where to put shovel to ground?"

"Let me try something," I said.

I logged on and entered, "The place of excavation is Tel Dan."

*Correct.*

"Where to dig? Hint."

*Dig at the wall.*

I showed the screen to Tal.

"Well, that helps quite a bit, but it's a pretty big wall. I've put in for a dig permit, and I'm pretty sure it'll come through in a few days. A guy I know is in the relevant office. He's even offered to help for a few hours every now and then. He's a groovy guy. Do they still say groovy there?"

"Not in many years, Tal. But I'm sure he's a groovy guy," Dad said.

"It's hard to keep up with American slang. You guys know I have a lot of work to do at the university—teaching, committees, office hours, and a lot of other things. And you know I do have a family. But this project intrigues me, and I'll devote as much time to it as I can. At present, that means weekends. Not every weekend but as many as I can possibly cram in."

"I appreciate everything you do, Tal," I said. "And I can be on WhatsApp with you whenever needed."

"He needs adult supervision," Dad said.

"Oh, well, maybe I can tell Ty some stories about—"

"Sorry, Tal. We have to go now!"

"Over and out, you groovy guys."

# Chapter 20

# Damascus

Months passed.

"I've found bits of pottery and an occasional beer can, but that's it," Tal reported over Zoom. "Not what we're looking for. Is there a possibility of getting another hint from that website?"

"I didn't want to press my luck, but it's worth a try."

I logged in and asked for another hint. To my surprise, I got one.

*Dig near the bench where the elders judged the people.*

Tal was relieved.

"That narrows it down a little. The wall, however, is rather long. I'll start looking there early next week."

And he did, sometimes with a colleague but usually not. Most of the time, I was on a Zoom call with him. Other times, he recorded parts of his work and uploaded them to his personal website. I was very eager to hear what he had to say, yet I was a little conflicted as well. I wished I could be there, doing this work myself. Waiting is hard. I had to go to school and act like I cared about normal things, but my heart was far away. Everything seemed to take a very long time.

Late one night, about three o'clock, I heard the chime of an incoming Zoom call. I was on it in a flash and clicked on camera. There was Tal beaming widely and holding a flat fragment.

"This looks promising! I believe it's what American fishermen call a keeper!" he said proudly.

"It sure does look promising!" I replied gratefully. "We have to get the information on it, then give it to a museum."

His head slumped in exaggerated disappointment.

"I see Aramaic characters but can't make them out. I'll have to clean it up at home. My guess is it's from the time of the First Temple!"

"Wow! That was …"

"That was three thousand years ago! Now you go back to sleep, and I'll go back to work. The other fragments might be just a few meters away!"

Tal was right. Over the next month, he and his friend came upon the three remaining fragments. From there, it was matter of assembling them correctly, which was easy, and figuring out what the Aramaic said, which was hard. But between Tal's expertise with languages and Sam's Cray DEROS, we got it. Well, most of it. There were damaged and missing places.

And]..[…………] war […….]
[… .] fighting against […]
[…] [Aram]
33 … [30] … [37.49] [04] … n
36 [16] [42.00].. [96] … e
the H[ouse of David. [……]
the land [……]

Fairly quickly, we figured out where I must go. The MIT computers were pretty strong.

I typed, "Damascus."

*Correct.*

*Find clues at Damascus site.*

"Damascus! Seriously? No way!"

I told Dad that evening.

"Damascus? Damascus? Who do those guys think we are? The Russian army? The Islamic State? Please tell me you have GPS coordinates."

"Got 'em right here."

"Well, let's see what we can do. This is way beyond our scope, and I am sure you know that."

"I know, but I need the clues that are there. If I don't complete it, there is no other way to avoid losing everything." It was hard to say that. I felt heavy, like I might even cry at the thought of not being able to continue my quest.

"We can try to look at the GPS coordinates from above again."

"Yes, I agree, but I am not sure this will do the trick. I don't even know what I have to look for. I assume again some writings on a stone or something similar."

"Do you have the exact GPS coordinates?"

"Yes. It's part of the old city of Damascus."

"I figured as much. Let's take a look."

Dad read, "'The site was built during the Aram-Damascus kingdom. It was part of an Aramean society that existed from the late twelfth century BCE until 732 BCE. It was bounded by Assyria to the north, Ammon to the south, and Israel to the west. The site sits alongside modern parts of Damascus.'"

We scrolled through the amazing photos of the place. Page after page of them. Some in black and white from the early twentieth century; others were clearly done with modern digital cameras.

"Ty, Damascus is in Syria. Do you know what that country's like today?"

"I know there's lots of fighting, especially in the north. Not so much in Damascus though."

"There are no fences or guard posts around the site. This is an important archeological site, yet it sits next to modern office buildings and paved roads."

"So it's safe! We're in!"

"Easy, Ty. See if we can get some help from the website."

I logged on and asked for a hint.

*There is great destruction of Jewish heritage in Jobar.*

*Go there to search for clues.*

Dad was searching in a flash.

"'Jobar is a district in Damascus. Its magnificent synagogue, Eliyahu Hanavi (Elijah the prophet), was destroyed a few years ago. It was built atop a cave traditionally thought to have served the prophet Elijah in hiding. The hall center was said to be the place where Elijah anointed Elisa. During the Syrian civil war, it was damaged, then looted.'

"We're going to need Tal," Dad said, exhaling loudly.

"I'll call him now."

The instant his camera came on, I laughed out loud.

"What's the matter, Ty? Haven't you seen a man enjoying a SpongeBob popsicle?"

"No, I haven't! You are the first!"

"They're quite good. Fruit punch on a stick. Somehow, I think this conversation is going to change to archaeology and travel to some exotic place in Israel."

"Not really," Dad said.

"Really? It's not … oh wait! You mean my next exotic place isn't in Israel."

"Correct, my friend. It's not far away though."

"Thank heavens for that. So is it in Egypt? Jordan?"

"Neither one. It's—"

"Oh no! You're not talking about going to Syria!"

"As a matter of fact, we are. But it's not Golan or Aleppo," Dad said calmly.

"Palmyra has magnificent Roman ruins—and a Russian airbase now," Tal noted.

"It's Damascus!" I said.

"Damascus! You think I'm in the Russian army? Syria isn't exactly hospitable to our people, gentlemen. You may have learned about the Six-Day War and the Yom Kippur War. You see long ago … okay, no lecture. But about going to Damascus. We're going to have to think about solving that problem. All three of us. Over and out."

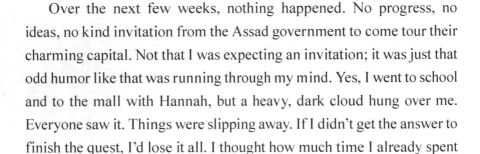

Over the next few weeks, nothing happened. No progress, no ideas, no kind invitation from the Assad government to come tour their charming capital. Not that I was expecting an invitation; it was just that odd humor like that was running through my mind. Yes, I went to school and to the mall with Hannah, but a heavy, dark cloud hung over me. Everyone saw it. Things were slipping away. If I didn't get the answer to finish the quest, I'd lose it all. I thought how much time I already spent on this adventure. And not only my time, the entire team's time, about two years. I couldn't stop now. I just couldn't!

But then my twelfth birthday arrived, and that distracted me for a few days. My parents threw me a big party with a magician who came to our home and amazed us with his tricks. My friends and I loved it. Dad invited Rabbi Shmuel, and he stayed for a short while. He gave me a special holy book called Tehillim. This book is a collection of 150 religious poems or songs that are traditionally attributed to King David.

Dad and I went to a trampoline park one Saturday. I bounced away for an hour or so and enjoyed myself a great deal, more than I thought I would.

"Let's have Asian food," my father said, and off we went to a Thai place down a side street next to a jewelry store. In between bites of pad thai and chicken satay, he said, "I might have a solution."

For a moment, I didn't know what he was talking about and kept eating. Then I dropped my chopsticks. "A solution? Oh, you mean—"

"Absolutely, I mean that. I was speaking with an old friend from my IDF days. That's the Israeli military. And we feel that he and I can get into Damascus for a few days."

"I want to go too!"

"Not on your ... I mean definitely not. It's dangerous. And if your mom found out I took you into Syria ... well, I'd rather be in a Syrian dungeon."

"But I know the site! I know what we're looking for. And Mom's communing with people in the Cascades. Please?"

"Oh, finish your pad thai, and we'll get dessert to go. We've got some work ahead of us."

---

We planned it for the Hanukkah holiday. My dad took a week off, and I had a school break. My dad's friend got us two British passports with our actual names. My dad would be an archeology professor, and I'd be his son. You might say I was born to play that role. Our residence was San Diego, but our birthplace was London. The passports were valid and issued by the British embassy with all the necessary IDs and details. We were to stay two nights in Damascus and then fly back to the US through Heathrow, just outside London. In case anything went wrong, my dad's friend would be in a Swiss embassy that operated secretly in the Syrian capital.

I wasn't afraid at all about going into a war-torn city. Maybe I should have been, but I was too excited about getting back on the quest and exploring a new dig. Who wouldn't be? I wondered just what my dad's friend did for a living, but I never asked. It was good to know he'd be nearby though.

---

On the flight to London, my father cautioned me about talking too much while in Syria. I might sound American or, what's worse, slip with a Hebrew or Yiddish word. That could cause *mishegoss,* or big troubles in English. Sorry, couldn't help it! We could become hostages, parts of international hostilities. I just wanted to learn about numbers, not start a war.

We landed at Heathrow, and after a short layover, it was off to Damascus on Emirates Airlines. We had to go to Dubai first, then basically make a U-turn to Damascus. That said a lot about the politics in the Middle East. We landed in the late afternoon and headed immediately to the checkpoint for recently arrived passengers. It wasn't anything like you'd see at Heathrow or JFK. It was more like something from a Chuck Norris movie. Guys in army fatigues and assault rifles were everywhere. I thought of my *Fallujah 2004* video game. No, the thought didn't make me come anywhere near to laughing. This was serious. It dawned on me. Guys like this hate guys like us. Anyway, it went well. The guards looked at our papers, asked a few questions in good English, and with a sudden head motion, signaled we could go on our merry way. A bouncy cab playing Arabic hip-hop music took us to the Old Vine Hotel, just a short walk from the Eliyahu Hanavi Synagogue.

The hotel had seen better days. The lobby had large planters with nothing in them and a fountain that wasn't turned on. Dad said that all the fighting over the years had reduced tourism a great deal. The concierge (that's like a hotel manager) said he hoped things would pick up in a year or so but was pleased to see the occasional guest interested in the old ruins. We checked into our room and hit the hay. I watched a little TV, but there were no subtitles. I'd picked up a little Aramaic over the years, but my Arabic was *bupkis*!

We awoke early and walked a few blocks to an old part of the city, turned a corner, and there we were in front of the Eliyahu Hanavi Synagogue, or what was left of it. Barefoot children ran and played in piles of rubble nearby. We heard an occasional explosion far away and rifle shots a few blocks away. I was not afraid at first. In the contrary, I felt the excitement of a new adventure. I think I simply didn't grasp the meaning of being in a hostile country. But when I noticed that my dad was quite worried, I started to feel unsettled. The synagogue itself was strangely quiet.

I made sure to stick close to my father. For the first time in our travels, I was in a place that left me feeling uncomfortable.

My father approached an old man with weathered face and dim eyes who stood nearby for no apparent reason.

"English?" my father asked cautiously.

"Little," he replied with a weak smile that caused lines on his face to come to life.

"We visit here for archeology. We from a British university. This is Eliyahu Hanavi Synagogue, isn't it?"

"Yes. Eliyahu Hanavi. Yes." His smile slowly vanished. "I had friends here ... they come here and pray. Bombs come here. Boom! Now you see. People come, steal and rob. Steal and rob."

"We are looking for anything of interest. Do you know where we can search?"

"People steal everything from holy place. Ilyās."

"That's Eliyahu's name in Arabic," my father explained to me.

The old man looked at us. There was a tense pause, and then I figured it out. My dad accidentally said Elijah's name in Hebrew. He looked at us for a few moments and then said, "A friend talk like you do. He was other faith."

"I see. There are things dividing people and things they have in common."

"My friend die here. Salman. Good man, good man. He prayed here. After he prayed, he come my house drink coffee. Good man, good man."

My concern eased as I saw my father come to trust this old man. You don't know the meaning of concern until you're in a dangerous land with loud noises every few minutes. I started to think my video games were childish compared to the danger that was here every minute.

"You come with me. Come with me. Show you. Maybe good."

"Okay. Thank you," Dad said. He looked at me warily, as though to say we should be prepared to make a run for the hotel at any moment.

We followed him down a side street to an old building with a rusty lock on the door, which he opened with a copper key. It was a one-room dwelling with a small carpet in the middle and a mosaic table.

"My home. Sit. Please sit. Coffee soon."

He boiled water on a hot plate, and in a few minutes, the smell of extremely strong coffee filled the room. He poured three cups.

"Drink, coffee. Please."

I didn't know much about the Arab world, but I knew that hospitality was important there, and although I was only twelve, I had to sip the concoction before me. I managed to do so without choking.

"Many years good here. Everyone lived good, everyone was friend. Holidays together, kids play, everybody friends. No war, no war. War come and nothing same. Jews leave. Most. My friend and family stay. Yes, they stay ... then ... soldiers kill them. Women cry."

"I'm sorry, sir. Truly sorry," Dad said.

"Thank you, thank you. Wait. I give you something. Wait."

He opened a padlocked wooden chest and brought a large basket covered with a red silk scarf. He handed it to my father and motioned for him to look beneath the scarf.

"Oh my, oh my," Dad whispered in astonishment.

I was dumbfounded. It was an ancient Torah scroll, yellowed and cracked in places but well preserved. Beneath it was a metal pointer in the shape of a hand used to avoid damaging old parchments with oils from human hands. Deeper in the basket were stone fragments, one of which had the Star of David engraved onto it, a Siddur prayer book, a stained tallit that enclosed a menorah. In better light, I could see it glow. It was made of gold.

"From the synagogue?" I asked.

The old man nodded solemnly.

"No steal. I protect. I protect until right time. Right people. For you. Right time, right people. I know."

He pointed to his heart and nodded.

"Not long. Not long for me. Gifts for you. Not long. You take. I wait many years to give this someone. I am sick." He pointed in his stomach. "Die soon. This is holy for Salman. Holy for you. You take it to other synagogue. Other synagogue. In Britain … or America."

"Can you show us back to the old synagogue? We want to search."

"I take you there, but all is stolen. Nothing there. But I take you."

My curiosity was awake. Now that I felt we could trust the old man, I wanted to explore the synagogue, to find more clues. This man radiated friendship, and I felt comfortable with him.

He led us down the side streets to the ruins. We looked around for several hours but found nothing. We stepped out onto the main street, but our guide was nowhere to be seen. There were only a few children playing. I didn't want to quit, but it was hard to see how to continue.

"I wanted to give him the prayer book."

"It might have been dangerous for him to have it," Dad suggested.

A burst of gunfire sounded a few blocks away, and the children stopped playing. Dad suggested we get back to the hotel, and I was not one to argue.

We didn't know what to do with the artifacts. If we were found with them, there'd be trouble. Big trouble. Dad suggested his friend could send them to us in a diplomatic pouch. They arrived in San Diego a week after our return.

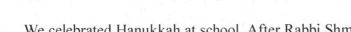

We celebrated Hanukkah at school. After Rabbi Shmuel told us of the Maccabees and the Temple, we went off to auditorium for *sufganiyot* and cider. Oh, sufganiyot are like jellied doughnuts without the holes. Afterward, it was just Rabbi Shmuel and me.

"Ty, I've never seen you with a briefcase before."

"Well, it's my dad's, and I brought it for a reason. You see, he and I were in Damascus last week."

"Damascus? It's so dangerous! What could possibly have made you go there?"

I opened the briefcase and removed the gold menorah. It glowed in the late-afternoon sun. My mentor's mouth opened, and his face took on the look of a child beholding a treasure.

"It's Hanukkah now, Rabbi Shmuel. It was used on the Festival of Lights at the Eliyahu Hanavi Synagogue in Damascus hundreds of years ago."

"Maybe thousands, Ty. Maybe thousands. And to think it was only a hundred and fifty miles from Solomon's Temple."

"A hundred and thirty-five miles. I measured it while we were there."

"Of course you did. Of course. I should've known you would find that number!"

"The Eliyahu Hanavi Synagogue was beautiful—one of the most splendid places of worship in the Middle East. We wept when we heard it was desecrated a few years ago."

I reached into Dad's briefcase once again. "I brought a few more artifacts." I placed the prayer book, stone fragment, and Torah scroll on the table. "We can keep them here or at Shul. I would like your help translating whatever we can. It may help on my quest."

"Somehow, Ty, I think these sacred artifacts will help you a great deal. This is an amazing Torah scroll."

"I hope so. I got stuck trying to connect all these relics. I mean, I want to think they're connected, but maybe I'm just too eager to think they are. Maybe they're just a handful of wonderful but unrelated things."

"Let's see." Rabbi looked closer at the artifacts. "At the time some of these artifacts were crafted, Israel was part of the Greek Empire. It was divided up when Alexander the Great died."

"That was in 323 BCE of course."

"Other artifacts are much older. Hence your puzzlement about connections. Kings Saul and David were many hundreds of years before Alexander. The menorah is especially interesting. It isn't a Hanukkah menorah, which has nine candles. This splendid work of art holds only seven. It can only symbolize one place."

"The Temple!"

"Yes, Ty, the Temple. Or the Beit Hamikdash, as it's known in Hebrew. Before the Maccabees revolted against the Greeks, the only menorah was in the Temple. It was gold and had seven candle places—three on each side and one on the middle. Each had its own oil source."

"Does each light stand for something?"

"The menorah as a whole symbolizes enlightenment. The central branch represents the light of G-d emanating to the other branches—a symbol of human knowledge. Light is often used in Judaism to mean wisdom and divine revelation. The seven branches symbolize completion.

"The number seven is sacred, and it appears often: seven days of creation, the Sabbath is the seventh day of the week, and other places as well. The Hanukkah menorah has eight branches—one for each day of Hanukkah, plus another for the *shamash*, the helper candle. We celebrate the eight days of Hanukkah to commemorate the miracle that took place during the Maccabean Revolt against Greco-Syrian rule."

"There's my Syrian connection!"

"Indeed. The menorah and the Magen David on the fragment point in one direction—the Temple. Let me go on, if I may. King David united the twelve tribes, conquered Jerusalem, and brought the central artifact of Judaism, the Ark of the Covenant. David chose Mount Moriah in Jerusalem as the site to house the ark."

"But G-d forbade him to build it because he was a warrior who had shed much blood."

"That is the case, young man. But his warrior history wasn't a black mark. It was simply incompatible with the peaceful nature of the Temple. David's son built the Temple."

"Solomon."

"Yes, yes. It was Solomon."

He studied me for several moments. He was looking for the right words.

"Ty, you have taken great risks saving these objects so sacred to our faith. With great risks, there are great rewards. I have only a small one for now. I've chosen you to lead a weekly discussion. It will give you more opportunities to discuss matters of our faith with your classmates and esteemed teachers, especially from a scientific point of view. Are you up for it?"

"I feel honored. But …"

"There's no extra homework involved!"

"Yes!"

---

I typed, "First House of the Sanctum, First Temple."
*Correct.*

*The Large Stone Structure is believed to be the remains of King David's palace. Go there, find clues.*

I knew it, I knew it, I knew it.

"What should I look for?"

*A code.*

"What code?"

*A code.*

I knew I'd hit a wall and decided to turn in right after I sent what I'd learned to Tal. I was almost asleep.

Just then, I remembered about the next day.

Monday brought my first presentation to the class. I couldn't have declined Rabbi Shmuel's offer. It was an honor, and in the back of my mind, I knew it would be good for me. That was the sort of thing parents said to kids. "Do it. It'll be good for you. You'll see. Someday you'll understand." I couldn't believe I was telling myself that now. My day had come, and I was as prepared as a boy my age could be.

"Class, today we have a special speaker. No, it's not Rabbi Mordechai or any rabbi for that matter. It's a member of this class who has gone to great lengths to learn aspects of our faith over the last year."

Hannah looked at me with a quizzical look. I nodded, and she smiled.

"Each of you will have the opportunity—the honor—of speaking before us; however, today we begin with Ty Lev."

Now everyone was looking at me, including the guys who thought I was just a goof. Well, I stood and proudly walked to the podium with a clipboard containing notes. Rabbi Shmuel sat at his desk next to me.

"Esteemed teacher and classmates, today I'd like to present my views on an interesting scientific phenomenon—our solar system."

"A phenomenon is something that's been observed by science," Rabbi Shmuel said.

He looked concerned, as though I was going to go off into taboo things. I was ready for that.

"My presentation will directly relate to biblical events and holidays."

He sat back in his chair, though still on guard.

"Our *hanukkiah*, the menorah we use during Hanukkah, has eight candles and a server candle, the *shamash*. According to tradition, all candles get their light from the server candle, which spreads the light to the others. Now, our solar system includes eight planets, and the sun provides the light to all. This is a direct analogy to the menorah. Is it a coincidence? Or is it the first model of our solar system?"

My audience was listening with great interest. Okay, one or two guys rolled their eyes, but Hannah smiled so very sweetly, and my confidence grew.

"Each candle has a twin on the other side. Astronomers see pairs in our solar system. For example, Mercury and Venus are called twins. They are similar—very hot and uninhabitable. Mars and Earth are similar in size and other characteristics. Same for the other planets. So the question remains, is our hanukkiah an ancient model of our solar system?"

I saw signs of wonder in my audience.

"Yes, I think it is!" Hannah said. "You just showed it to us all!"

"The Torah has it all," said a classmate who typically didn't talk much.

"A fine presentation," said Rabbi Shmuel. "Now let me say a few words, if I may. We already know that our Torah contains vast amounts of knowledge and wisdom. We can see it in any part of our lives. We are told to wash our hands before we eat. We are told not to mix certain foods. And we are told of forbidden foods. Modern medicine justifies these rules. This is not only in medicine. Ty has nicely presented the knowledge of the universe contained in our ancient texts. The connection between the hanukkiah and our solar system had not occurred to me before this very day. I have to thank Ty for this. And so should all of us."

My classmates applauded, and I bowed my head modestly.

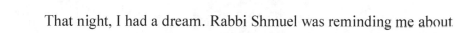

That night, I had a dream. Rabbi Shmuel was reminding me about my quest.

"You are doing great things, Ty, but don't hold back now. Remember, you have to finish your quest before your Bar Mitzvah."

He stopped abruptly, and his face looked strangely puzzled and sad—something I'd never seen before.

"Your time is my time. Your time is my time."

I woke up in fear and confusion. What did it mean?

# Chapter 21

# City of David

I needed to find information about the Large Stone Structure that is believed to be the remains of King David's palace. The archaeological site was on the eastern side of the City of David, Jerusalem. I asked for Tal's help, but he was busy with work and unable to get to the site for two weeks. Two long weeks. Additionally, he had to get an archaeologist permit, and that took more time. Finally, after a few weeks, he could start searching at the site but didn't find anything. Well, we also didn't know exactly what we were looking for. Maybe inscriptions, codes, or signs? After about a month of no results, I rethought everything—all the previous finds and hints and searching around. I closed my eyes and thought. Was this site the proper place to look for the next item? My mind swirled, and a thousand images flashed before my eyes—the island in the Nile, the cave in Turkey, Iraq, Jericho, and Damascus. They all blurred into one image, one thought. Then I remembered the discussion with Rabbi Shmuel after I returned from Damascus. Yes, all hints led to the City of David. I was on the right track, in the Jerusalem site.

I got back in touch with Tal in the morning.

"There must be something there. I'm sure of it. Please look again for an inscription, letters, signs, something. Please?"

"I'll do my best next weekend."

<hr />

Unfortunately, he was unable to make it that weekend or the next one. The time until my thirteen birthday was slipping away every day. It was still seven months away, but it no longer seemed as long as it once did. You know how kids think a few months is eternity? Well, I used to think that way but no longer. My time was limited.

I read up on the Jerusalem site and many others. I thought it might help with my quest, but it was interesting anyway. Learning stuff is interesting. The more you learn, the more you want to learn. Like that German guy who felt it was his mission in life to find the ancient city of Troy. That's the place where the Trojan Horse was. He eventually found the ruins of Troy in Turkey. But I was more interested in the holy City of David. I found this:

> The Stepped Stone Structure is the name given to the remains at an archaeological site on the eastern side of the City of David. It is a curved, 60-foot (18 meters) high, narrow stone structure that is built as a series of terraces. It was uncovered during a series of excavations in the 1920s, the 1960s, and in the 1970s–1980s.
>
> The archeologist who found more details in 2007 believed that the Stepped Stone Structure connects with and supports the Large Stone Structure. She presented evidence that the Large Stone Structure was an Israelite royal palace in continuous use from the tenth century until 586 BC. Her conclusion that the Stepped Stone Structure and the Large Stone Structure are parts of a

single, massive royal palace makes sense of the biblical reference to the Millo as the House of Millo, describing it as the place where King Joash was assassinated in 799 BC while he slept in his bed. The Millo is described in the Bible as having been built by Solomon and repaired by Hezekiah, without giving an explanation of what exactly the Millo was. However, it is mentioned as being part of the City of David.

So I came to the conclusion that the site was indeed the remains of King David's palace. I launched a web search for Eilat Rosen, the archaeologist who wrote that stuff about the palace, and emailed her. She got back to me! A professor in Tel Aviv actually got back to me! I'm just some guy in San Diego with odd ideas, and she got back to me! She gave me her WhatsApp name and a time to call. I couldn't wait.

"Hello, Eilat? How are you this … well, I guess it's morning there in Israel."

"Good evening, Ty. It's a pleasure to get in touch with you."

"Same here—and thank you for taking the time to help me."

We talked about where we lived and where we'd been, but I was eager to get down to business.

"I need to know if you found any particular inscriptions in the site we believe was King David's palace."

"Well, we found quite few symbols and Aramaic and ancient Hebrew. Some were in good shape, and some were worn and chipped. That's simply something we have to expect. Time wreaks havoc on all things."

"Even stones?"

"Yes, even stones. Sandstorms, freezing water, millions of feet."

"Where are they now?"

"It was many years ago, so I don't remember exactly, but all the materials we found were given to museums or the local authorities. I can look it up if you like."

"That would be awesome!"

"I still have my excavation diary. Let me look through it. I digitized it a few years ago. Okay … okay. Yes … yes. I see in here that we did find something out of the ordinary on one of the stones. It seemed to be a number of some sort. At the time, we didn't know what it meant, so we simply recorded it. We just couldn't figure it out."

"That might be just what I'm looking for. What were the characters?"

"It was actually three numbers: four, seven, one. We weren't sure if it was individual numbers, part of a message, or something else entirely. There were no other symbols, which was odd to us. It appeared on a small stone that seemed made of white rock. But wait—how do you know about it?"

"Oh, I'm doing research regarding architecture in ancient Israel."

"Pretty heady stuff for a lad your age. I don't understand how you knew to look for a number or a combination of numbers. I find it fascinating. We never talked about these findings with anyone besides the antiquities authority."

"I dunno. It was just a lucky guess that came from my vivid imagination. Thank you very much, Eilat. You've been amazing. I need to go to sleep now. It's very late in here. Many thanks again."

"Okay. Glad to have been of help. Shalom."

"Shalom!"

I pulled up the computer screen with the question on it. I typed "4 7 1" and hoped for the best.

*Correct.*

*We will get back to this number later.*

*You are starting now the second part of stage twelve.*

*King David planned to build the First Temple, but the task eventually fell to his son, Solomon. King Solomon was married to many women from many countries. He also had children with some of these women. In one of these countries, his son created a dynasty, and that country considers King Solomon as its father.*

*Which country is it?*

Hmmm. This would be interesting. I did a web search.

It looked like King Solomon had seven hundred wives and three hundred concubines. Seriously? Seven hundred? He must have been a busy man. How did he manage to get anything done? Oh, and how would I find information about all those kids?

A few hours of fruitless searching brought me nothing. So it was back to the screen.

I typed, "Hint."

*Hint: The relevant country relates to a shofar.*

A shofar? That's like an old bugle. It didn't help a bit.

# Chapter 22

# The Wise King

First I asked Sam. He put a workstation on the job because the Cray DEROS was booked and a search for Solomon's children wasn't supercomputer work anyway. A day later, he got back to me with scores of names and countries but nothing really noteworthy. Nothing tied in with a shofar.

Off to school to speak with Rabbi Shmuel. He had nothing to add except that Rabbi Mordechai would be in for a visit toward the end of next week. I posed the matter to him as soon as he set foot on school ground. He nodded his head, polished his glasses, and stroked his beard as he listened. He sat silently for a minute. I thought he was baffled. But then he spoke.

"Yes, King Solomon was known to have had many wives. Some of his marriages were made to establish peaceful relations with neighboring tribes and nations. Your question is which son went on to create a dynasty, presumably one other than the House of David. A very interesting question."

"Ty, you believe there's a connection to the shofar," said Rabbi Shmuel.

The two rebbes were baffled. Something came to me—something that would never have crossed my mind if they weren't present.

"What is a shofar made of?" I wondered.

"From a ram's horn," Rabbi Shmuel replied matter-of-factly.

"Does that lead us anywhere?" I asked. It certainly led me nowhere.

"The ram caught in the bushes … Abraham saw it as an alternative to sacrificing his son," Rabbi Shmuel said.

Rabbi Mordechai spoke up instantly. "The ram represents the power to penetrate, overcome, and achieve. It symbolizes the assertion of strength in creative ways to achieve a breakthrough. It's also associated with sacrifice."

I quickly searched on my phone and read aloud. "'According to the Talmud, a shofar may be made from the horn of any animal from the Bovidae family except that of a cow, although a ram is preferred. Bovidae horns are made of a layer of keratin around a core of bone, with a layer of cartilage in between, which can be removed to leave the hollow keratin horn. An antler, on the other hand, is made of solid bone, so an antler cannot be used as a shofar because it cannot be hollowed out.' Okay, how do we connect this to a country?"

We sat in silence for several minutes. Rabbi Mordechai shrugged his shoulders and said, "Ikh veys nikht!"

I looked to Rabbi Shmuel.

"That's Yiddish, Ty. Rabbi Mordechai says he doesn't know."

"Oy!"

---

That night, Tal called me out of the blue on WhatsApp.

"How goes it, my friend?"

"I've hit a roadblock. Another one. I can't find a connection between the shofar and the country Solomon founded a dynasty in. Even my two most scholarly and helpful rabbis are baffled. All we have is shofar, ram's horn, and country."

The line was silent, but I could hear scribbling on paper and sipping from a glass. He was on the case.

"I'm getting something, Ty. Maybe. Maybe it's not related to the animal at all. Sometimes the clue is in the question. A shofar is a horn. Let's focus on that word. Do a web search of horn and country."

I read the results, and one got my attention immediately.

He read, "'Horn of Africa, a region of eastern Africa. It is the easternmost extension of African land and for the purposes of this article is defined as the region that is home to the countries of Djibouti, Eritrea, Ethiopia, and Somalia.'"

"Hmmm … I remember a group from Israel visited our school. They were from Ethiopia and told us many fascinating stories about the Jewish community there."

"You are correct. There are many Ethiopian Jews in Israel today. They immigrated here a few decades ago. Apparently, there was a large Jewish community in Ethiopia for thousands of years," Tal said.

"That's it, Tal! I just searched 'Ethiopia son of king Solomon' and got the answer. Let me read it. 'According to Kebra Nagast, a fourteenth-century Ethiopian national epic, in the tenth century BCE he is said to have inaugurated the Solomonic dynasty of Ethiopia, so named because Menelik I was the son of the biblical King Solomon of ancient Israel and of Makeda, the queen of Sheba.

"'He was conceived when his father, Solomon, tricked his visiting mother, the queen of Sheba, into sleeping with him. His mother raised him as a Jew in her homeland, and he only traveled to Jerusalem to meet his father for the first time when he was in his twenties. While his father begged Menelik to stay and rule over Israel, Menelik wanted to return home. Solomon sent many Israelites with him to aid in ruling according to biblical standards. One account holds that King Solomon gave the Ark of the Covenant to his son as a gift, while another states Solomon attempted to regain the ark but was unable to due to its supernatural properties. Menelik was crowned king of Ethiopia and founded the Solomonic dynasty.'"

"It sounds to me like you've found your answer."

"*Toda Raba*, Tal!"

"It was nothing!"

Tal bowed in an exaggerated way and disappeared from my phone.

I was already logged into the website.

I typed, "Ethiopia."

*Correct.*

*The Ethiopian Orthodox Tewahedo Church claims to possess the Ark of the Covenant in Axum. The ark is currently kept under guard in a treasury near the Church of Our Lady Mary of Zion. Replicas of the tablets within the ark, or Tabots, are kept in every Ethiopian Orthodox Tewahedo Church.*

*Your task is to go Axum and find the final clue.*

Oh man, oh man, oh man!

The final clue!

# Chapter 23

# The Final Clue

I presented the task to my father over dinner. Mom was still off in Washington.

"This is the last task I have to do, Dad. I think."

"Ethiopia? This is becoming a very expensive venture, Ty. As much as I want to help, it may not be possible financially."

I stuck my eyes in the floor. I knew he was right.

That night, I couldn't sleep. I mean, I tried everything. I tried to console myself by thinking back over the great adventure and even the miracles I had witnessed. I guessed that had to be enough.

Still, I hated leaving the quest undone. Six months. I had six months until my thirteenth birthday. And I didn't see any way to get this done.

A few days later, Dad said he changed his mind. "Well, at least it's off the beaten path. We've never visited that part of the world, I'll say that. Plus, we want to complete that quest, right?"

"Off the beaten path and fascinating! I'm not getting any younger. I need to go. Please?"

My father released a long sigh. Sometimes those things are signs of frustration and an approaching scolding. Sometimes they're signs of throwing in the towel. Dad was involved in my quest. Not as much as I was but a little more than Sam and Tal were. I thought I had him. Nonetheless, I held my breath. Then he smiled with wit.

"Well, I have to look at the bright side. You're giving us a world tour. Without your quest, I would never have seen all those exotic places. At least it's not a hostile country. And to be quite honest, I am starting to like worldwide exploration. I'll see what I can do. Passover will be here soon."

"Great! Thank you, Dad."

I didn't mention there was a civil war going on in Ethiopia. I had researched the country quite a bit. Fortunately, the fighting had for some reason stopped near our destination.

Our guide explained that being in the town of Axum was like stepping back into ancient times. It was said to have been founded by the great-great-grandson of Moses. In its heyday, the empire it governed was a great power. Today, Axum is most famous for ancient granite obelisks, the queen of Sheba's palace, and the church of St. Mary of Zion. And if that weren't enough, it's also said to be the resting place of the Ark of the Covenant, one of the most precious relics of three religions.

The Tewahedo Church had an unusual type of architecture. It looked a little like the old gray buildings at English universities, at least to me. The columns were straight and simple, and on top there were several domes and crosses. Inside was a museum with lot of crowns, clothing, paintings, and artifacts of emperors of Ethiopia. A long corridor led to a huge iron door.

"Behind that magnificent doorway is the Ark of the Covenant," our guide said reverently and proudly.

"Can we see it?" I immediately asked.

Our guide smiled. He had probably heard that question a thousand times.

"Only on very rare occasions are people allowed behind the door, and only for a minute or two. Needless to say, guards are inside, and they will prevent any trespassers."

I couldn't stop myself from knocking on the door. My dad was irked, but our guide remained calm.

"I assure you that no one will open the door. The guards have strict orders, and they obey them to the letter."

I stared at the door, trying to visualize what was behind it. The sound of clanking metal came from the secret chamber.

"This cannot be," our bewildered guide said. "This simply cannot be!"

We stepped backward as the giant door swung toward us, opening only slightly. A tall monk, dressed in a long black robe, gave us a stern look, as though to say, "Who dares disturb me?" He stared straight at me.

"Can I see the ark please?"

"No one can see the ark," the monk said. "Absolutely no one."

"I came from very far away. I'm on a quest."

His eyes now looked more like they were studying me than rebuking me. "I'm afraid not, young man."

"Please," I said with sorrowful eyes.

The monk closed his eyes, maybe searching for an answer, then spoke softly. "Only you can enter with me—for a few minutes only."

I couldn't believe my good fortune.

Dad looked deeply worried. "I am not at all sure about going in by yourself. We don't know what's inside. It could be dangerous. Isn't it said that no one should touch or even get close to the ark?"

"I know. The rabbis have told us that. I won't touch anything. Promise."

"This is an extraordinary privilege, sir. Most extraordinary. I've never heard of such a thing!" our guide explained with a bewildered face.

"You can go in but only for three minutes," Dad said as he looked at his watch. "Three minutes."

The monk motioned with his hand, and I headed immediately for the huge door. I was frightened at first, but curiosity and faith took hold, and I entered the dark chamber. The door closed behind with a loud clang. The air had the scent of old wood and exotic spices.

"That's the scent of frankincense, which comes from a special tree, young man. Follow me and do exactly as I say."

He opened another door, smaller than the outer one and painted red and gold. The inner chamber was dark except for candles and a circular window about two feet in diameter near the ceiling that sent rays of light through the hazy air. We walked a few steps in, and the monk pointed ahead.

There on a massive slab of black marble was an ancient wooden chest with long arms extending from front and back. Two large gold birds adorned the top. The sun brightened, and the ark and all its detailed engravings shone brilliantly. The birds seemed to be soaring in midair.

"No closer, young man. No closer."

His words, though whispered, reverberated in the sacred chamber and sounded like a gentle wind in a forest.

"This is it? The ark?" I asked softly.

"We have replicas in every church in Ethiopia."

The answer was no answer.

"But is this the real one?"

He smiled softly.

"That is not for me to say. This is the way we protect the ark. No one really knows which is real and which is replica only."

"I see. So no one knows which is the true ark. Even if it's a replica, it's a great privilege to see it. And who knows? Maybe it is the real one. Imagine that, seeing the sacred Ark of the Covenant."

My mind returned to my quest. There was a clue here, and I had to find it before time ran out.

"Do you know if there are any inscriptions or fragments?"

"I know of nothing in here besides the ark."

"Is there anything you can tell me that you never told anyone? I need to find something."

He looked at me with a strange expression. It was part puzzlement, part wonder. Yes, a look of wonder same over the stern monk's face. "For generations, there was the puzzle of where the ark is. It's claimed that it's here, as King Solomon gave it to his son, Menilek I, the king of Ethiopia."

I listened intently. We were on to something.

"The Old Testament records that in the seventh month of the year, at the Feast of Tabernacles, the priests and the Levites brought the Ark of the Covenant from the City of David and placed it inside the holy of holies of the Temple." The monk paused and looked over to the ark. "So the question remains, is the ark really here or is it somewhere else entirely?"

"Somewhere else *entirely*?"

"I can tell you this. Under the old city in Jerusalem, where King David used to walk from his palace to the Temple Mount, there is a passageway. It is not well known. Not at all. There are waterways nearby. Some of the monks here believe with all their hearts that the ark is buried somewhere along that passageway."

"Not here? Not in Ethiopia? In Jerusalem? And it's been there all along?"

"I did not state that as fact. I merely said that some holy men here believe it." He turned again to the ark. "My life has been dedicated to guarding this sacred place. But I've never had the certainty that I should have. That would be deemed blasphemous by some of the monks here. They stand watch, as their forebears have for thousands of years. They cannot have doubt. They cannot have it for one moment. That one moment of doubt would be their end. If this is not the true ark, I hope one day someone finds it. It would mean so much to so many. Perhaps one day that person will come to us."

I was baffled. I didn't know what to say or ask or think anymore.

The monk knew exactly what to say. "Your time is up, young man. We are done in here. Please. You father is waiting."

He motioned for me to follow him, and so I did. When we reached the giant outer door, something came to me. "I don't know your name."

"My name is Isayas. It's an Aramaic way of saying Isaiah."

"And my name is Ty."

"Perhaps you will let me know what you find. I will write a number for you. It is my sister's. Please let me know through her."

"I will. Thank you for allowing me to see this."

He nodded and began to swing open the door but stopped and pondered something. "There is a legend among us that is told for many generations. One day a child will arrive and will discover wonders. I was thinking of that legend when I heard your knock. Ah, but enough. It's time to leave. Your father awaits."

Indeed he was waiting—and rather anxiously too. "Did you see it, Ty? Did you see the ark?"

"Ikh veys nikht."

"What?"

"That's Yiddish."

"I know full well it's Yiddish, Ty! My grandparents spoke it all the time. But what do you mean you don't know?

"I'll explain on the way home."

# Chapter 24

# The Most Sacred

Rabbi Shmuel stood up suddenly and paced around the office. "You were in Ethiopia, entered that church, and actually saw the Ark of the Covenant?"

I couldn't tell if he was angry at me for telling him a tall tale or amazed at what I'd done. To tell you the truth, I don't think he knew either, at least not at that moment.

"Yes … I suppose. I mean maybe. I saw something in that church, but I can't say for sure it was the real thing. No one can."

"So you have some doubt about its authenticity. You're not sure if it was the most sacred object for every Jew, the ark that archeologists and researchers have searched for over many centuries, the holy treasure that was built in Har Saini. Why do you doubt it, Ty?"

"I doubt it because the monk at the church said he himself wasn't sure."

He stopped pacing about and stood next to me.

"A monk entrusted to the site expressed doubt?"

"Yes, he did. He most certainly did. But he suggested a place where the real ark might be."

"Oh, this is too much for me! Much too much. Okay, Ty, where do you think it is?"

"Somewhere under the city of Jerusalem. In the tunnels beneath the Western Wall to be exact. I'd like to go there."

"The Western Wall tunnels? David walked there. This is too much to be just coincidence. Something … Ty, Yeshiva University in New York is sending a team to the Temple Mount next week."

"Can we tag along?"

"Tag along? One doesn't *tag along* on such a thing, but yes, I think with Rabbi Mordechai's help, two more can take part. The school can find the funds for us. Do you think your parents will permit it? One of them will have to sign authorization."

"Oh, I think I can convince my father to let me go. I mean, what's another trip to the Middle East at this point?"

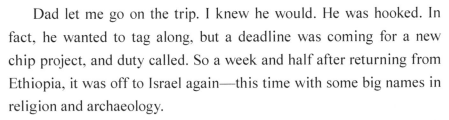

I read some neat information about the tunnels underneath the Temple Mount. They were discovered in the 1850s, but serious exploration didn't happen until after the Six-Day War in 1967. The tunnels were fairly long and had many side passages. Maybe too big?

I typed, "Hint—where to search?"

*After the Guy Street gate, six meters forward, you'll find a niche. Follow the slit.*

I wrote it down.

Dad let me go on the trip. I knew he would. He was hooked. In fact, he wanted to tag along, but a deadline was coming for a new chip project, and duty called. So a week and half after returning from Ethiopia, it was off to Israel again—this time with some big names in religion and archaeology.

Rabbi Shmuel and I sat in JFK in New York waiting for our EL AL flight. The three guys from Yeshiva University had caught an earlier flight and would meet us in Jerusalem. Rabbi Shmuel was trying to nod off after grabbing a bite, but I had a question—as usual.

"Rabbi Shmuel … Rabbi Shmuel …"

"Ah, what? Yes … what did you say? I'm listening."

"I'm thinking about the ark."

"As are we all, Ty."

"Moses received instructions about building it while on Mount Sinai for forty days and nights. Then he instructed the Israelites. First, were the instructions highly technical?"

"Indeed, my young friend. There is no doubt that there were technical instructions conveyed to Moses. The Torah tells us that it was built with specific dimensions and sizes. It was made of several materials, among them gold."

"We also know that it was forbidden to touch the ark, and it was always stored away. While the nation of Israel roamed the desert, wherever they camped, the ark was placed in a special tent—the Tabernacle. As King David was bringing the ark to Jerusalem, Uzzah, one of the drivers of the cart who carried the ark, put out a hand to steady the ark and was struck dead by G-d. The place was subsequently named 'Perez-Uzzah,' literally 'Outburst against Uzzah.' David, instead of carrying it on to Jerusalem, then placed the ark in a house. It stayed there for three months."

"Yes, Ty. The holy of all holies. No one was allowed to make contact with it."

"The ark was used in wars. It was brought into battle in the hope it would bring divine aid. It worked many, many times but not always. In fact, after a defeat at the hands of the Philistines, they seized the ark. But they were stricken by illnesses, and many of them died. So they returned it to our people."

"I am pleased that you have become so learned!"

"So all these facts, in my humble opinion, point toward the

possibility the ark contained some type of technology that could strike people. Maybe radiation? Maybe a transmitter of some kind? There must be numbers involved too."

"I see you are baffled and eager to know more. And that is a pleasing sign that tells me you are on the way to higher knowledge. But we don't need to explain everything in the Torah in terms of science. We *cannot* explain everything in the Torah. Sacred objects are forbidden for all besides those who need to be in their presence. We don't question if science is involved in here."

"I understand."

I didn't.

"But it does make sense, Ty. You know, the Torah doesn't rule out science or contradict it. On the contrary, it supports it in many accounts. It may not provide us with deep details, but science is definitely there."

I sat back in my chair and listened to the PA system announce that our flight would be boarding in forty minutes.

*Forty again.*

I stared out into the New York skyline and thought of its magnificent buildings. I tried to imagine the science and equations needed to build even the simplest of buildings.

"I can't wait to see the tunnels, Rabbi Shmuel. Think of it. A maze and mysterious sites under the Temple Mount."

"It's very exciting. This will be my first experience underneath the Temple Mount. I'm pleased that you and I will be there soon. One thing to keep in mind. This area is a source of conflict between Muslims and Jews, so please always stay with me. Do not leave my sight. This area is a powder keg ready to explode from a small spark."

"Yes, I read about it, and there's stuff on the news every now and then too. I'm almost at the end of my quest. I believe after this hurdle, I'll be given only one more task to do. And then the secret of numbers may be revealed to me."

"I hope so. I truly hope so."

The PA system came to life.

"El Al Flight 440 for Tel Aviv is now boarding ..."

"C'mon, Ty. They're calling us."

"They sure are!"

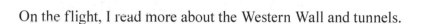

On the flight, I read more about the Western Wall and tunnels.

> The Western Wall of the Temple Mount is one of the
> most magnificent and significant remnants in Jerusalem
> from the days of the Second Temple. It was destroyed
> by the Romans about two thousand years ago. The wall
> once stretched almost half a kilometer, but today only
> seventy meters remain. The tour of the tunnels allows
> visitors to see segments of the wall out of view and to
> touch stones that tell the story of the Jewish nation. Most
> of the tunnel is a continuation of the open-air Western
> Wall and is located under buildings in the Muslim
> Quarter of Jerusalem's Old City.

We rented a car at Ben Gurion and headed immediately for
Jerusalem, where the others were. We had an early lunch near the
Western Wall, then learned the others, eager to see the tunnels, had
entered hours ago and more or less finished for the day. That was fine by
me, as my interests were not the same as theirs, and if I had questions, I
could get in touch. Besides, I didn't want to tell them what my research
was all about.

Rabbi Shmuel and I stood at an archway above the tunnel entrance,
not far from the north side of the wall. We were supposed to be part of

a tour group, but we had other plans. We paused and let them go ahead of us.

"Something extraordinary awaits us, Ty."

"I'm sure of it! Let's go!"

We descended into the tunnel. Though underground, it was nicely illuminated by modern lighting so we could read the signs that gave information. But we were looking for other signs. Rabbi Shmuel and I walked on wordlessly. We could hear the steps and voices of the people ahead of us reverberate off the cold stone. Parts of the tunnel were wide, but some ... oh man, were they narrow! We had to turn sideways in a few places and practically shimmy through. It wasn't for nothing that a sign above ground warned of claustrophobia!

After about forty-five minutes, I heard the tour guide a hundred feet or so ahead of us say this was the Guy Street Gate.

"This is it!" I whispered.

I felt excitement and then sudden dizziness.

"Are you well, Ty? Should we rest a while? We could go back and return tomorrow if you like."

"No! I'm fine. Really. I see a passageway off to the side. It curves off to the right."

The guide realized we were behind and started coming back.

"Go ahead, Ty. I'll delay him."

I walked slowly down the passageway, using my phone to light up the walls. I heard Rabbi Shmuel engage the guide in a conversation about Herod and his dynasty—the Hasmoneans or something like that. I came upon a rusty gate and walked eighteen feet to the exact spot. I shone my light on the walls and above but couldn't see a niche. Then I saw a pillar sticking out of the wall. When I touched it, small pieces about the size of grains of sand fell off.

*Where is it? Where is it?*

I felt a slight breeze, and I noticed a hole behind the brickwork near the pillar. I reached into the hole and felt around until I came upon a metal bar. It was cold, and I felt engraving on it. I tried to pull it, then push it, then move it up and down, but it wouldn't budge. My index finger found a hole in the metal that gave me a better grip.

*Now I got it!*

I pulled and hoped. The sound of heavy stone moving slowly and grudgingly grated my anxious ears. An opening appeared only a little larger than my hand.

*"Follow the slit."*

*There has to be more! There just has to be!*

A dim light appeared in the opening and grew brighter. There was something in there! I shimmied up the wall, sticking my feet into whatever crevices and brickwork I could find. Good thing I wasn't too big and heavy. I poked my head into the hole and saw and felt a warm glow. There was a chamber, maybe the size of a classroom.

*Oh! Oh! I can't believe it!*

There it was. In the middle of the chamber, seated on a stone altar, lay a chest with long arms and two magnificent birds almost fluttering above it in the warm glow. It was the most sacred object of religion and archaeology and human yearning. Yes, there before me was the Ark of the Covenant!

*Right under the Temple Mount. Where else would it be?*

I thought of everything I'd learned in school and synagogue. It was the worldly symbol of G-d's love for his people, built by Betzalel out of acacia wood and adorned with pure gold. It hadn't lost any of its luster and majesty. I was what Rabbi Shmuel called "transfixed"—paralyzed by a sense of beauty and wonder and oneness.

The glow surrounding the ark pulsed like a heartbeat, and symbols began to form. I'd seen things like them. It was Aramaic! I reached into my pocket for my phone and took picture after picture. With pencil and paper, I sketched the symbols just in case.

My feet began to slip, and I slid down to the ground. I sat down, leaned against the ancient brickwork, and caught my breath.

"Ty? Ty?"

"I'm down here, Rabbi Shmuel. Come quick!"

"What is it? Are you okay?"

"I'm perfectly well. Take a look for yourself," I said, pointing to the opening.

He stood on his toes and craned his neck for a look, but he too had to clamber up a few feet.

"No … no … it can't be! It can't be!"

"But it is! I'm sure of it!"

He looked into the chamber for several minutes and began to pray. He climbed down more gracefully than I did and sat beside me.

"It was here all along," he said quietly and solemnly. "I don't understand why it was never found until now. Did you get the message you were seeking?"

I looked at my phone.

"I did. And I took photos. They're still on my phone too. I'll send them out for translation tonight."

"Yes, yes. The sacred images are there."

We both sat there, trying to grasp what we had just seen.

A voice came from down the tunnel.

"Rabbi Shmuel! Rabbi Shmuel!"

It was the tour guide. He'd taken a head count and come up two short. Rabbi Shmuel looked at me and pointed above. I shimmied back up to the opening and pulled the lever, closing off the chamber from any more eyes.

"Oh, we just saw an interesting artifact. Sorry to have caused worry," Rabbi Shmuel said as we stood up and dusted off our clothes.

"You two look like you've seen—"

"We just came across some interesting brick and stone down here,"

Rabbi Shmuel replied in an offhand way. "At least we thought they were interesting."

"But we're amateurs!" I said.

The guide shone his light all around.

"Interesting? Oh, I suppose. There's a lot of brick and stone like that down here, I assure you. Listen, we have to exit the way we came in. There's been a lot of tension about these tunnels in recent weeks, so it's best we do not go out near the Muslim Quarter."

We exited the tunnels where we'd entered an hour earlier, near the Western Wall, and said goodbye to the guide. We wanted to stay a little longer, but the sun was coming down, and security concerns were going up. Rabbi Shmuel faced the wall, donned a tallit, and began to pray with more devotion than I'd ever seen. I joined him. I didn't need a prayer book that day and never did again.

We met up with the Yeshiva University team at Ben Gurion. They were proud of their findings. We said we enjoyed our visit immensely and found our faith strengthened by it. They nodded approvingly.

"I know just what you mean," said one of them.

Rabbi Shmuel and I smiled and thanked them.

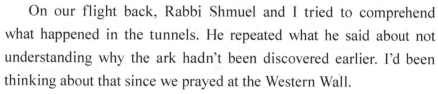

On our flight back, Rabbi Shmuel and I tried to comprehend what happened in the tunnels. He repeated what he said about not understanding why the ark hadn't been discovered earlier. I'd been thinking about that since we prayed at the Western Wall.

"I don't know. Maybe because it doesn't need to be found. It doesn't want to be found. Like Noah's Ark. Some things in life simply are not meant to be found. They are meant to remain hidden and cause wonder and appreciation and urge us on to better things. And ways are found to prevent discovery, like telling us that the ark is in a church in Ethiopia."

"Young man, that is profound, wise, and commendable!"

"Should we keep what we saw to ourselves?"

"Honestly, I'm still confused about what we saw, but I'm almost sure it was what we think it was. This thing needs to be a secret, and I am sure it will be. The ark is protected from discovery. That's all there is to it. Let it remain undiscovered and cause wonder and appreciation and urge us on to better things, as a wise man once put it."

I almost cried. I really did.

"I did get the clue though. And I took pictures of it too. See?"

"I see the opening in the wall, Ty. I also see symbols in there. But I'm afraid the larger object is hidden by the glow."

I looked at the photo again, enlarging it. "You're right, Rabbi Shmuel. You're absolutely right."

"As I said, the ark is protected from discovery, except by a tireless, resourceful young man."

"Thank you!"

"But don't think for a minute you don't have to study for school anymore, especially for my class!"

"Right again!"

The cabin attendant stopped at our seats and asked if we wanted a meal.

"Yes!"

We finished our salmon and rice dinners, and in a few minutes, he nodded off. I looked out the window and gazed at the horizon.

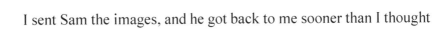

I sent Sam the images, and he got back to me sooner than I thought he would.

"Where did you take these?"

"Oh, in a tunnel underneath Jerusalem."

"Globetrotting again, I see. What's the strange light around the symbols?"

"Well, I can't say for sure. Same with Rabbi Shmuel. I just aimed my camera, clicked, and hoped for the best. I think it's related to my quest. Can you make out any numbers?"

"Here's the message that I translated: 'Father planned, son built.' Then comes a weird sentence: 'Four seven one is what I am.'"

"Four seven one? That's the second time we've seen it. The first time was on that stone, but we didn't get any explanation for it. It sent me to Ethiopia eventually."

"I've run that number through a lot of biblical and archaeological data. More than you can comprehend. I got nothing though. Sorry, Ty. I've done all I can. If you get any hunches, maybe I can work from there."

"You're a mensch! That's a—"

"I know a little Yiddish and Hebrew now, Ty. Believe me I do."

---

I thought of the monk in the Ethiopian church and his request to be kept up to date. Without him, who knows where I'd be. He gave me his sister's contact info, and I found her on WhatsApp.

*This message is for Isaiah. Please tell him that it's from the young man that he helped in the church a few weeks ago. Please send my thanks for his help and the following message:*

*"I found the real one."*

*I'm sure he will know what I mean.*

*He and the others will continue their sacred duty in the church. It's their faith, and I love them for it.*

*Thanks and shalom,*

*Ty*

---

I called Rabbi Shmuel.

"I need your help—again."

"Ty, look out the window. It's almost sundown, and the Shabbat begins within an hour. I have my hands full."

"We translated the message. It has two parts. Part one is 'Father planned, son built.' Part two is 'Four seven one is what I am.'"

"Father … son … four seven one … I'm not getting anything. I have to prepare my presentation and do countless other things. Let me call you back, probably on Sunday."

*Call ended.*

I think he was ticked. But I got the first part. Father planned / son built was of course David planned / Solomon built. No matter how hard I tried, no matter how many times I opened the Bible to a random page in the hope of getting a clue, nothing helped. I had to wait until Sunday. So close, yet …

The phone rang.

"Okay, Ty, busy as I am, my mind went to work for the quest. Four seven one is 'Har HaMoria' הַר הַמּוֹרִיה in Hebrew. It's the site where the Temple stood. It's exactly above the passageway where the ark was. Now, I got to run. The sun is almost—"

"Wait! Please! How did the number lead you to Har HaMoriah?"

"Har HaMoriah in the Gematria practice of assigning a numerical value to a name translates to four seven one. Try it, and you'll see. Shabbat Shalom."

"Thank you! I'm going to research Gematria. I hope I don't get in too deep!"

"I trust you not to go in deep at all."

A small research led to more knowledge.

Gematria, גימטריה, is a practice that assigns a numerical value to a name, word, or phrase by reading it as a number, using an alphanumerical cipher. The letters of the alphabet used have standard numerical values, but a word can have several values if a cipher is applied. Hebrew gematria is commonly used in the Talmud and Midrash and by many post-Talmudic commentators. It involves assigning numerical value to each letter of the Hebrew alphabet, instead of its phonetic value, and reading words and sentences as numbers. When read as numbers, they can be compared and contrasted with other words or phrases.

I had all the information I needed. I felt elated. I knew that I had accomplished stage twelve.

I typed, "Temple Mount."

*Correct.*

*You successfully accomplished stage twelve.*

# Chapter 25

# Stage Thirteen— Har HaMoria

*B*efore moving to stage thirteen, the last stage, you'll be asked a key question about each stage. You must answer each one correctly. Otherwise. you cannot go on to stage thirteen.

Stage thirteen?

*You must dedicate time to this. Some questions may be answered fast; others may require time. You may choose a time to perform this. Now or later?*

I had to think.

*Now or later?*

I looked at the time. It was Friday evening. I had a few hours.

"Now."

*Stage one. You were asked to read the weekly parashah and think about a number. You passed the stage but not because of correct numbers. The numbers you provided were incorrect but not important for the task.*

*What do you think was your important achievement in this task?*

I thought carefully and then typed, "Dedication."

*Accepted.*

Whew!

*Stage two. Here you were directed into the idea of science in the Torah. Abraham received an instruction from G-d to go to the land of Canaan.*

*What did you learn from this stage?*

"Science and faith do not contradict."

*Accepted.*

*Stage three. Today we know about the Prat and Hidekel Rivers, and you found the other two rivers, the Pishon and Gichon, in Egypt. What did you learn from this task?*

"The importance of research and common sense."

*Accepted.*

*Stage four. Here you found that Joseph was the Pharaoh's Imhotep, great vizier. What did you learn here?*

"Joseph's importance in history."

*Accepted.*

*Stage five. Here you learned about Joseph but what else?*

"Israelite-Egyptian relations were good in Joseph's time."

*Accepted.*

*Stage six. You had to go to the Island of Sehel and find clues. What did you learn?*

"The power of a team work."

*Accepted.*

*Stage seven. You found coordinates on the Island of Sehel. You went to this location. What did you learn there?*

I wasn't sure, but I couldn't stop then. I thought back on how I went there. Oh!

"Miracles happen."

*Accepted.*

*Stage eight. Noah's Ark. How did you feel about the experience?*

How do you describe what it's like to see the ark like that? The beautiful blue glow of the ice.

215

"Amazed."

*Accepted.*

*Stage nine. The Tower of Babylon and the most sacred location in Judaism. Describe this stage in one word.*

"Technology."

*Accepted.*

*Stage ten brought you to the most sacred site of all, where the Ten Commandments were given. How did you feel there?*

"Holy."

*Accepted.*

*Stage eleven. You went to Jericho, where a great victory was won. You searched for a clue to lead you to the next destination. What one word describes this mission?*

"Archeology."

*Accepted.*

*Stage twelve. Here you saw something that no one had seen in thousands of years—the holy of the holies. How did you feel about this experience?*

"A lot happier than that guy who found Troy or the wreck of the *Titanic.*"

I was on a roll, and I typed in that answer without thinking much. The screen paused. Suddenly, I thought I'd blown it.

*Accepted.*

The screen went blank, and the cursor blinked silently.

Maybe I had blown it …

*You have done well. You are ambitious, dedicated, and courageous.*

*Stage thirteen is your last task, and it will have to be done on a specific day. It'll be the riskiest of all and will require faith. You'll be asked to obey exact instructions, even if they seem dangerous.*

*You have seen great wonders and traveled through history and time. Now you can get the answer to your question—do numbers end?*

*There is much more meaning to numbers. It will be revealed to you after a successful completion of stage thirteen.*

*Stage thirteen is all about faith in the face of danger.*

I stared at the screen. I felt elation and curiosity. I was no longer playing child games. I was on the verge of something big, something out of the ordinary, something with deep meaning—something that would have importance for the world. I was ready to give everything to achieve it.

I had faith.

Text appeared in seconds.

*Har HaMoria,* הַר הַמּוֹרִיָּה *in Hebrew, is a hill in the Old City of Jerusalem venerated as a holy site in Judaism, Christianity, and Islam. It has particular religious significance for Judaism and Islam. The Muslim community of Jerusalem manages the site. The Israeli government enforces a ban on prayer by non-Muslims.*

*The Temple Mount is considered the holiest site in Judaism. According to Jewish tradition and scripture, the First Temple was built by King Solomon, the son of King David, in 957 BCE, and was destroyed by the Neo-Babylonian Empire in 586 BCE. The Second Temple was constructed under the auspices of Zerubbabel in 516 BCE, renovated by Herod, and destroyed by the Romans in 70 CE.*

*Orthodox Jewish tradition maintains it is here that the third and final Temple will be built when the Messiah comes. The Temple Mount is the place Jews turn toward during prayer. Jewish attitudes toward the site vary. Many Jews will not walk on the mount to avoid unintentionally entering the area where the holy of holies stood, since, according to rabbinical law, there is still a divine presence there.*

*Among Muslims, the site is revered as the Noble Sanctuary. The courtyard can host more than four hundred thousand worshippers, making it one of the largest mosques in the world. It also includes the location where the prophet Muhammad is said to have ascended to heaven.*

I had never seen the machine give so much information. I read it carefully and made notes because I didn't know if it was going to disappear. The Temple Mount is important to three great religions, but it's also a source of great tension between Judaism and Islam. Okay, where's this going?

*Eid ul-Adha (Festival of the Sacrifice) is important in the Islamic calendar. It celebrates the completion of the holy pilgrimage of Hajj. The holiday is spent with family and loved ones.*

*The Israeli police do not allow non-Muslim visitors on the site that day.*

*Your final task is to go to Har Habait on the day of Eid ul-Adha. Enter the compound and go to the Dome of the Rock.*

*Enter the compound and wait for a message.*

You just said my people weren't allowed there that day, and now you're sending me there? Are you kidding me? You're not kidding me. You're dead serious.

Oh man, oh man, oh man.

An unexpected message popped up on the screen.

*Over the time you've been with us, we have developed confidence in you.*

*Know this.*

Emboldened, I read up on the Har haBayīt, and yes, it's another name for the Temple Mount. That's a dangerous place, especially in these times. Passions are high, and so is security. Sometimes rocks are thrown, and sometimes riots break out. It's an unforgiving place and no place to do anything foolish.

I researched further about it.

> The Temple Mount, or Haram al-Sharif, is a site of profound religious and historical significance located in the Old City of Jerusalem. It is revered by both Muslims and Jews, housing iconic structures like the Al-Aqsa

Mosque and the Dome of the Rock. While it is a site of great spiritual importance, it is also a place that can become particularly volatile and dangerous to visit, especially during religious holidays like Eid ul-Adha.

One of the primary reasons the Temple Mount can be perilous to visit during Eid ul-Adha is the potential for heightened religious sensitivities and tensions. Eid ul-Adha is one of the most important Islamic holidays, commemorating the willingness of Ibrahim (Abraham in Judeo-Christian tradition) to sacrifice his son as an act of obedience to God. On this day, Muslim worshipers flock to the Al-Aqsa Mosque in large numbers, increasing the potential for overcrowding and frictions, especially when coupled with the presence of Jewish visitors or religious events nearby.

Moreover, the Temple Mount has long been a focal point for the Israeli-Palestinian conflict. The competing claims and disputes over control and access to the site have led to sporadic violence and clashes, particularly during times of heightened tension. These tensions can easily escalate during religious holidays, leading to confrontations between various groups.

Security measures in and around the Temple Mount are stringent and can contribute to the sense of volatility. Visitors, especially during Eid ul-Adha, may encounter checkpoints, metal detectors, and a strong security presence. These measures are intended to maintain order and prevent violence but can sometimes lead to friction between visitors and security personnel.

While the Temple Mount is a place of immense cultural and spiritual significance, it is also a location where the convergence of religious, historical, and political factors can make it dangerous to visit during Eid ul-Adha or other times of heightened tension. Visitors should exercise caution, stay informed about the current situation, and follow the guidance of local authorities and travel advisories when considering a visit to this historically and emotionally charged site.

The more I read, the more worried I was. This was dangerous, even more so than our other visits.

Okay, I admit. I was scared.

---

There was also the not-so-small matter of swinging another trip to the Middle East. My back-and-forth mom was off at a New Age seminar near Crater Lake in Oregon. Good vibes, I suppose. Dad and I went hiking in the foothills an hour drive from San Diego. Afterward, we grabbed late lunch at a mom-and-pop place just off Ry 67. Corned beef sandwiches and root beer.

"My birthday's coming up, Dad."

"I know. I was there."

"Hah! And you know which birthday it is too."

"Number thirteen. It's time for your Bar Mitzvah. Rabbi Shmuel will have you recite a Saturday prayer."

"The Aliya La-Torah. Yup, he already discussed it with me. I'll start studying my parashah one month beforehand."

"You've become quite the expert on our religion over the last year."

"Well, it's a major part of my quest. Things run into one another in research—religion, math, archaeology, travel ..."

"Travel? Oh no. Another trip. Where this time? Timbuktu? Katmandu? Why am I hoping it's Israel?"

"Because you know your son! Yes, I want to go to Jerusalem again."

"That's an appropriate trip for someone about to be Bar Mitzvahed. Your mother and I would love to visit the Old City."

"I need to do this journey alone."

"Oh, I see. Forget the folks, eh. All grown-up."

"It's part of my quest. The last part, I believe. I have to be in a specific place in Jerusalem and on a specific date."

"We have relatives there. You can …. From the look on your face, I get the distinct impression you have this all planned out. You're not going alone, Ty. You're just not."

"I was going to ask Rabbi Shmuel to join me."

"Well, I'm okay with that. He's a responsible person. One question though. What's this special place you have to be at?"

"It's a holy place. I hope we can leave it at that."

"A holy place. Well, the whole city is holy to one religion or another. They're safe. Most of them anyway. Security is excellent."

"Yeah, most of them are quite safe."

Off to school.

# Chapter 26

# The Temple Mount

"Do what? On the Temple Mount?"

I'd never seen Rabbi Shmuel so alarmed. He was always calm and in charge. Not that afternoon in his office. He sat down, mopped his bald spot, and shook his head.

"Ty, sometimes I think the website is giving you ... then again, it helped us find the ark. But going to the Temple Mount and doing some deed? That could bring trouble—for us and for the whole region. The Middle East is a powder keg, and this website wants you to light a match. Maybe the website had some keen insights, but this one? I just don't know."

"I've been reading about the Temple Mount, and I know the problems. But the website is leading me to do something important—and good. It's not going to get me to start a riot or a war. I know it."

"Possible, possible. Nothing that led us to the ark could lead us into something evil."

"You're right. So very right. This task calls for faith. And I do have faith. I've learned so much about so many things in the world, but I've also learned about faith—about our Jewish faith and my personal faith. I now know that nothing bad will happen to me or the Temple Mount. There's something urging me on, and it will protect me."

My mentor sat back and smiled.

"Yes, Ty. I've seen it grow inside you. It usually takes a much longer time to see it blossom in people. We both know that most students are here because their parents send them here. They'd much rather be in public school or a private school that let them have more time and leeway. Am I right?"

"I'm afraid so. Most of my classmates prefer popular things. But my quest has put things in order for me."

"Religious study isn't important to most students. We teachers know that. We hope to plant seeds that they'll better appreciate as they grow older. You, on the other hand, have come to see the beauty and truth in Judaism. And that has given you faith. Without faith, where are we?"

"We're lost in a confused world."

We both fell silent. Rabbi Shmuel stood suddenly and paced around the office.

"This day you want to go on the Temple Mount is a holy day for Muslims. Not just in Jerusalem. Around the Middle East and around the world. It's called Eid ul-Adha, and it commemorates Abraham's willingness to sacrifice his son. The Israeli police close off the Temple Mount to Jews that day. The Muslims have come to expect that, and violators will not be treated well."

I'd read all that but nodded along as he spoke.

"How do you propose to get on the Temple Mount that day, Ty? Oh, I see now."

"I need your help getting there. Do you know anyone who could find a way for me to do it?"

"It would be easier to reach the top of Mount Everest in winter."

He paused. He was thinking. A good sign, unless he was thinking about finding me a shrink or a Sherpa guide.

"Rabbi Mordechai has a cousin living near the Muslim Quarter. Rabbi Menachem. He's old and wise and very committed to a Jewish Jerusalem."

223

"Great! Would he take a chance on helping me?"

"Ty, he's already taking chances living near the Muslim Quarter."

"I need to find a way to enter the compound without using the official access points. I see there are many buildings right next to the Temple Mount. They're old, and old buildings have passageways that not everyone knows about."

"I'll get in touch with Rabbi Mordechai and his cousin. But there's a condition."

"Yes?"

"If you want my help with this operation, I am coming with you. You are not trying this alone."

Well, I was about to ask him to come along and was prepared for some pleading. Now he was thinking it was his idea. How things work out sometimes!

"Come along? Oh, that's a good idea. Please do come along!"

———————————————✦———————————————

A week later, Rabbi Shmuel dismissed the class but sent me a glance that told me to hang around. After the others were gone, he closed the door and sat down at his desk, and I stood next to him. He pulled a map from his black leather briefcase and spread it out on the desk. I knew most of the details, though I was puzzled by three red circles that had been drawn on the map.

"We know the Western Wall and the Temple Mount. Let's look at these smaller streets. Rabbi Mordechai's cousin, Menachem, lives … right … here."

"Not far from Herod's Gate."

"Right. Rabbi Menachem and a handful of friends live dangerously. They pray together in a small yeshiva in that part of Jerusalem. More importantly, they do something else."

"They pray at the Western Wall? No, it must be something more. You mean they pray atop the Temple Mount? That's forbidden, isn't it?"

"Indeed, it is. Very much so. So they put on Muslim attire, ascend the stairs with others of that faith, and pray."

"They pray Jewish prayers right next to al Aqsa and the Dome of the Rock?"

"Right next to al Aqsa and the Dome of the Rock and hundreds of Muslims. I know, I know. It's dangerous. I warn them, but they do what they feel they must."

Rabbi Shmuel shrugged his shoulders and rolled his eyes. I shivered for a moment. At first, it was out of fear, but then out of excitement. I imagined myself in Muslim attire! And I imagined Rabbi Shmuel in similar getup. Wow! He was no longer the dull scholar and teacher. He was a fellow adventurer, and we were about to go on a secret mission.

"Ty, I see a look in your eyes. I didn't say you and I were going to do anything like that."

"I see. You are speaking ... oh, what's the word?"

"Hypothetically."

"That's it! You were speaking *hypothetically*. Okay, but what are these three red circles?"

"I was getting to that. These are the three places where, according to Rabbi Menachem, one can secretly enter the compound. Two of them are beneath Arab residences. The owners receive handsome benefits. The third is from the small yeshiva I mentioned. It's thought to be watched by those who oppose a Jewish presence. Nonetheless, Rabbi Menachem thinks it's the best place for someone to use."

"I love the old architecture there. I've looked at tons of pictures and maps. I know every street and alley. I know it as well as I know downtown San Diego."

"It's much more dangerous than San Diego, Ty, especially on that day."

"The Temple Mount is large. Thirty-seven acres. Once someone is up there ..."

Rabbi Shmuel looked at me. He peered into me, gauging me, judging me, wondering about me.

"Okay, Ty. Rabbi Menachem senses you have a special mission in the world. He prayed on the matter and had a dream. He agreed to help us get up there. Just you and me. We'll dress in Arab garb, ascend the steps to the Temple Mount, and do what we feel we must do."

"I knew it! I knew we'd find a way!"

"Does your father know what your mission is?"

"He believes in my quest."

"I see, I see."

"Rabbi Shmuel, do you believe I have a special mission in the world?"

He smiled and clasped a hand on my shoulder.

"Yes, Ty. I do. Very much so. I too have prayed on the matter."

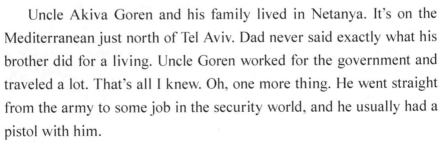

Uncle Akiva Goren and his family lived in Netanya. It's on the Mediterranean just north of Tel Aviv. Dad never said exactly what his brother did for a living. Uncle Goren worked for the government and traveled a lot. That's all I knew. Oh, one more thing. He went straight from the army to some job in the security world, and he usually had a pistol with him.

He and his wife welcomed me, showed me the sea, and kept me happily fed. Their son was doing his time in the army along the Golan Heights overlooking Syria, but we managed a short phone chat. He urged me to move back to Israel when the time came for my military service.

"You and your dad were in Syria not long ago, from what I hear," Uncle Goren said.

I didn't think Dad told too many people about that particular trip.

"Yes, we were in Damascus exploring an old religious site. He and I are amateur archaeologists."

"And now you're going to the Temple Mount for more research. Well, that's a wonderful place. Very important to our religion and to Christians and Muslims."

"But ... how do you know that? I never told you where I am going to go."

"Ah, I know things ... I know it's a place of tension at times."

"Very great tension. The Temple Mount has tremendous significance to all three faiths. For many, it has importance for the end-times."

I must have looked confused by that term.

"The end of days can mean different things, Ty. The coming of our Messiah, the return of Jesus to Christians, and the triumph of Islam to the Muslims. It's not always a pleasant occasion. For most, it's a time of peace and rejoicing. For others, a time of violence and death comes beforehand. And the Temple Mount is the center."

"I didn't know about that. It sounds more dangerous than I thought."

"It's very dangerous, Ty. In my work, we learn of people who want to take command of the Temple Mount or even blow it up."

"Blow it up? Why in the world would anyone want to do that?"

"The end-times, Ty. It will cause a huge war that causes great death and destruction."

"Oh, I think I see. In order to bring about a new world, the old one has to get blown up."

"And not everyone wants to wait for the heavens to do it. They want to do it themselves. It's their mission. Their calling. I've arrested and interrogated some of them, Ty."

I think my jaw dropped at what Uncle Goren revealed.

"So I need to be careful when I'm there."

"Very careful, Ty. We all do. It's an explosive device, and we don't want anyone playing with matches there. Let's let a higher power handle when the end comes! Now, come on. We have to get you to the station. Your bus leaves in an hour."

I was wondering if he'd be there, but I dared not ask.

---

I took a bus from Natanya to Jerusalem. We traveled up winding, tree-lined roads that had burned-out hulks of tanks as monuments to the 1948 War of Independence. My grandfather fought around here but never spoke much about it. I arrived at the King David Hotel, just west of the Temple Mount, where Rabbi Shmuel and Rabbi Menachem were waiting.

"Hello, young man! It's a pleasure to meet you at last!"

Our host was well into his seventies and had distinguished lines across a weathered face. He spoke English with a very noticeable accent, more European than Israeli, I thought.

"Rabbi Shmuel told me a lot about you—and only good things, only very good things. I understand that you are his student in Torah classes and doing wonderfully. Well done, young man, well done."

It was high praise, and I felt my face turn red.

"My car is nearby. Let's go before the traffic gets bad."

We hopped into his car, and off we went. He maneuvered his small Fiat 500 through traffic and small streets with vendors on the sidewalks not five feet from us. He said he was from Brooklyn, but his accent was from his Hungarian parents and extended family. He studied at Yeshiva University and fell in love with Jerusalem as a small boy. He was determined to move there, so he did.

We arrived at the steps leading down to the wall. Above, a blue-orange sky was cradling the city as day gave way to night. Floodlights came on to illuminate the holy site. I'd been there not too long ago and got the note that fell from Western Wall. I loved the place. It had some type of magic. It was less crowded than during the day, so we made our way to the wall and sank into our thoughts and began to pray. I touched the stonework and felt its warmth from the fading sun.

*Thousands of years ago, people from the tribes of Israel came here to pray and congregate. They were shepherds, merchants, priests, artisans, and many other things, but they shared beliefs. Their destinies were tied to those of their people. Maybe a great elder or king touched this very stone and prayed. Maybe the people who hid the ark a few yards below me prayed at this exact spot.*

Yes, I was on the verge of something. Just what I didn't know. There were dangers coming, but I had to go on anyway.

"Ty? Ty? It's time to go home," Rabbi Menachem said, calling me away from my thoughts. "Did you pray?"

"No, yes … I don't know."

"In one way or another, you were praying."

We walked back through the same streets. They were less crowded now. I remembered something.

"Wait here! I'll be right back," I said.

And before they could stop me or even ask questions, I dashed down a side street. I knew exactly where I was going. Two blocks down and just off to the left. In a flash, I reached my goal and stood in front of the best falafel place in Jerusalem. Customers were walking out with satisfied faces and aromatic takeout. Suddenly, a great tragedy occurred. The store lights went out, curtains were drawn, and a sign in Arabic and Hebrew was put in the window.

*Closed for the holiday.*

"Oh yeah," I murmured. "Forgot about that."

Discouraged and a little hungry, I sauntered back to find my elders. I came upon a man speaking to a dozen people gathered around him. I couldn't understand what he was saying, but he was greatly agitated, and he pointed frantically every now and then to the Temple Mount. The crowd was fascinated, and more and more gathered to hear him.

His voice climbed to a shriek, and he tossed a handful of flyers high into the air. The crowd eagerly grabbed them. One fluttered down into my hands. I couldn't read it, but the image was striking—the Dome of the Rock and behind it an immense nuclear explosion. It struck something side me. The Temple Mount, so sacred to me and millions of others, was in danger. I folded it up, put it into my pocket, and returned to my companions. They needed to know what I found.

"No falafel tonight. I'm afraid the place was closed."

# Chapter 27

# The Remarkable Thing

In the morning, I saw Rabbi Shmuel sitting on a stone bench in the courtyard between buildings. He was ordinarily a serious man, but that morning he was especially so. I sat next to him. No one spoke for quite a while. Finally, he did.

"Today is the day that we are going to do this remarkable thing. I don't have a good feeling about it."

"Rabbi Shmuel, you don't have to come with me. It's my quest."

"Yes, I do. Of course I do. I can't let you go up there alone. I feel responsible for you. No, I *am* responsible for you. Ty, did you know I don't have any children? I'm sure everyone at school knows. Having children is a great mitzvah according to the Torah. It means one's life carries on to another generation. It seems every rabbi has at least eight or more children! In that matter, I've been ... oh, not very successful. Ty, you've become my son, my hope for carrying on to another generation."

"That makes me feel very special, Rabbi Shmuel. But I sense there's more."

"There is, Ty. There most certainly is more. I've thought about it and prayed about it. More than I have for anything in my life—except before I chose to become a rabbi. It was my calling, and I feel that this quest is my new calling. It's my destiny to ascend the Temple Mount and find sacred meaning."

"We'll climb the steps together. And we'll find sacred meaning."

"In one hour, Ty. In one hour."

The rabbis and I gathered in the living room.

"Today is the day. The hour has come. You have an urgent matter that calls upon you to pray on the Temple Mount. That's *haram*, as the Muslims say. Absolutely forbidden. Jews are not allowed to pray on what they call the Noble Sanctuary, where al Aqsa and the Dome of the Rock have stood for centuries. I will help you. But you must listen to me, and you must be careful. We live in perilous times."

"I believe I can learn much from you," I said.

"Such a good young man! It's best you dress like simple Arab visitors. Not flowing robes, just shirts and trousers that a working-class father and son would wear. As observant Jews, you will want to wear yarmulkes. That of course presents problems but not insurmountable ones. You will simply have to have another form of head cover atop your yarmulkes. I've done it countless times, and so have others. Now go change in the other rooms. The hour has come."

Rabbi Shmuel went into the dining room, and I headed for the bathroom. Out we came in simple clothing and plain cap hats. I almost laughed when I saw him.

"Not the time for humor, Ty," he said sternly.

"Well, you look passable! Very passable! Remember, do not talk. You know English and Hebrew but not Arabic. And your accents are clearly American. Now, when you reach the Temple Mount, you will of course want to pray. Every Jew does. But you must not let words slip out. It's best not to even let your lips move. It's a Muslim holiday, and we're not supposed to be there at all, let alone praying there. It will be crowded with many anxious people, and we don't want to start anything."

"Anxious and vigilant people," Rabbi Shmuel added.

"Very vigilant people. You know the layout of the Temple Mount. Do not enter al Aqsa or the Dome of the Rock. Do what you must in the courtyard and come back down. Agreed?"

We nodded.

"Now, let us go to the yeshiva. There's a mikvah there."

"That," Rabbi Shmuel explained to me, "is a bath of sorts for a cleansing ritual."

"Because we're going to a holy place."

"Such a good student you have!"

Rabbi Menachem led the two Arab pretenders through the narrow streets to his yeshiva—a smallish, old building of brick. We entered a sparsely decorated room down a hallway, where a young man in his twenties sat quietly.

"You have phones in case of trouble. I can get Israeli security to help immediately. I hope. Blend in and say nothing. Text me when you are on your way back. We'll be waiting for you. Now, my student will take you to the next room, and from there, your journey begins. May it serve you well."

"May it serve all," I said.

The young man motioned for us to follow. The room was dark and smelled of old, moist stone. He lifted a painting of the old city from its hooks, revealing a window, which he opened as quietly as the old wood allowed.

"Climb out and push the bushes and branches aside. Slowly. As little noise as possible. You will see a small passageway that leads upward. Upward to your destination. Now go. We'll be here waiting. Text us."

Out we climbed and through the brush we walked. In a moment, we found the passageway that led to one of the main stairways. The sides were narrow and the overhead low. We had to shimmy through tight passages.

We came upon the entrance to a main stairway. We crouched in the dark as group after group of Muslim faithful passed us. A large group went by, and the next one stopped as a baby cried insistently. We casually walked out from the opening, looked straight ahead, and began to climb the stone steps. There must have been several dozen of them, and Rabbi Shmuel was winded. Finally we saw light ahead and heard the sounds of prayer. A moment later, we stood in bright sunlight.

We were on Har HaMoria, the Temple Mount. It was no dream, no online experience. We were there, standing where Solomon's Temple once rose above Jerusalem and dominated the skyline for miles. Rabbi Shmuel's look of awe quickly vanished as he tried to remain calm and not draw attention. I too remembered Rabbi Menchaem's instructions.

Around us were hundreds of the faithful, some walking reverently around the mosques, others enjoying meals with families on blankets spread out beneath tall trees that swayed with light breezes. Security forces, Israeli ones, were all about but not especially close. They scanned the crowd for signs of trouble, and from their determined expressions, they were prepared to deal with it.

At one end was the Dome of the Rock. I'd seen it from far many times, as I was visiting the Jewish Quarter. It always seemed beautiful but foreign and unappealing. Now, however, its majesty struck me and called to me. Now I was at a close distance, and it looked huge and shiny. As we approached the amazing Dome of the Rock, my eyes widened with excitement and wonder. The golden dome shimmered in the sunlight, making it look like a magical castle from a fairy tale. As I explored further, I noticed the intricate carvings on the walls. The words in Arabic were so beautifully written, like an art form in themselves. I couldn't understand their meaning, but they felt important and sacred.

That's where I had to go to get the final message that would end my quest. The time was near, and I had to go to the appointed place. I looked over and saw Rabbi Shmuel with eyes fervently closed. He was praying. His lips were moving! I nudged him gently and pointed to our objective.

"To be in this place of our Temple, our Beit Hamikdash, where our ancestors worshipped … it's overwhelming, Ty. I've never felt more humble and holy than this instant."

We headed for the Dome of the Rock. The closer we got, the more intricate the blue-green mosaics were, the brighter the gold dome, the more excited the faithful. No one thought us any different from the others.

"Remember, Ty. We're just ordinary visitors."

"Yes, ordinary visitors."

*But with an extraordinary destiny.*

We stood at the appointed spot and looked about for signs, symbols, anything. I saw nothing.

"Keep looking, Ty. I'll look occasionally, but I'll also look at the dome, like everyone else."

We casually walked silently toward the main area. Rabbi Shmuel looked stressed but kept a calm expression. I was transfixed by the magnificent, golden structure of the Dome of the Rock. I didn't know where exactly to go or what to expect. I assumed that things would reveal themselves as they had until now. Every place that I went on the designated date and time had some discoveries, and I expected the same today.

It was the Muslim holiday, a forbidden event for Jews, and I was not supposed to be there.

I had done lots of reading about this place and thought it was fascinating. Now I was seeing it in front of me. Now I was walking on holy ground. The courtyard, Sahn in Arabic, could host more than four hundred thousand worshippers, making it one of the largest mosques in the world.

For Sunni and Shia Muslims alike, it ranks as the third holiest site in Islam. The plaza includes the location regarded as where the Islamic prophet Muhammad ascended to heaven, and served as the first "qibla," the direction Muslims turn toward when praying. As in Judaism, Muslims also associate the site with Solomon and other prophets who are venerated in Islam. The site, and the term "Al-Aqsa" in relation to the whole plaza, is also a central identity symbol for Palestinians, including non-Muslim Palestinians.

We stopped in front of the Dome of Rock. The structure was amazing, and we both were transfixed for a few minutes. The crowd around us was noisy, and I looked everywhere as slight fear crawled up my back.

We walked to a spot that was fairly empty of visitors. I could see metal gates in the main entrances to the compound and numerous armed Israeli military and police standing with helmets. I well knew why. This was just in case there were riots. But today seemed a calm day, and people around us seemed to be praying or simply walking around, enjoying the holiday.

I looked around and wondered what should I look for. Where were my answers? But nothing was shown to me. We were both calm since we had gotten used to the fact that we looked like typical celebrators, and no one paid attention to us.

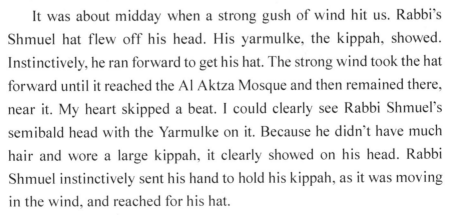

It was about midday when a strong gush of wind hit us. Rabbi's Shmuel hat flew off his head. His yarmulke, the kippah, showed. Instinctively, he ran forward to get his hat. The strong wind took the hat forward until it reached the Al Aktza Mosque and then remained there, near it. My heart skipped a beat. I could clearly see Rabbi Shmuel's semibald head with the Yarmulke on it. Because he didn't have much hair and wore a large kippah, it clearly showed on his head. Rabbi Shmuel instinctively sent his hand to hold his kippah, as it was moving in the wind, and reached for his hat.

Fearfully, I looked around me.

People noticed. I saw people pointing toward Rabbi Shmuel and yelling in Arabic. I didn't understand what they said, but I figured out the content. They saw a Jew there during their holiday. Quickly, the yelling got louder around us. I ran to Rabbi Shmuel. He put his hat on his head, and we started to quickly walk away. But it was too late. Like a fire in a dry field of thorns, an angry crowed ran toward us. I could see Israeli guards and soldiers talking in their radios and running in our direction. They were far, too far. In a matter of seconds, we were surrounded by a mad crowed yelling at us in Arabic. One man pulled our hats and pointed at our kippahs.

"Jews, you are forbidden to be here today!" the crowd yelled in Hebrew. I knew enough Hebrew to understand.

"Please ... leave us alone," I cried in English. My heart raced, and I was terrified.

"Please, leave the child. He is just a child." Rabbi Shmuel protected me with his body by leaning above me.

"You are not allowed to be here! You are not allowed!" someone from the crowd yelled in English. Then the crowd pushed on us. I felt Rabbi Shmuel being beaten by dozens of people as he was covering me.

Dozens of people screamed at us. The loudness was horrific and scary, and I covered my eyes in fear.

A clap of thunder almost shook the ground. The crowd's attention turned to the skies. It was a sunny day.

Another loud thunder sounded, and a dark swirl of clouds started to form above us. There was a hum in the crowd, and they moved a few steps backward. Rabbi Shmuel and I were on the ground. A swirl of dark clouds grew larger above us. It spanned slowly, and we could see flashes of lightning inside it. The crowd became silent and watched in fear. The rest of the skies were completely sunny; only above us were the storm-like tornado clouds.

A gunshot shattered my concentration.

The crowed pulled farther away. Rabbi Shmuel sent his hand to his chest. It was covered with blood. He looked at his hand in great disbelief.

"No ... no ... no!" I cried loudly.

He lay on the ground.

A red bloodstain started to grow on his shirt.

"No one's supposed to have weapons in here! No one's supposed to have weapons." I sobbed. "Look what you did!" I screamed at the crowd.

Israeli soldiers came running.

"Are you well, Ty? Stay with me until the soldiers arrive. They'll take you home." Rabbi Shmuel held my hand tight and tried to smile.

Another thunder rolled through, and a flash of lightning blinded us all for a second.

A voice spoke from within the lightning clouds. Everyone in the world could hear it. Everyone in their own language. The world stopped and became silent. A halo was seen in the stormy clouds.

The crowd fell on their knees. Rabbi Shmuel and I looked at the skies. Something extraordinary was happening.

"There shall be no more wars, no more bloodshed. Share your world together. Share it in peace. Share it with love."

The crowd was astonished. Many prayed in Arabic.

"Move, move aside!" One of the people pushed the crowd away and leaned near us. "I am a doctor. Let me check you."

He examined Rabbi Shmuel. "Not good. By the blood, one of his arteries got hit. He needs an immediate evac to a hospital. Otherwise ..." He put pressure with his hand on Rabbi Shmuel's chest but seemed unhappy with the results. Blood continued to gush out. "What are you both doing on the mountain today? Don't you know it's forbidden?"

He turned around and yelled in Arabic to the crowed. They moved backward and watched silently.

There was another lightning and thunder from the clouds. "There shall be no more sorrow and no more killings. You will respect all beliefs peacefully. There shall be no weapons among you and no evil actions."

"I am so sorry, Rabbi Shmuel! It's all because of me," I cried.

"Are you crazy?" He laughed, but I could see that it cost him vast effort. "I wouldn't miss this event for anything. To be on Har HaMoria, to see what … we saw. I'd never want to miss this. Thank you for taking me here, Ty. It's worth everything. I've been honored … honored with the greatest honor that a Jew could ever have. You make sure to get out of here safely with the soldiers."

I held Rabbi Shmuel's hand. It shook.

"I can't stop the blood. How a weapon got into here?" The doctor shook his head, frustrated at being unable to help Rabbi Shmuel.

"Thank you, friend." Rabbi Shmuel smiled at him. "Please make sure the child is safe."

Rabbi Shmuel turned to me. "Ty, I want you to know that I am very proud of you. You brought the world peace. You are a tzaddik."

I couldn't say anything.

"Now don't you forget to attend the Shul at home. Even if I am not there, it doesn't mean you can skip holidays and festivals. I am so very proud of you for your journey and what you learned the past few years. Who knows? Maybe you'll attend a yeshiva one day …" He tried to laugh but gave up. It was too painful. "You did good, Ty. You did good."

He leaned backward, looking at the stormy clouds above. "Look at those beautiful clouds above. It's a miracle. A miracle … I am going to rest for a little bit here now. Do you see the clouds above, Ty? Do you?"

"Yes, I do see them." I sobbed.

The people around us seemed to be touched by the scene. I could hear whispering, and one woman brought me a bottle of water.

Rabbi Shmuel's hand became lifeless, and he closed his eyes.

"No, no, no," I cried and raised my eyes to the clouds. "Please help me ... please! Rabbi Shmuel is my good friend. He helped me to get here! Without him, none of this would have happened. Please ..."

There was a sudden silence in the world. All seemed to stop moving. I had never experienced such complete silence. It was like everything in the world had stopped. No wind, no birds chirping—nothing.

Rabbi Shmuel's hand moved. I looked at him. He opened his eyes. Then I noticed. The blood on his clothes and hands disappeared. There was no wound anymore. He lay there for a moment and then slowly stood up. I was so happy.

"Rabbi Shmuel, you're okay! You're okay!" I hugged him in a burst of joy.

The doctor looked at him in awe. The crowd watched in awe. No one said anything. In front of their eyes, a miracle had happened.

Then the people looked up. The Israeli guards and police lowered their weapons and placed them on the ground.

The halo became larger. Lightning and thunder were followed by a voice. I was not sure if the voice was for the entire world or only for me.

"The numbers will never end. It's a sign from me for you to remember who you are and that you have to live in peace. The numbers conceive the ultimate secret of your universe and will never end as a reminder for you not to create means to destroy yourselves. I've been watching you too long and have seen too many horrors. No more. All your weapons and evil technology will be eliminated, and I'll be watching you from now on. Make peace. Live together. Love your fellow as you love yourself.

"וְאָהַבְתָּ לְרֵעֲךָ כָּמוֹךָ"

# Chapter 28

# The End and the Beginning

The world went through unbelievable transformation. Weapons of mass destruction were destroyed, and every country created rules for keeping minimum operational weaponry. Any efforts to create sophisticated weapons failed. It was like technology had been disrupted by a greater power. Engineers couldn't design and produce any superior technology anymore to create destructive weaponry, and the world learned that it was being watched and monitored for its own safety.

An international world government was established to ensure all lived in peace with global cooperation. Countries shared territories. Arabs and Israelis shared holy places, and there were no more wars. The world focused on providing food for the hungry, fighting crime, and make efforts to save the planet's environment. Investments turned from weapons and destruction technology to medicine and space exploration.

Against all odds, the world became a better place.

---

As for me, I got my answers. Turns out numbers never end after all. I had my Bar Mitzvah in the Kotel a few months after the great event. All my friends were there, including Rabbi Shmuel. I am thinking of joining a yeshiva maybe later in life. After the yeshiva, I'll go to engineering school. There is no contradiction between religion and science. For now, I am enjoying my childhood.

Yes, I became famous and was offered lots of money to do a feature films or write books about my experience. I liked the idea and now am working on my first book. After I complete it, I want to make a movie. I love these types of things. I still have to convince Rabbi Shmuel to join me, acting in the movie.

Many months have passed since that great world event, and somehow, deep inside, I am not convinced that we were given a complete answer.

---

It was one late evening, about midnight, when I sat in front of my computer. On an impulse, I went to the website that had given me the quest.

"So the numbers really never end?" I typed.

*You already got your answers.*

"Yes, but do numbers truly never end?"

There was a blank screen for a while.

*They do.*

My heart raced.

I knew it! I knew it! I had a feeling all along.

I typed, "Can you show me how?"

*Because you showed such great dedication, good intention, and purpose, I'll show you only once that numbers can end. You have to reach a certain number, which is not too large, but you have to do the addition in a slightly different way.*

I thought about my good friend Sam. He'd love to know about this. The website like read my mind.

*Yes, you will need your friend's supercomputer, but you have to inform him that this demonstration will be done once and only once.*

I typed, "Okay."

*Follow the exact next instructions on screen. Give them exactly as they are shown to your friend to execute on a supercomputer. The computer will work exactly ninety-nine minutes, and in the hundredth minute, you'll get the answer.*

I typed, "Thank you."

*You did a good job, Ty. You deserve to know that numbers can end, but this information cannot be given to humanity.*

I copied and pasted the given instructions into a document.

I had the top secret in the world.

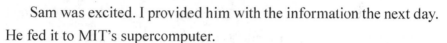

Sam was excited. I provided him with the information the next day. He fed it to MIT's supercomputer.

"This is a very odd sequence of operations. I've never seen this technique before. It looks absurd. It can never work. It doesn't make sense."

"Just do it, Sam. In the hundredth minute, you'll get the results."

His face looked skeptical on the Zoom call.

After about half an hour, everything was ready. Sam clicked on the button, and the word "Executing" showed on screen. Sam started a timer.

The computer started to add numbers. Quickly the value reached numbers of high exponents, and the supercomputer continued.

On the hundredth minute, it happened.

The computer added one more number and stopped. A finite number showed on the screen.

Sam looked at the screen in disbelief.

"Wait—something is not right." He manually added one. The number remained the same. It didn't grow.

"There must be some malfunction. The computer typically reaches a much higher value. Let me check."

Sam spent a few days checking the computer system, its hardware and software, but couldn't find any flaw.

---

We met on Zoom a few days later.

"I don't know what to say, Ty. "It seems like there is an end to numbers. It has to be counted in a different method in order to witness the phenomenon."

"I was right." I felt victorious. "I had a feeling all along."

"But ... I don't understand why we didn't reach it before."

"My guess is that this type of discovery may lead to great knowledge and the destruction of humanity. So it's been eliminated from us so that we don't harm ourselves, exactly as a parent takes hazardous toys from their children."

"Really, that's bull ... I don't believe that this is the case."

"Sam, this opportunity to see how numbers end was given to me once. It will not happen again. Enjoy this knowledge. It's a token of gratitude for your help."

"You forgot that now I know the technique. I have all the documentation. I can reproduce it again and again and will become the most famous scientist in the world." Sam was joyous.

"Nope. You won't. As I said, this privilege was given to us once only. Have a great evening, Sam."

---

As I had been told, the privilege was given to us only once. As the supercomputer reached the end of the numbers, it couldn't continue, and the only way was to reboot it. Sam used the exact same information I had given him, but the computer never reached that result again; it didn't matter how many time Sam tried.

I tried a few more times to access the website that had given me the quest, but it seemed to disappear from the cyber world—like it had never been there.

———◆———

Today, I am eighteen years old. Eventually, I decided to go to college to study archeology. I like digging into the past and finding facts that may be related to the present or the future.

During my first year, I traveled to Tibet to dig in a new site that was estimated to be thousands of years old. My classmate and I found a piece of stone with some inscriptions on it. Now I had the knowledge to translate it.

Later that night, after cleaning the stone, I translated the inscriptions.

*This is not to be given to you since it may bring the end of humanity. For generations, humankind brought Armageddon upon itself. A code is going to be released to cause chaos and limitations on humanity's progress. So you all shall live.*

"Hmmm," I mumbled to myself. "What is this code they're talking about?"

*This world is yours. Share it together. Share it with love. Share it in peace.*

Printed in the United States
by Baker & Taylor Publisher Services